A
HUNDRED
SMALL
LESSONS

A HUNDRED SMALL LESSONS

a novel

ASHLEY HAY

ATRIA BOOKS

New York   London   Toronto   Sydney   New Delhi

ATRIA
BOOKS

An Imprint of Simon & Schuster, Inc.
1230 Avenue of the Americas
New York, NY 10020

Originally published in Australia in 2017 by Allen & Unwin

This project has been assisted by the Australian Government through the Australia Council, its arts funding and advisory body.

The quote on page 118 is from "The Story" by Michael Ondaatje. Copyright © 1998 by Michael Ondaatje. Reprinted by permission of Michael Ondaatje.

First Atria Books hardcover edition November 2017

ATRIA B O O K S and colophon are trademarks of Simon & Schuster, Inc.

For information about special discounts for bulk purchases, please contact Simon & Schuster Special Sales at 1-866-506-1949 or business@simonandschuster.com

The Simon & Schuster Speakers Bureau can bring authors to your live event. For more information or to book an event contact the Simon & Schuster Speakers Bureau at 1-866-248-3049 or visit our website at www.simonspeakers.com.

Manufactured in the United States of America

10 9 8 7 6 5 4 3 2 1

Library of Congress Cataloging-in-Publication Data

Names: Hay, Ashley, author.
Title: A hundred small lessons : a novel / Ashley Hay.
Description: First Atria Books hardcover edition. | New York : Atria Books, 2017.
Identifiers: LCCN 2017011046 (print) | LCCN 2017016301 (ebook) | ISBN 9781501165153 (eBook) | ISBN 9781501165139 (hardcover) | ISBN 9781501165146 (softcover)
Subjects: LCSH: Families—Fiction. | Domestic fiction. | BISAC: FICTION / Literary. | FICTION / Family Life. | FICTION / Contemporary Women.
Classification: LCC PR9619.4.H38 (ebook) | LCC PR9619.4.H38 H86 2017 (print) | DDC 823/.92—dc23
LC record available at https://lccn.loc.gov/2017011046

ISBN 978-1-5011-6513-9
ISBN 978-1-5011-6515-3 (ebook)

For Nigel Beebe, and for Hux

. . . the people we were
who said
or omitted to say
the appropriate words . . .
The shapes we mistake
for love . . .
the shapes we mistake
for ourselves
at the edge of the water.

—JOHN BURNSIDE
"III. DE LIBERO ARBITRIO"

A
HUNDRED
SMALL
LESSONS

1

Elsie's house

IT WAS early on a winter's morning when she fell—the shortest day of 2010, the woman on the radio said. From where Elsie lay, quite still and curled comfortably on the thick green carpet between the sofa and the sideboard, she could see how the sun coming in through the back door made a triangle on the kitchen floor. The light caught the pattern on the linoleum and touched the little nests of dust that her broom had missed under the lip of the kitchen cupboards.

The bright triangle changed as the minutes passed, disappearing from the kitchen to pop up first in the back bedroom, then across the busy pattern of Nile green and white tiles in the bathroom. Later, in her own bedroom, it reached almost all the way across the floor to the thick rose-colored chenille of her bedspread, before it swung around further towards the west in search of the sunroom. The pile of the carpet, from where she lay, looked like neatly sheared blades of grass, the tidy job of mowing that Clem would have done.

There was something comforting about being this close to the topography of the house. She knew this place so well. She wasn't sure if it was an extension of her, or she of it. So this was a new kind of exploration, noticing the way the floor sloped a little into the spare room, and how the beading sagged slightly on one segment of the ceiling.

Topography: she counted through the letters—ten. Geography; landscape. The answer to fourteen down in that morning's crossword, where she'd been trying to make "projection" fit. She was losing her touch.

From outside, she could hear the kookaburra; he'd be looking for his food. *You could set your watch by him*, she thought. There were cars on the road, the squeak of the swing in the park, the rich buzz of aeroplanes climbing up from the airport, the chatter of lorikeets, corellas. All that activity; it was nice to lie still among it—although the kookaburra would be disappointed she'd put nothing out today. And then the house muttered a little too, its boards creaking and stretching as the day warmed.

It was a consoling sound.

They'd had a long chat, Elsie Gormley and this house, more than sixty years of it. It had witnessed all her tempers, all her moods, and usually improved them. It held her voice, her husband's, her children's, and now their children's in turn—echoes and repetitions lodged in around the baseboards, around the window frames like those pale motes of dust that had wedged at the edge of the kitchen floor.

"Reverb," one of Don's young boys had told her—Don's own grandson, she supposed: her great-grandson then. The one with the noisy guitar. "Imagine it like this, Nan: layers of echoes arranged to make it sound like you're in a great big space."

Well, 'reverb,' she thought clearly. A nice word. She liked to keep abreast of what they knew, how they lived—their magic gadgets, their shiny new phones. *Like this, Nan: one swipe and it turns on.*

She swiped her fingers now against the thick green carpet. Yes, she could almost hear it. All those voices; all those years.

It was lunchtime, and then afternoon, and as the sun sank lower, she wondered how cold it might get, there on the floor, overnight. She was eighty-nine years old, and her bones were brittle and tired.

The neighbors came then, one to the front door, one to the back. "Elsie," they called, "are you there, love? Are you right?"

"I'm not here," she said, and lay still, wondering if she could turn her head far enough to see the fiery clouds of the sunset through the windows at the front of the house.

There were sirens in the street—she could see the reflections of blue and red flashing lights on the wallpaper above her head—and then a policeman broke in through the door. *By whose authority*, she thought she said, but no one seemed to hear and she was onto a stretcher and into an ambulance before she had time to realize she didn't have her shoes.

Imagine leaving home without your shoes.

It was cold in the back of the ambulance and too bright. She wanted her cardigan. She wanted to sleep. If she could move her head slightly, she might see the steps, the porch, the battered front door. If she could lever herself up a bit more. But she couldn't.

"Rightio, love." The uniformed man was far too cheerful for his job.

Elsie closed her eyes. "I don't think I'm ready to go." Her voice, this time, quite loud and clear.

In the hospital, a fortnight later on, she thought they said she was going home, but it wasn't her home they took her to. Some other place, with a bright new apartment for her, a view down to the river, a bell she could press for attention, and meals, if she preferred it, in a hall. She had her shoes now, and her cardigan—they were bringing her mountains of stuff for such a short stay.

"What's that word? 'Respite?'" she said to Donny when he came one day at lunch.

"Sort of, Mum," he said. "In a way."

She'd signed some papers about some people she'd never heard of, a pair called Ben Carter and Lucy Kiss. Donny's wife Carol said they had a little boy. But what was that to do with her? Were they tenants for her house while she was here?

"Sort of, Mum," said Don again. "Yes. In a way."

"Well, make sure they keep up the garden. Your father will never forgive me if that rockery goes wrong."

Clem Gormley. Now, where was he? When did they say he'd be here?

"Ben Carter," said Don, squaring the papers. "Lucy Kiss. I think we've made the right choice."

Of course, she knew what was happening; she knew where she was. The *facility*, she'd always called it, with its apartments for the well ones, and rooms—then wards—for those who weren't. It was just a stop or so on the bus along from her place, and its back fence butted the sports fields where Donny's grandkids played. She could walk home from here, she thought. Be back in no time.

She'd lived in that house more than sixty years—nearly sixty-three, she worked out as she lay the first night in her new room in her old bed and her old, cold sheets. She could remember the day they moved in, the size of their loan so cripplingly vast that she never dared to speak of it to Clem. To even put it into words. Back when the house was fresh and new. The house whose lawns her husband had so carefully tended. *Rest his soul*: yes. That was it.

And yet in spite of so many years, the day she fell, the day she lay there on the floor, was the first time she'd seen the way the light moved from one room to another, tracking from the back of the house to the front, calling into corners, illuminating space.

Such a lovely thing to have seen, she thought. *Such a lovely day to have spent.*

~

The modest house was sold, as the real estate agent had promised, in next to no time. "A big block like this, with the park at the back, and the shops, and so close to the city—no trouble at all," the agent had said.

Elsie's children, the twins, Don and Elaine, came to empty the house for the sale. Elaine swept shelves of items into bags, disposing of them in the gaping maw of a dumpster emptied once, emptied twice. Don went through things piece by piece: cutlery drawers, button boxes, the old letter rack from the high kitchen shelf. Some of its receipts and notes dated from decades before. There were photos in there too: a gallery of grandkids, an image of Elsie before her own children were born, and the house up to its windows in water during the '74 flood. He stood a while, wiping the dust off this last image.

"That bloody flood—you know, I don't think she ever got over it. We should have made her sell the house back then."

"And made no money on it—who'd have bought here, after that? We're lucky that people forget." Elaine had the fridge door open and shoveled jars and packets into a garbage bag. "Look at this—all out of date."

"Carol used to take her shopping once a week; some of it should be all right." Don slipped the flood photo underneath the other pictures, and stared a while at a tiny black and white of his mother, taken almost seventy years ago. "She was so pretty, wasn't she, when she first married Dad? This must have been when she was working at that chemist's in the city, before we were born. She always said she felt important, behind the counter in her starched white coat." He turned the photo over: "January 1941," he read. "The year we were born—and that'll be seventy years ago, soon." He shook his head at this impossible thought. "So strange that she'll never come home. Do you mind if I take these?"

"This milk's two *months* past its date." Elaine dropped it into the bag, bursting the carton so that the room filled with a terrible, sour smell. "I wonder why she never went back to work—she must have been so *bored*. God, we should have got a cleaner in and—oh!" Her hand at her throat as a crow, big and shiny black, landed on the threshold, cocking its head to look through the door.

"You don't mind if I take these, Elaine?"

Elaine tied the bag with a savage twist. "Whatever you like." She glanced across at him. "You were always more sentimental than me—here." One of the pictures had dropped on the floor. "Here's another." She reached down and passed it across.

It was a photo of a portrait, and Don frowned. "It's a painting, but it almost looks like Mum." He held it close to get a better look.

"A painting of Mum? Let me see." His sister took it from him and went out onto the deck, studying it in the sun. "It can hardly have been her," she said at last, folding the print—in half, then half again—and stuffing it into her pocket. "As if she'd get a portrait done like that."

Most of the furniture went to a thrift store, along with the clothes and almost everything from the glass-fronted kitchen cupboards: the crystal, the crockery, the pots and the pans.

"Of course, she's not dead yet," said Elaine, which made Don wince as he set aside a painted vase he thought was his mother's favorite and a book he remembered her reading, years ago, around the time that his father had died.

She looked small in the new place, he thought. She looked lost.

"I must get back to reading to your father," she said when he next visited, patting the old paperback with its spotted pages and crumbly cover. "And did you bring my house keys? How will I get in when I go home?"

In each room, there was something Don balked at removing. The sideboard in the lounge where his own school sports trophies still sat arranged on one end. A plastic fern in the sunroom. The velvet-covered stool in front of his mother's dressing table.

"Your father did that upholstery—lovely rose-colored velvet; a present one birthday," Elsie said when he mentioned it. "He said it was fit for a queen." She smiled. "But you're right: I won't need it while I'm here." She'd watched her reflection change through the decades as she'd sat on that elegant stool, her hair fading from a warm chestnut brown down to grey and the skin under her fine chin loosening. All those crystal canisters on the dressing table; the vials of perfume she'd never quite finished. Who was keeping up the dusting and the sweeping while she was away? Was Elaine chipping her nail polish pulling out the little weeds that grew between the white pebbles in the front garden? She doubted it.

When she visualized her daughter, she saw a younger version of herself. She was always astonished when the real Elaine arrived and looked, and was, so very different.

~

When the new people came, they put the stool and the fern into a dumpster along with all the wallpaper—"a different pattern in every room," said the husband, Ben, laughing—and the thick green carpet. "Last vacuumed . . ." He shrugged, glancing down at his small son. "I think Tom's found a cockroach to eat." Ben was taller than he stood, his shoulders curled from years hunched over writing. His dark hair was greying and he kept his glasses on top of his head, ready to read things at a moment's notice. He looked down at his son, his hands busy with the desiccated insect, with a detached kind of appraisal.

"But these floorboards are going to look lovely," said his wife, Lucy, taking the cockroach out of the boy's hand. "It's such beautiful wood. And look, they've left a pile of pretty doilies." They were bundled together behind the door, and she paused for a moment, stroking the patterns on the delicate white linen runners and mats—a suite of flowers and fruit and elaborate twirling curls.

"Look at this—" holding up a star-shaped doily for her husband to admire. "So fine: the stitching's as neat on the back as it is on the front. I wonder if they meant to take them; seems a shame that no one wanted them. Or maybe they meant them for us."

Sitting on the floor, Tom unpacked small white pebbles from the back of a brightly colored plastic truck.

"Star," he said, pointing to the shape his mother held. "Star."

"That's a beautiful word—and a whole new one." Lucy smiled so much she was crying.

"See, Lu?" said Ben, brushing her deep red hair away from her forehead. "I knew we'd be all right here."

~

They spent three weeks stripping, painting, moving. The first night they slept in the house, Lucy woke at three, disoriented by the map made by the beading on the ceiling. Which house was this? Which city, which country? In the past years they'd been all over the place— to Washington, to London, back to Sydney, and now to Brisbane.

Where they seemed to have bought a house.

"First step to feeling settled," Ben had declared—and Lucy thought she ought to trust that he was right.

Brisbane: the place where he'd grown up. Now it was where Tom would grow up too, while Ben went off to his new job with the paper. Gadgets, inventions, and discoveries had always been the things that piqued his interest (Lucy preferred more seriously to describe it as science or technology), and he'd at last been approached to cover that round.

"I'd be mad not to give it a go—all those magnificent stories," he'd said in Sydney when the offer was first made. "We'll stay here until Tom turns one, then we'll go. Come on—the next adventure!"

She had jobs that she did—administration, management. He had a job that he loved. That was how they both defined their working lives.

"You're mad to go," her sisters had said. "Tom's so tiny. You need your networks."

"Get back to work," her mother had said. "Best way to settle into a new place."

"You'll have a ball," her father had said. "A whole new city—and take your time."

Their standard difference of opinion, thought Lucy, *and here I am*. She stared at the ceiling. *Old bed, new house*. It was the first house they'd ever bought. They'd been in Brisbane a month or so—and back in Sydney barely a year before that. She was unpacking boxes in this house that she'd packed in London, in Washington before that. She'd never thought of it as moving but as arriving, and there was a trick to arriving somewhere new—a person or a place that made it easy, or a sliver of coincidence that made her think they'd landed precisely where they ought to be.

"And now, the great Australian dream," Ben had joked. "The kid, the house, the mortgage." How very fast they'd made that real.

Now, in the night's light, she looked at her husband's face as he slept—he was always smiling, home each night with some great story, some great new moment from his day. While she made spaceships for Tom as she emptied their boxes, and began to work out where they were.

Their names had looked so slight against the weight of all that mortgage.

"In at the deep end," she'd said to her sisters, trying to laugh. And they'd laughed too.

The floorboards felt warm as she walked to the kitchen. She liked the rich glow of the newly polished jarrah, and she liked how they felt underfoot. There was something warm about the whole house at night—perhaps it was the soft light from the streetlamps. She stood by the kitchen window, filling a glass with water, and watched as rain started to fall, smudging the reflection of the lamps in the park into patches of brightness on its concrete path. She walked into the living room with her glass, patting a doily that she'd left on the arm of a chair.

"I know we're not really doily people," she'd said to Ben, "but it seems wrong not to keep some of these—they're exquisite." Now, as her fingers felt the stitching, she knew the tiny mats would probably hang around for as long as they lived in this house.

Elsie's house, thought Lucy. Elsie Veronica Gormley. She'd seen the woman's name on the contract, and she'd pressed the neighbors for any more details. Elsie must have been around ninety, they'd said, and she'd lived here a very long time. She and her husband had bought the house when it was built, back in the forties, and they'd lived here with their twins, a boy and a girl. Her husband had died—no one could quite remember when; no one had been here that long.

And then she'd fallen. And then she'd gone.

"I think they chose to sell to you because you're a family," the estate agent had said as she'd slid the contracts across her cluttered desk.

"We'll look after it," Lucy said as she signed her name and passed them on to Ben.

"Meant to be," he said, squinting through his glasses as he signed.

There was a tiny whisper in the darkness from some of the seventeen circles they'd found drilled into the different rooms' floors when the carpet had been taken up.

"Circumference of a broom handle," Ben had said. "We should stopper them up." But he hadn't done that yet, and the wind sometimes caught at them, stirring puffs of air like little breaths.

Lucy checked on Tom and headed back to bed, rattling the front doorknob as she went by.

"We should change the locks," she'd said to Ben earlier that day. "You should always change the locks when you buy a house."

"What?" Ben had laughed. "What do you think is going to happen? Elsie's going to let herself in?"

"Elsie's family—how many keys might there be in the world?"

Now, in the darkness, her fingers fiddled with the door lock's button. *Safe and sound, safe and sound, safe and sound.* It was like a line from a lullaby.

In the quietness of the middle of the night, she turned these words end over end in her head, dropping back into sleep beside her husband and his warmth.

~

Elsie woke at three, disoriented by the hum of an air conditioner nearby. *Three in the afternoon*, she thought, looking at her watch. *How could they have let me sleep so long—I've missed breakfast and lunch, and there was a bus I wanted to catch.*

She buttoned her cardigan, and as she felt around for her shoes, her handbag, her hat, she knocked the vase that Don had brought for her, cracking it into four or five pieces as it smashed against the floor. She'd never liked it—it had been a present from one of Clem's friends when they were first married. She dropped the pieces into the rubbish bin, wondering why it was so dark. Then she heard the rain against the window and nodded. This time of year, you could expect a thundery shower on a Brisbane afternoon.

She looked into the street: it was very quiet, and although she watched and watched, no cars or buses came. Perhaps there was a strike she didn't know about. Still, it wasn't far to walk: through the park towards the river and then along the road.

She'd see her garden, her lilies, her hydrangeas, her azaleas. She'd see how they'd fixed the front door—Donny said it was bright red now, which she wasn't sure about—and how the walls inside had all been stripped of their carefully papered patterns.

She smiled: there and back in an hour. She'd feel like herself again once she was home. She'd let this strange dark rain ease up before she went.

≈

The next morning, taking Tom into the garden, Lucy paused at the top of the stairs, registering the stray flecks of the new front-door paint spattered on the porch's balustrade. Such a strong color, somewhere between vermilion and scarlet. Fire engine, Lucy had called it, but Ben revised it—"lipstick"—with a smile. Lucy loved how brazenly bright it was.

She scratched at a splatter, then levered the color from under her fingernail and rolled it into a ball. Their new place. Leaning out from the top of the stairs, she saw the park, the busy through road beyond that, the streaks of shiny color as the cars zoomed by. Hours of entertainment: Tom would love it.

There was a shimmer of movement and a kookaburra landed on the power line, its feathers soft and furry and its head tilted to one side, expectant.

"Hello," said Lucy. "Are you a regular here? Look, sweetheart, isn't he beautiful?" She turned Tom around to see the bird's smooth feathers, its still trust.

A car came around the corner then and the bird took flight, before settling itself farther along the wire. Lucy raised her hand, uncertain if she was waving to the car, to the bird, to the house, or the morning itself. Then she helped Tom down each step.

The kookaburra sat, watching.

"Well done, love," Lucy said as Tom reached the last tread. "The first step in being somewhere new." She smiled. "And later, we'll head out and explore."

As she turned to herd his steps across the lawn, she saw footprints, smaller than her own and closely set, already pressed into the still-wet grass.

2

The clock

IN THE morning, Elsie slept through the time for breakfast and for morning tea. She slept through the time she could have joined the garden club and the time she could have joined a game of lawn bowls. When she woke, the sun was near its midday peak, blasting the flowers on the jacaranda tree by her window to an impossible luminosity. It looked hot out there: she waited for the day to dim.

In the old days, she and Clem had walked the streets at dusk this time of year—October and into November—inhaling the color of these flowers. Had they been walking again? She rubbed at her calves and her shins: what had she been doing to make that ache?

Then her mind slipped into another time and place. It made perfect sense. It reminded her of reading *Alice in Wonderland* to Donny and Elaine, and then to the grandkids. It was like following Alice down a rabbit hole. She heard a bell ring nearby and knew that lunch would now be served. Might as well eat in the dining room as fuss about with cooking.

"I think it's chicken, Mrs. Gormley," said the Cheshire Cat, sliding a plate onto her placemat as she sat down. "Lovely to see you today."

It was quite a pleasant way to pass the time. In some moments, she thought her mind might just be wandering—that was the phrase people liked to use—but wasn't it nicer to wander off into your memories, instead of holding them at arm's length? Surely it was nicer to feel yourself back in the moment when your husband was ten minutes away from home than to remember that he'd been dead for thirty-seven years now, and would not be home again?

All this nonsense about which day of the week it was and who was the prime minister—Elsie had never cared much for politics. Everyone shouting at everyone else and not a skerrick of manners in sight. Here was Clem, coming through the park; here were Elaine and Don, kitted out for their first day at school—way back in the summer of 1947.

Little things; her little things. Swinging their big bags up onto their shoulders and setting off through the school gate. Donny so quick with his numbers—she didn't know where he got that from—and Lainey always top with her reading. Elsie could have burst with pride at the pair of them: and here they were, running back across the high-school yard, twelve years later, straight past her and into their lives. Ah well, Donny had made a happy go of it. But Elaine: no matter how muddled the stuff of all her memories, Elsie tripped up on Elaine's disappointments. One of the last talks she'd had with Clem (here it came, unspooling like a length of film) was about his worry that they hadn't done enough to encourage their girl.

"But her baby—she had Gloria," Elsie had said. "What more could she have wanted than that?"

"I reckon she'd a head for learning," Clem said, reaching over to turn off the bedside lamp and finishing the conversation in the dark. "I reckon we did her a disservice, not pushing her more towards that. I reckon we could have done more." Those last words eaten by his horrible cough.

Elsie braced against the side of the table, almost pushing herself to standing to get away from this memory. *No, I don't want that today.* She looked at her chicken and found herself hungry, wolfing it down, while she let herself imagine gliding along the river in the handy boat that Clem had always talked of building, scavenged from bits and pieces he'd found in the swampy dump by the back of their place. That was better than hearing sharp words from long ago.

On the shelves in her new bedroom Donny had set up the bracket clock that Clem's great-grandfather had brought around the world from Kent to Brisbane. Clem had loved the sound of the clock's tick, and after lunch, Elsie lay on her bed again, her ears attuned to the beat of its pendulum. It was a drum. It was a footfall. It was the rain. It was her life.

"You'll have that clock when I go, Donny," she said to him when he came in to see her later. "You'll take good care of it. It's all that's left now of your father's family."

"All that's left, apart from us," he said.

She smiled, reaching up to pat his faded ginger hair. "You look just like your father, young man." She could say anything to her son—a stray memory; a sudden segue; a question from the depths of distant time—and he took it in his stride.

"Young man!" He gave her a smile in return. "We're seventy next year, Elaine and I." He held her hand tight for a while. "Carol will love the clock," he said then. "I remember her talking to Dad about it—years ago, when we were first married. They were fond of each other, you know."

Bless him for reminding her; she couldn't tell him that his wife entwined sometimes in her mind with his sullen sister, and she could spend a whole morning wondering why her Donny had married such a woman before she unknotted the mess, located his real life, and settled herself back into some happiness with his world.

"I was thinking about your first day at school, love," she said in a while. "How little and brave you looked—how it all went by so quickly."

"Your next great-grandchild will be at school before you know it, Mum—we'll have to bring you along for that day."

And bless him for imagining her future.

"Wind it for me, Donny?" She nodded to the clock on its shelf. "I don't like the idea it might stop." And she watched as he fitted the key into its clean white face and turned it; she loved the sound of its gears. She loved its buffer against the silence.

"You know I'm going to marry Clement Gormley," she said above the mechanical crick of the clockwork. "I met him the other week—just when war was declared. I was coming through the city on a tram and decided to hop off in Adelaide Street. He's a lovely man, very gentle. I think you'll like him, when you meet him. Should we have a little drink in celebration?"

"I'll put the kettle on," said Don, emptying her bedside jug of water into the potted plant that stood on the sill. It was an orchid and so perfectly white that she wondered if he was rubbing its petals to see if they were real. "Who brought you this, Mum?"

Did they ask these things to be polite, she wondered, or to check how much she knew?

"Gloria sent it—from London. It came the other day. Lovely girl, that Gloria. A shame she and her mother never found a way to be friends. A shame she never had kids of her own. I thought Glory's kids would be my first great-grandchildren. And she'd have been such a good mum."

"I'm sure Elaine and Gloria are friends in their own way," said Don carefully, heading over to the kitchen. "It's not everyone who takes to mothering like you did, and like Carol. Gloria was lucky she had you to make a fuss of her. All our kids were."

"I remember walking you and Elaine to school one morning,"

said Elsie. "She was so little—but she wouldn't hold my hand. And she saw this girl, the little sister of someone in her class, I think, all pigtails and a pretty frock. 'Do I have to do that, Mama?' she asked me. I always thought she meant wear her hair like that, or the frilliness of the dress—but maybe she meant having a child. Maybe I never heard them right, the things Lainey tried to tell me."

Elsie's hand was stretched out, as if to hold the hand of her tiny daughter. In this memory, the jacarandas were so thick and rich overhead that they seemed to make a canopy as wide as the sky. From beyond the footpath came the sound of hinged windows as a veranda was opened up. Elsie began to hum the music she could hear now from inside the house.

"In the old days," she said as Donny came back with the tea, "they held dances in one of the houses by the school; all the women in pretty dresses, twirling and spinning in the night. I used to walk up in the evenings trying to catch the breeze at the crest of the hill. It was like peeking into a jewelry box, watching them all at their fun."

"Did you ever go, you and Dad? Did you ever go to those dances?" Don was holding out a teacup, its china pure white against the sun-spotted skin of his hands.

"Did we ever go?" Elsie frowned at her son's hands; how old they looked. "I wanted to—I can't remember. I had a silver dress I wanted to wear: did anyone pack that? I can't remember seeing it since I came here. Although I suppose there's not much call for dancing. I still see your father sometimes, over there by the dressing table." She pointed to the corner where a single armchair sat. No mirror. No dressing table. No stool. "He comes home from time to time."

"Give him my love, and I'll head off now," said Don then, downing his tea in a gulp. "I've got to take one of the boys to his swimming—a full-time job, these little ones." He rattled his cup against its saucer. "Pop in again tomorrow. I drove past the old

17

place yesterday; someone's done the front garden—I thought you'd like to know how neat it looks. They're already planting trees; Dad'd be complaining about the mowing. But it's looking lovely."

"Yes," said Elsie, wistful. "Yes." She blew him a series of kisses as he went, her lovely bright boy. He looked older now than she was, although she didn't suppose that could be true. Such a surprise, when Lainey had slipped out in his wake; she hadn't known she was having twins. *Like all my Christmases had come at once*, thought Elsie. She'd been poleaxed by how utterly and completely she loved them.

She'd look up sometimes when she was bent over helping them with their homework, entranced with the idea that she was guiding them towards some solution, some new piece of knowledge— entranced that she might have that power—and she'd catch sight of a softness in her husband's face and she'd smile.

"You make such a lovely mum, Else," Clem had said, and she said it was all she could do.

It was all she'd ever wanted.

She blew another kiss as she watched her son cross the garden to his car, and he paused, looked up and waved—for all the world as if he'd felt it.

We've got something special, you and me. It used to scare her to even think such a thing about her son, but she'd always known it was true. And there he went, two toots on the horn as always, and a cheery wave through the window.

Whereas her daughter—Elsie frowned. Never so much as a backwards glance. She shook her head: how had she gone wrong with her girl? In the forties, when Elaine was just tiny? In the fifties, when she was at school? In the sixties, when she did what Elsie had always hoped for—found a husband, had a child.

"Be the making of her," Elsie had whispered to Clem. But he shook his head.

How right he had been. When all Elsie ever wanted was her daughter's happiness.

The way Elaine spoke to her: so cold, Elsie sometimes waited for her to call her "Mrs. Gormley."

It was the puzzle of her life. *What else could I have done? How else should I have been?*

The hands of the clock inched around to three—they'd be in from school soon, and ravenous. Elsie looked around her new rooms—the clock, the orchid, the spackled ceiling, the shiny sink and bench—thinking of her old kitchen, with its heavy, rounded fridge and its cream and green enamelled biscuit barrel. But her world, her real world, had gone, submerged by a strange wash of time. She drank the last of the tea her son had made for her, stone cold now and in the wrong cup. Even Donny hadn't found her favorite one to bring.

In the bathroom she stood splashing water onto her face—she must have splashed through a riverload of water in her years in this city, keeping herself cool through Brisbane's summers. Now, she knew, another summer was on its way. Elsie loved the way the heat pressed against every plane of her skin.

She sized up the image in the mirror. Age seemed to have come on so quickly. "I have no idea who you are or why you're here," she said clearly, and she took a mouthful of water and sloshed it around, then spat it onto the troubling reflection.

When she tried the door to the hallway—the one by which Donny had left—it seemed jammed, somehow, or locked.

She closed her eyes, determined to think herself through.

3

The pendulum

FROM THE long couch in the middle of the living room, Lucy watched the closed front door. For the first time in as long as she could remember, she had a house to herself. Ben had taken Tom to see the purple brilliance of the jacarandas along the river, and she'd walked awkwardly through the handful of empty rooms in the little cottage, unsure what to do, before slumping on the sofa for a while, still and quiet. It was bliss just to be on her own—no one she had to pay attention to.

Houses could feel so different when you had them to yourself. She remembered, long ago, being home on her own after school— she was seven years old, her three sisters busy in other places, and her mother still at work. Most days, Lucy hadn't minded her mother being at work—her mother was a doctor, a "general practitioner." Lucy had loved the sound of so many syllables, such very long words. And most days there was something exciting about being home on your own. Something grown-up.

But that day, when she was seven, the house had felt different—lonely and bare. Lucy didn't want her mother to be working; she wanted her mother to be sitting at home waiting for her, like her friend Astrid's mother did. She wanted her to be sitting at the kitchen bench, like Astrid's mother did, with a glass of milk poured and three homemade peanut-butter biscuits laid out on a small plate with a striped edge.

Lucy had looked at the empty kitchen. She looked at the full milk bottle in the fridge, and the mug her mother had left ready for her on the table. She looked at the biscuit barrel, full of plain biscuits bought at the supermarket. And then she ran away to Astrid's house, where she was exhilarated to be gorging herself on seven of the famous biscuits, and asked for two refills for her glass.

"My pleasure—any time," said Astrid's mother, Linnea, as she filled the glass again. "It's always lovely to see you."

And then Lucy and Astrid played in the garden—a complex game where each separate path was a different room in some enormous mansion—until the light dropped and Linnea sent Lucy home.

She was letting herself in at the back door when her mother came in at the front calling, "Hello? Lucy-Lu? How was your day, sweetheart?" And she realized that the whole excursion had been secret. She'd run away, and no one had noticed.

Now she sat inside this new house. It felt friendly. It felt good. Of the five offers made, theirs had been chosen. Maybe it was because they were a family, as the agent had said, but Lucy took it as a sign, as if the house had chosen them.

In the time since they'd moved in, she'd busied herself with the usual tasks and rhythms of Tom's days—the good ones; the great ones; the ones that sparked with pure frustration, hers or his. There was a perpetual motion to parenting; no one had told her about that.

There was so much new life here. The yard was full of new birds, new bugs, new butterflies. Lustrous beetles glowed on the doorstep, and a python had crossed the road beside the river, right there in front of her and Tom. The spiders' webs spanned entire footpaths, wide and strong and golden in the light, with their residents as big as saucers in the center.

Hanging out their welcome, Lucy thought, watching one glisten through the window from her spot on the sofa. It was exquisite, but who knew which ones might bite?

"Our little home," Ben said sometimes at the end of the day, when Tom was tucked in and asleep. He was remembering so many things about the place he'd left almost thirty years before, somehow alive with its history, its geography, its heat now that he'd returned. It was as if he was pulling out the pieces of an old jigsaw puzzle, turning them over and recognizing how they might all fit together. She'd never heard him speak so much about this place—and the jigsaw's picture was mostly mysterious to her.

"I'm still not so sure where I am," she'd said to each of her parents, ringing her mother at her busy doctor's practice, her father in his studio by the beach. She was used to settling quickly somewhere new.

But if she was honest, she hadn't quite known where she was since Tom was born. Nothing dramatic, just a kind of wrong-footedness from moving too quickly through different sensations: anxious, joyous, watchful, bored, and back.

"A whole new life," Ben had whispered when they'd brought their baby home. She saw now that was about them as much as Tom.

"Take your vitamins," her mother told her. "It's exhausting, moving cities, and with Tom."

"Get Ben to take you to the beach for the weekend," her father said. "That's all that's wrong with Brisbane: there's no beach."

In the garden now, two crows cawed, their calls harsh and sudden, and Lucy jumped with surprise at the noise.

She was differently attuned to sound these days. Even when Tom slept, she was aware of and anticipating the moment he'd wake up. Crying. It seemed he mostly woke up crying—another thing no one had mentioned as a possibility of motherhood and one that made her heart ache.

Now, in the house, in its silence, she wanted a different kind of sound. Standing with her arms stretched high, she pulled a CD down from the shelf and put it into the player. It was an old compilation of nineties songs; she couldn't remember where it had come from. She waited for the disc to load, and cranked up the volume.

She couldn't remember the last time she'd danced either—unless you counted swaying through a lullaby. Her father had told her once that she looked like a tree in a breeze when she moved to music, and she'd held onto that compliment, loving the idea of herself stretched out, sinuous and moving free. She wasn't tall—"average everything," she always joked—and she was rarely graceful. Now, just a year shy of forty, and always a little bit tired, she felt slower and duller sometimes, as if she needed to urge herself forward.

But when her body, her arms, her legs began to move in time to music, any music, she was a different being, extended and alive. It was as if the movement was drawn out of her, one long fluid line pulling her up and away. She scooped her long red hair up onto the top of her head, watching her reflection in the window. Her arms made a canopy over the space in which she moved.

A staccato four-beat drove on beneath song after song; she loved its insistence. It reminded her of the little pendulum that had marked out the tick and the tock of music lessons in her childhood, reliable and clear, while the melody played and curled across the top. She loved the predictable and perpetual beat of that plumb, the regular and contained arc it made from one side to the other, on and on. She tapped it out, that safe sound that kept music in check.

And then she started to sing along.

She'd always sung. Her mother had sent her off to singing lessons for years, and she'd won prizes in eisteddfods and talent shows. Her mother had thought she should try for the music conservatory, but she didn't. She did an arts degree, a couple of drama subjects, and took a touch-typing course on the side. She took short contracts to work in university offices, traveling in between—and she became known for her knack of unraveling any problem, reorganizing any mess, meeting the most impossible of deadlines.

Fixing things.

"I thought you'd make more of yourself," said her mum.

"As long as you like what you do," said her dad.

What she loved was standing in a crush of people at a gig, the whole darkened room shouting the words of a song straight back at the performer on the stage. That was power; that was life. That kind of communion she loved.

It was a long time since she'd felt that: the last gig she'd been to, before Tom was born, she'd suddenly felt scared among the bodies—felt him kicking hard inside her as if he were afraid too.

"I need some air," she'd shouted at Ben and gone outside, not knowing she wouldn't go back.

Now, there was a thrumming silence; the music had stopped, and the crows were quiet too. Across the street, someone was knocking on a door, and then she heard a cheery greeting called.

It was funny; she must have filled thousands of hours before there was Tom—all the things she'd done, on her own, for herself. Now she fought to keep herself away from the washing that needed folding, the dinner she might start to cook. No. She wanted sound. She wanted movement. She wanted to feel like her old self. She notched up the volume, sent the CD around again.

Perhaps Elsie had danced here, in this room. Perhaps she'd sung too. Could you sense that, the traces of earlier moments? She waited, but could hear only the slam of the back flyscreen and a corresponding thump somewhere outside—something knocked down by the wind. There were often things moving and bumping in the crawl space, above and below. She tried not to think of the python: this whole city seemed wildly alive.

Or maybe it was a bit of Elsie, left behind. Lucy raised her hand to the empty room. "Hi," she said aloud, feeling foolish all the same. *As if Elsie would come back and let herself in.*

The songs looped again, and Lucy felt them beat into her body. She drifted into the kitchen, still humming along as she flicked on the kettle to make tea.

"You even lived in London and you never drank the stuff," Ben had marveled that morning. "I wonder why you've started now—some late-onset postpartum tastebud glitch?"

"You and your grown-up descriptions." She'd laughed at him. The answer was behind the beveled glass of one of the kitchen cabinets. A teacup, saucerless; a slightly fluted cream cup with a big blue floral blaze.

Peonies, thought Lucy, *and something like a fuchsia.* She'd found it forgotten at the back edge of the deck, the sludgy-mud rime of its last cup of tea still coating its bottom. For a few days, washing it with every load of dishes she thought of returning it to Elsie—ringing the estate agent, or looking up the address on the settlement papers. Then, on a whim, she'd taken it from the kitchen bench and made herself a cup of tea. One of Ben's teabags. Weak, no milk; sharpened with a small slice of lemon. You could tell it was the drink the house was used to—there was no room for a coffee machine on the narrow bench top, and the decor predated anything hippie and herbal (as Ben liked to call such things) by several decades.

Now, she drank her tea, savoring its warmth as she stood by the kitchen table, until the beat of the music made her set down the cup to tap the bass line of the song with both her hands. Her wedding ring clinked a kind of percussion, and she jibed and swayed to its beat. There was a particular shape to this music, something low and funky that made her feel at least a decade younger.

And then she was back there, in a dark room thick with people. She was wearing a long red dress that left her back bare and she was tracing shapes across the skin of her neck, her chest, her collarbones with an ice cube that dripped, delicious, down her skin. The room was hot and the audience pressed in closer. She was shouting this song back to a singer six feet away on a tiny stage.

She was standing on her own. She'd never felt more completely alive.

The music. The cool wetness. The dark room and the close air. It was summer and she was on her own for the first time in years. She had left Ferdi Klim and just about felt as if she could fly. Ferdi Klim. Their names hooked together for years on end, and then she'd walked off to find her own space. And felt invincible—even now, her body stretched higher, straighter with the memory of ice tracing her warm skin. That was who she wanted to be, the woman who reached out for more.

It took a moment for her to realize that there was another noise nearby, and it slammed her back to the present. She grabbed at her loud ringing phone.

Another thing she hadn't understood all the years before Tom came along: motherhood's terror—extremity, catastrophe, terror. The crazy swing from love to dread that could disrupt the most nondescript day. No mother she'd known had talked of it: not her sisters, nor her own mother, nor the friends she'd left behind in every place they'd lived.

There were so many things to worry about—Tom himself, and the spiders in the garden; the planet; and everything in between. She couldn't bear to watch the news. Some twins, she'd heard the edge of a report just this morning, had been starved to death by their own mother in this very city. She'd broken a plate in her hurry to switch off the radio.

Now, she scooped her phone off the counter. Ben was ringing to tell her something dreadful. Something had happened. By the river. Something had happened to Tom.

And then the ringing stopped, just as suddenly as it had started, and Lucy stared at the silent screen. There was no number listed.

All the smoothness, all the music's joy fell away from her body.

She hadn't been like this before. Easy come, easy go; easy even with the randomness of life. Now, every hiccup, every unknown, was a crevasse into which she could fall.

In other countries, she'd read once, there were spirits who traveled ahead of you in time, doing the things you'd do next. Alone in the house, she stood still to remember their name. Not a doppelgänger. Not an alter ego. *Vardøger*: that was it. It was Norwegian. She'd typed a paper for someone once—a professor in London, who specialized in Norse mythology—and she'd liked the sound of these creatures. "They never threaten, never frighten," he told her. "Some people hear the *vardøger*; some people see them. Perhaps you hear something busily going about its business and doing whatever it does. And then, a short while later, the person themself arrives, and does all those things. It's like a premonition, a future self."

The security, the comfort, of a version of yourself gone on ahead.

The Vardøger of Lucy Kiss: Ben had joked about taking the phrase as the title for a novel. But what would her future self be doing? She'd loved this game when she was pregnant with Tom, holding onto an idea of herself somewhere ahead, with her baby safely delivered. She'd always be calm, always fabulous, the kind of mother who could take a toy, a snack, from an elegant tote bag at a moment's notice. Instead of her current self, lugging Tom's stuff jumbled together in an old conference bag of Ben's, in the bowels of which she could rarely find a thing.

From outside, she heard footsteps pounding along the bitumen: if that was her *vardøger*, it was running away.

Then there were voices in the street, and laughter. Rinsing her cup at the sink, Lucy leaned forward to try to see the speakers. The cup clattered onto the draining board as her phone rang again, and she grabbed it, registering Ben's name on its screen.

"Hello?" Her heart pounded; the line was completely silent. "Hello? Ben? Hello?"

4

The wedding

EARLY IN the morning of her daughter's wedding day, Elsie woke with a jolt in the darkness, holding tight to her husband's left hand. It was the excitement, she told herself. She'd been married just ahead of her own twentieth birthday, in the spring of 1940, and now here was her daughter, twenty years old herself and taking the same big step as 1961 tipped into winter.

There was a symmetry to it, thought Elsie as she watched the silver-mauve light before sunrise. Perhaps it would set something to rights—because there was no doubt that Elaine had never been as happy a child as Elsie had hoped she might have been. Not that Elsie usually voiced this, even to herself. But this marriage, to Gerald—the most equable of men, and already doing well for himself in something to do with the mines—this would be the making of her.

Following in my footsteps and *I'm very proud*, Elsie practiced, imagining the ladies who would offer their congratulations after the ceremony at the church beyond the ridge. It was a pretty place, with a spire on the roof and a small pipe organ inside. A young man would play the Mendelssohn wedding march, with its short, sharp, declarative beginning, and all would be as it should be.

I'm very proud, Elsie practiced again. She would stand with her husband, beside her daughter and her brand-new son-in-law. They would smile for the photographs. She squeezed Clem's hand and he snorted a little in response.

"I'll put the kettle on," she said as he stirred, as he woke. "Might as well make a start on the day."

"Come here, Else." He reached for her but she was buttoning her dressing gown.

"Things to do. Things to do."

The rest of the house was quiet. The door to her son's room stood open, as always, while the door to her daughter's was shut. On her own wedding morning, Elsie remembered, she'd been up before the birds with the excitement of it, nudging her sister, and getting in and out of her frock—a pale green one that she loved, overlaid with a new chiffon skirt embroidered with tiny pink roses—three times before breakfast.

Her mum and her sister had come down from Bundaberg on the train and she remembered the laughter of their preparations ahead of the service on that bright spring day. They were neither of them with her today, her mother dead a dozen years, and her sister away on the other side of the country; she missed their chatting and their humor. She'd never found other confidantes quite like them, although she'd hoped Elaine might be one. It would have to be enough to sit and write a letter about it all in the quiet of this evening, while Elaine and Gerald spent the first night of their honeymoon at a smart hotel down on the Gold Coast.

The start of a new life for them: what a thing.

Elsie stood at the kitchen window, rocking the teapot as its leaves steeped and watching two lorikeets busy in a bottlebrush. There was a soft noise behind her and she turned to see her daughter turning away from the doorway and heading for the bathroom.

"Good morning to you, Lainey—I was going to bring you a cup," she called, ahead of the bathroom door's click.

"I'll fix one for myself," her daughter called, and then came the noise of running water.

Rightio, thought Elsie. Nothing was going to rankle her—until she carried the tea through to Clem and caught sight of Elaine's room, packed into suitcases and boxes as if ready for evacuation.

"Did you know?" she hissed to her husband. "It's not just her holiday she's packed for—she's moving out."

Clem took a deep draught of the tea before he answered. "Of course she's moving out, Else—she's getting married. She probably thought she'd save herself the bother of having to do it when she came home, or save you the bother while she was away. I told her I'd drive her things up to their new place tomorrow."

Elsie shook her head, her hand unsteady as she held the pretty cream and blue cup. "As long as she's happy," she said. "What more could I want?" But her voice sounded small and defeated.

"He's a good man, that Gerald," said Clem, setting down his empty cup. "We've got nothing to worry about there." A curse came from the bathroom on the other side of the wall. "And she won't miss our tiny tank of hot water." Clem laughed, and Elsie did her best to smile.

She didn't mean to be standing by the bathroom door when her daughter came out, but she was.

"Was I that long?" said Elaine, reaching for the handle to close her bedroom door behind her.

"Oh, love, no. Of course not." She was wrong-footed by whatever her daughter said, nine times out of ten. "I just thought you might like a hand—with your hair, or your dress?"

But Elaine shook her head. "I can manage. You just look after yourself. Gerald said your car would come at ten."

Smart cars, and a reception with chicken and champagne. *What more could I want?* Elsie nudged the water heater into action, waiting until the flow ran hot again.

But while Clem and Don ate breakfast and put on their suits

and sat waiting on the back deck for the fuss—as Donny called it—to begin, Elsie sat in the quiet of her own bedroom, conscious only of the similar quiet in Elaine's. *I should take her something—I should do something—I should be there.* Her own mother had brushed Elsie's clean hair to a shine on her wedding day, then twisted it into an elegant chignon. Her sister had made pot after pot of tea. And there'd been laughter, so much laughter.

Today, she didn't know how to cross her own hallway.

She watched the different angles of her reflection in the three-paneled mirror of her dressing table; there wasn't a flicker of movement or emotion on her face in any of them. She looked neither happy nor sad, more stern. It usually calmed her, sitting here, still, the house quiet around her. Today, her stomach roiled and caught, a mess of unknown things.

It was a funny idea, handing your daughter into marriage—did it make you less of a mother somehow? Who would she be now, her daughter grown up and gone away to a smart little flat up the hill? Would her own life change too?

She didn't want that. She didn't want anything else. Was she supposed to?

Well, she still had Donald—although he was getting earnest about that Carol. And perhaps there'd be grandchildren soon.

More than enough to go on, she thought. *And around the great loop we all go.*

She zipped up the new dress she'd chosen for this day. It was a deeper green than her own wedding dress had been, worn with a loose coat of rich green shantung. She patted a fine dust of powder across her face, lightly combed her set hair, its brown starting to fade and mottle, and glossed her lips with as bright a shade as she'd let herself choose in the chemist's. When Gerald's sister came—a pretty girl a year or so older than Elaine, and in a lilac version of Elaine's wedding dress—Elsie was standing on the front steps to welcome her.

"Mrs. Gormley, you look so lovely," the girl said, her arms filled with flowers, a single pink rose for Elsie's lapel, and a pale orb—creams, whites, the softest pinks and yellows—for the bride. Its stems were bound together to make a kind of floral lollipop. "Have you seen her? She won't be nervous—I've never known anyone as self-assured as Elaine. It's marvelous, isn't it? I dream of having that kind of confidence."

Elsie smiled and held out her hands for the flowers. "And you look lovely too, dear," she said. "I'll take those in for Lainey before I go on in the car." She'd never thought of Elaine's stillness as confidence.

As she pushed open the door to her daughter's bedroom—registering it as the last time it would be her daughter's bedroom—she swallowed the salt edge of tears and stepped forward. She held the flowers at her waist as if she was walking in a procession. Elaine stood, a straight slip of a thing in a white dress by a sunlit window, and her mother did cry then.

"Did you want something else?" Her daughter's voice was flat and Elsie stumbled.

"Just the flowers—here, your flowers." Pushing them forward.

She wiped at the tears on her cheeks and stood, her hands working around each other like a machine.

Elaine held the flowers in front of her body, turning them slowly like a great pastel-colored wheel.

"I thought there'd be more to it than this," she said at last.

The way the pulse throbbed, fast, beneath her daughter's skin; the way the tendons in her neck stood out, taut.

"Oh, love—I think they're gorgeous," Elsie said at last. "A bigger bouquet and you'd quite disappear."

5

The call

LUCY STARED at the phone, at the timer ticking on: ten seconds, fifteen, but every time she raised it to her ear, there was only the same entire silence. She stabbed at the red hang-up button with her thumb, and the screen changed again.

She pressed the phone against her belly and felt her stomach churn. Why was it so easy to be alarmed? Why assume it was bad news? Why assume anything?

And she made herself take a deep breath.

Perhaps, before, it was Elsie, trying to ring to introduce herself. That was a better fantasy than disaster. *Perhaps it was another me, just ringing to tell me I'm fine.* But where was Ben? Where was Tom? She dialed Ben's number and it went straight through to voicemail.

Lucy shook her head, hanging up the call and pulling up the browser on the phone. Distraction. She wanted distraction.

This word, *vardøger*: she wished she could hold it in front of herself like a shield. She typed it into the search engine. *A form of bilocation*, she read. *Déjà vu, but in reverse.* Scrolling down, she focused on phrases that underscored what she remembered. *A*

Norwegian word defined as the "premonitory sound or sight of a person before he arrives."

Or she, thought Lucy, fumbling the phone as it began to ring again.

"Ben? Where are you? What's happening?"

She heard him this time, safe and sound and asking, simply, for a water bottle. He'd forgotten to take one for Tom. "Don't know what happened last time—I was shouting at my end. You didn't hear?"

"I'll come now." The sound of her heartbeat surged in her ears—fast, then dropping back. A drink of water: the most basic request. She could do that. Of course they were fine.

"Take your time—take a break—there's no—"

"No. I'd like to come and find you now." On the brink of saying she hadn't known what to do with herself; on the brink of saying she'd been scared.

In the bathroom, she watched herself in the mirror as she ran the water hot to wash her face and melt away the last memory of that long-ago ice with one of Tom's soft, fluffy washers. As if she needed to return to being a mother walking out to meet her husband and her son. Sometimes Ben left the cabinet's mirrored door slightly open and when Lucy looked up, expecting to see herself, she found she'd been erased from the room by its angle. It surprised her every time.

She dried her face, filled Tom's drink bottle, and tapped at the screen of her phone, calling up the map of her new local streets. No matter how much she concentrated, she couldn't get her bearings in this place—as if the city were always shifting; as if its landmarks were always in play. She plotted her course: left, right, left, right, right, and then over the bridge. Really, how hard could it be?

She set off, humming one of the songs from the CD. Her footsteps fell in time with the beat as she jogged along, and she stumbled once or twice—on a gutter, on the rough and rocky path of the cemetery beside the bridge.

Crossing over, running on, she had the strangest sense of someone keeping pace beside her, until she turned and saw that it was her own reflection, tracking along in a bus shelter's wide sheets of glass.

～

At the other end of the day, coming into the kitchen after settling Tom, Lucy leaned against the doorjamb with a sigh.

"Did I ever tell you, before Tom was born, that I was scared I'd put him down in a room full of babies and not be able to recognize him when I had to pick him up? I didn't know if I'd know who was mine."

Ben swirled two Moscow Mules, mixing their ingredients with the wrong end of a knife, and passed one across to her. He made an elaborate drink each evening, imbuing its choice and presentation with a kind of ceremony. "You really had no idea, did you, Lu?"

"None at all." She sipped the drink, licking the spicy sweetness of the ginger beer's bubbles from her lips as she reached around to the stereo and flicked its switch. Her songs were there, waiting, and Lucy clicked along. "Sometimes, later, I'd catch a glimpse of myself and Tom in a window as we walked along a street, and I'd look around for the lady with the baby before I remembered it was me. At least I knew what he looked like then."

"God." Ben laughed. "You can make yourself sound crazy." He nodded with the music, his fingers tapping to its tune. "I haven't heard this song in years."

She took another sip. "The nineties. This is what I was playing today in my hour of solitude—don't you love the beat? The way the rhythm folds into itself? The beat ticks away like those little pendulums they have in music class."

"Pendulums? Don't you mean metronomes? It's no wonder you're terrible at crosswords." He tilted his drink at her—a fake toast.

Lucy blushed. She hated it when Ben corrected her; he never got words wrong. "Pendulum, metronome, whatever. I remember hearing this song at a gig," she said, "years ago. I'm not even sure where it was—but it was summer, and it was great."

She put her arms around her husband, humming the chorus and singing a phrase here and there as they danced around the kitchen.

"Anyway, who cares about words?" she said, pulling him along, until the song stopped and they paused.

"Who cares about words?" Ben dipped her in mock outrage, leaning in farther to give her a kiss. "I don't know about that."

Later, when he was in the shower, Lucy clipped on a set of headphones and piped the songs into her head. Lying on the living room floor with the lights off, she scanned along the spines of their CDs and picked out the shapes of their possessions: the sofa from London, the rug from Tashkent, the photos she'd bought by the Seine. There was a story for every thing they owned. Elsie's bleached and starched white doily glowed on a chair's arm like a burst of starlight. *How sad that something made so carefully ends up thrown away.* Now it was just another story Lucy would tell.

All the things they'd brought into this house; all of Elsie's things, packed up and taken away. A world delineated by this ebb and flow of items. The stuff of people's lives.

Her mind drifted as the song went round and round. And now there were so many people. *Maybe we're out of originals. Maybe these days most of us are* vardøger, *living versions of a finite set of lives.*

I wonder what the other Lucy Kisses are doing tonight?

Did you have just one *vardøger*, scurrying ahead, or did new iterations of yourself peel off whenever you made a decision? All the other incarnations of Lucy Kiss who'd traveled to different places, met different people, taken different jobs, different lovers, different paths.

She pushed her fingers against her eyes and watched the darkness sparkle. Perhaps all the Lucy Kisses were lying on their living room floors right now, listening to this song, tapping along to its bass line, remembering when they'd heard it, years ago, one summer, on their own. Surely one of them was standing in a pub right now, singing and dancing. Surely one of them was still living that life.

She hoped so.

She pulled off the headphones and sat up. No time for nostalgia. She had five hours, six at the most, before Tom would wake up for another day.

At the other end of the house, he coughed as if he'd heard her. And she crept into his room, where she kissed him and rested her hand against his head for a while. This person who remade, recast every single piece of her life: no wonder that she sometimes tripped up.

In her own bed, she waited for Ben. And when he climbed in and reached out his hand, she grabbed it and held on, holding fast to this here and this now.

6

The sitting

IT WAS a quiet Sunday morning. Clem was busy with some project in the garage downstairs, and the bells from the church on the ridge had just stopped ringing. If Elsie thought of religion—of churches, of believing—she thought of bells: a pretty sound that drifted in from somewhere else but which didn't have much to do with her world.

After nine, she thought as the chimes faded. *Rising ten.* She'd give Elaine one last quick call—bless Gerald for these telephones—and then she'd get ready for her strange morning meeting.

Three days earlier, Elsie had been standing on an empty curbside watching a big dark car speed by. It was a shiny black Mercedes with huge oval headlights and two neat little fins pinched onto its tail, just like the cars they'd hired for Elaine's wedding ten months before. A man was driving, with a woman sitting in the back. Elsie caught a flash of something like the deep green color she'd worn to her daughter's wedding and almost raised her hand to wave at herself in her frock, heading off to the church last July.

And now she's having a baby, she wanted to call to her passing double. Here she was, on the brink of becoming a grandma. The thought made her beam.

"Mrs. Gormley? It is Mrs. Gormley?"

The voice by Elsie's elbow had made her start. She'd seen no one on the street a moment before, but here was someone standing by her on the curb.

"I'm Ida Lewis," said the woman. "Up the hill from you. You're the blue house on the corner, aren't you? I always love it in the springtime when your amaryllis bloom, the red ones above the white."

Elsie nodded. Everyone knew Mrs. Lewis. Up on the hill. In a house full of windows. With a husband who'd left his first wife for her. Ida Lewis was the most famous person in their little nest of streets. She was a painter, and someone had told Elsie that she even had pictures hanging in galleries down south in Sydney and Melbourne.

"Of course I know who you are, Mrs. Lewis." Elsie was grateful for the bags that stopped her having to hold out her hand, since she wasn't quite sure if she should.

"Well, good. I have a business proposition for you. I see your parcels there, and you're on your way home. But if you have a moment next weekend—maybe Sunday morning—I wonder if you'd like to come up to my place and we could have a chat."

"Mrs. Lewis." She took care to clear her throat first to sound more businesslike; as if she, Elsie Gormley, were in the habit of making new acquaintances on the roadside. "Of course, Sunday morning. Around ten? I do a bit for some of the other ladies around here—cleaning and mending and so forth—" There wasn't much of it, just helping where she could, but that must be what the artist had in mind. "Whatever it is that you need doing, I'm sure we can work something out."

"I'd appreciate it," the other woman said, raising her hand to shade her eyes from the glare and staring at Elsie so hard she felt the force of the gaze like a magnet. It wasn't entirely unpleasant. "It's often awkward to ask," Ida Lewis went on, "but there you are. Come and have a cup of tea, and we'll see how you feel."

And she was gone, darting into the butcher's before Elsie could take her leave. She'd walked home with a sensation that swung between a giggle and a frown. *What a thing*, she thought, *what a funny thing.* She hadn't had another house to clean for a while—not really since the children had left home, if you could call two twenty-one-year-olds children. But there was a bolt of some beautiful silver fabric she'd seen in town. A little extra in her purse, and she could buy a length to sew into a dress. Something elegant, she thought; *a sheath.* Maybe Clem would take her out for a meal in that nice beer garden by the river, and she would wear it then.

You don't have to be a grandmother all the time, she thought. Even so, she was giddy with the idea of Elaine becoming someone's mum.

A beautiful baby. That would be the making of her girl.

Perhaps she and Elaine might even become friends when this baby came; the two of them mothers together. Of course, her daughter had her own set of friends, some from school, a couple from the secretarial college she'd attended for those few months, and now her husband's sister, of whom she made a great show as her dearest sister-in-law; her friend.

"The sister I never had," Elaine said.

Which had broken Elsie's heart in a whole new way.

Now, on this quiet Sunday, before she walked around to see Ida Lewis, Elsie listened as Elaine's unanswered telephone rang out, and her stomach jagged. She remembered the sensation from the first days of knowing Clem. Excitement and fear all at once. The baby. It was the baby. Coming soon.

In the bathroom, Elsie checked her hair, her dress, her stockings. It always helped to look your best. There'd been nothing strange or unusual about the way the artist looked, or what she wore—no paint spots on her fingers or in her hair—which had been a bit disappointing. Clem carried his work as a janitor at the university under his fingernails and in the grain of his skin. And as she looked in the mirror, she wondered how her own work sat on her—the children, the house, her odd jobs. Did they mark her in some way?

The painter's husband was a professor; he did something with flies, the lady in the bakery had told her once, and had been in New Guinea in the war. Working with flies: Elsie sniffed. Give her a swat and she'd work the blighters out. The dark buzz of them that used to hover around the swamp in summer—let him turn his attention to that instead of punting over to the university to do who knew what. She slapped at an imagined incursion on her arm, to make her point.

Beyond the back fence, children were playing in the swamp, their calls echoing around its culverts. The incandescent blue of hyacinths spotted the water's dark shadows. From under her feet, then, came an almighty crash and a curse—"damn it!"—as blue as Clem's language ever got.

"You right, love?" she called down through the floorboards. She'd make him a cuppa and take it down to the garage. She liked to see him at work there: it let her imagine the decades of old age they might have—being together, busy in their different ways.

It was one of the things she liked most about him, the way he could putter. Looking for him, she'd call, "Where are you, Clem?" and he'd say, "In here, love, just puttering." While he dismantled the rusted parts of something, or reglued something else, or rebuilt the entirety of some machine he'd hauled out of the dump's morass, bringing it home flecked with mud.

Coming into the garage, she balanced the two cups of tea on the edge of his vast green-baize billiards table and admired her husband's industry. The look on Clem's face when he was sunk into busyness: it was the kind of trance she felt when she was kneading dough, satisfactory and rhythmic. He rummaged through a toolbox for a screw, weighed one in the palm of his hand, held up another to check its thread. After a moment, he drew another from a different compartment and set it into place. And it was perfect.

"There," he whispered, a look of pure contentment on his face. "Have this working good as new," he said, brushing imagined dust off a mangle's smooth wooden rollers. "I promised it to that lady up the hill, that artist. Guess even artists have to get the water out of their wash, don't they?"

She passed him his tea, steadying her own. "I didn't know you'd been talking to Mrs. Lewis," she said. Something about it irked her, as if the artist was her secret. "And what a curious thing, to talk about a mangle."

"Met her on the train back from town," he said. He took half the cup of hot liquid into his mouth at once, puffing his cheeks out like a toad before he swallowed. "Can't think how it came up, but I knew I'd seen one in the dump, and I promised her I'd fix it. Should have it done by the end of the day." He was all dust and grease and sweat from the exertion. His ginger hair was speckled with oil spots and fluff.

Elsie took up a broom that was propped against the wall, and swept wide arcs across the floor. "Our mangle's a bit rickety, if it comes to it," she said. "I don't miss it so much now the children have gone, but I could do with something a bit more useful when it comes to doing the sheets."

And there'd be Elaine's new baby too. She'd be needing to help out with that.

"Be nice to have a little one around again," said Clem. Sometimes he said things that made Elsie wonder if he could read her thoughts. Was that how a marriage might go? "I miss fixing up Donny's carts and Lainey's dolls."

"They weren't children long," said Elsie, setting the broom back and brushing the detritus into a pan. There were days when she still felt almost young herself. And then there were moments when she felt impossibly old—like when her son started enthusing about men being fired into space and about bombs, bigger and bigger, being detonated somewhere out there, east of Brisbane, over the ocean.

Not in front of the baby, she wanted to say if his sister was there, her belly stretched like a ball stuck onto her wiry frame. *Let's keep the world safe still for its sake.* Reaching for her husband's teacup now, she saw that her hand was shaking. Surely she was never so superstitious about her own children, even though they were born in the middle of the last big war. But perhaps that had something to do with there being two of them. Two little ones, and then they were gone. Elaine looked like a child in her wedding photograph, so slight in that white dress—Elsie was sure she hadn't eaten for a month.

"I'm off to Mrs. Lewis's now," she said. "She wants some help with cleaning."

"Well, you go on," said Clem, "and I'll get on with this mangle. You know I can't think if you're fussing about." It was his place, under the house, as exclusive and singular as he thought of the kitchen as being hers. "Tell her I'll bring it round when it's done."

~

It was a strange room, so busy. Elsie had never seen anything like it. The house itself was not dissimilar to her weatherboard cottage, except that each room was slightly larger and set with wider windows. And then tacked on at the back there was a cube, three sides half-glass from the roofline down, and with deep eaves to the north and the east. Beneath each windowsill were stands of shelves, thick with jars and vases, with bottles and boxes and enough shells, Elsie thought, to furnish a beach.

"I don't get round to doing much cleaning—" she heard Mrs. Lewis say.

"Well, it would be very easy to pop up for a morning once a week," Elsie said, wanting to save her the embarrassment of asking.

"Hmm?" Ida Lewis was holding two lengths of fabric, one a dark and bloody crimson, and the other a deep, rich blue. "The cerulean, I'd say—would you call it cerulean? Or is it more towards ultramarine?"

Cerulean. Ultramarine. It was a foreign language to Elsie, and she felt it sink into some deep and hidden section of herself. Poetry, it was like poetry. Those words that could make you feel.

I always knew there had to be more to it than blue, she thought, and was surprised to hear herself saying this aloud.

"More to it than blue—you are right, Mrs. Gormley." Ida Lewis looked up at her and smiled. "But what are you saying about cleaning? I wanted to ask if you would sit for me—if I could paint your portrait."

Elsie had never known that so much of her could flush: she could feel the heat around her ankles, her knees, stretched right across her stomach and fingering its way up her neck and onto her face. "Mrs. Lewis," she said, brushing at the air in front of her face. "Mrs. Lewis, I thought you were going to ask for some cleaning. But painting, a painting, I don't—"

"I only require that you can take a pose and sit with it." Ida Lewis arranged the blue fabric around an empty chair—pulling it this way and that. "There. And I can pay you, of course. Probably more than you'd get for some cleaning. But this would be of far more use."

Elsie looked around the cluttered room. She saw the cobwebs in the corners of the ceilings, the patina of dust on the few flat surfaces that remained clear, the way the front covers of the books, and some of their pages, had yellowed in the light and were curling too: that's how it was in these tropics with their humidity. A dead fly lay under the lowest rib of the slatted blind; another clung to the lip of the baseboard. Elsie wondered if they belonged to the professor.

Ida Lewis stood behind a wicker chair, her hands set firmly on its back. She was looking hard at Elsie; she was waiting for a reply.

That gaze: it was like a hot knife sliced through butter—so smooth, so easy. It was like basking in some unknown sun.

And I could sit with this.

Elsie coughed: what a notion. Who was she to sit still when there was work to be done?

"Mrs. Lewis," she said quickly, "I've never done such a thing—" And as she waited for her own voice to demur, she heard it rattling on. "I'd be curious to do it for you." And then another blush. "But I would like to clean your room first. It does need it, you see, and otherwise I'd be sitting here all morning marking out what I'd be better employed to do."

The words so unexpected, she thought another speaker must have come into the room.

Ida laughed, a full, round sound. "Good for you, Mrs. Gormley: well, all right. Come tomorrow morning and do your wretched dusting—I won't be here; I'll leave a key in the box. Then come again the next day, at nine, and we'll see how this painting gets on. I should have a couple of weeks before the dust starts to mount up and your cleaning hands get twitchy again. I'll pay you as we go—a pound per sitting. Agreed? Now, a cup of tea?" And she was gone into the kitchen before Elsie could reply, calling, "My sister-in-law brought cake the other day, so it's a good day to have morning tea in this house, and a rare one."

Elsie smiled, brushing the two dead flies into her handkerchief and shaking them out through the window, hoping the professor wouldn't mind.

She looked around the jumble of the studio. A pound a week: it felt too generous. And in this extraordinary room—she noted the way it pushed out into the garden, its glass letting in the greenery and the light.

"It must be lovely to work in here when it's raining," she called in reply. "To have the garden so rich and so close." Clem hated a busy garden: their own block was bare save for a poinciana in the back corner, an umbrella tree at the front, and a rockery he'd built around the porch. But this garden was so thick and lush, with oleanders, crepe myrtles, lilly pillies and acacias, a huge poinciana, a jacaranda *and* a mango, and the pretty trunk of a leopard tree pushing up above the rest.

"There's a story that some minor member of the royal family planted that leopard tree, you know," said Ida, "a prince or something, when he visited the colonies late last century. All this way, to dig a hole in the ground. But isn't the foliage magnificent?" She stood at Elsie's elbow, holding the tea tray for want of anywhere to set it down. "Could you—" Ida nodded to the bookshelf running along the eastern window. "Just push those out of the way a bit, and try not to mind the dust. Now, milk? Sugar? And a piece of this cake?"

~

Walking back to her own house, Elsie felt the blush creep up her body again. She'd never had such a morning. "Ida, please call me Ida," Mrs. Lewis had said, and Elsie had found herself giggling.

"Just come as you are on Tuesday," Ida had said at last. "Don't worry about your dress or anything like that—just come as you are, and we'll see how we go."

Every extra bit helps, that's what Clem always said, and Elsie thought about how proud he'd be. And then she would sit in that lovely light room. And someone else—a painter—would make a whole new version of her.

Imagine that.

Elsie stepped onto the road and startled as a truck rattled past— she hadn't noticed it coming. *No*, she thought, *no, I won't tell Clem about it. I'll wait till it's done, and then he can see it. I'll tell him there's a lot of cleaning that needs doing, to set the house to rights before the professor comes home. And the other, the other thing*—the blush again. She'd keep that secret for herself.

Letting herself into the artist's house the next day, Elsie stood a moment in the middle of the kitchen, her bucket of rags and detergents in one hand, her housecoat in the other. There was a handwritten card propped on the table—*Morning tea*—next to another slice of the sister-in-law's cake.

She paused in the quiet of the kitchen. It felt strange to be alone in someone else's house. Usually, when she whipped round with the duster, there was a young woman, lying in, with a new baby, needing a hand—or an old one, at the other end of time, no longer able to keep up her work. Elsie walked through the rooms: the floor plan might have been an enlarged echo of her place, but here was different furniture, so many shelves of books, a heavy desk with a green lamp, and stack after stack of papers, journals, notes. Here were paintings and strange ornaments—from New Guinea, she supposed. And here was a bed—its legs holding it higher off the ground than she'd ever seen before; its two ends delineated by great strips of dark wood.

She touched the quilt cover, a heavy velvet, and couldn't stop patting it. It had a supremely soft nap and she wanted, for an instant, to be lying facedown on the pale-blue expanse, to feel its rub against her cheeks, her bare arms, even the tops of her feet. This overwhelming desire for sensation: her own house did not make her feel like this. Nothing that she knew of ever had.

Back in the studio, her body skewed with the weight of a bucket of hot water in one hand and the shaft of a mop in the other, she pulled up: there was carpet on the floor, where she had remembered—or imagined—bare boards. It was brown and ridged, like corduroy, flaring with every color imaginable around the space where Ida's easel stood. Elsie crouched down, feeling the way the paint had set rigid onto this surface, feeling its smoothness against the rough fibers of the matting. She rocked back on her feet, looking around the room from this shrunken height: shelf after shelf of books, and against the one solid wall, a stack of pictures set in on their ends as if they were slightly taller, wider volumes. Crossing the room, she pulled out one at random: a man's face, a dark room behind him—perhaps it was the professor. Another showed the very garden outside this window, and another something like a mess of mud on a seashore somewhere. She stared a while, then slid them back into their nook.

It must be strange to be an artist. How did you know you wanted to be one? Elsie wondered. How did you even know to try? She scratched her nail through the grime on the cabinet's top— she was etching a sort of leaf, or a boat maybe, into these leftover particles of stuff—and then sponged it into nothingness with her cloth. There had to be artists, she supposed, if people were to have paintings on their walls. And museums, too; she'd found herself once in the gallery on Gregory Terrace, escaping from the rain, and spent a morning staring at the pictures in their ornate frames, wondering how long she was supposed to look at each, and what she was supposed to see.

"What do you make of that one?" It was an elderly man who'd spoken to her. He was leaning towards a picture of an old woman, one hand propping her chin, the other holding a letter. "First Australian painting this gallery ever bought," he said, "and it's by a woman." He shook his head. "None of your Robertses. None of your McCubbins. Just an old woman reading a letter—what do you make of it, miss? What do you think?"

And Elsie, whose children had recently started school, had blushed a little at being mistaken for someone so young they warranted "miss." It wasn't even clear to her from the picture whether the letter had brought the old woman good news or bad.

"What's it called?" she asked at last, leaning in towards the frame. "*Care?*" She paused, not wanting to sound ignorant. "She's made the scarf very pretty," she said, gesturing towards the canvas. "Blue, but silver; I suppose there's a proper word for that."

But the old man coughed into his handkerchief and stepped three frames ahead of her. "By a woman—by a woman!" she heard him mutter once more before he reached the door and went away.

Elsie had stood a while then, alone in the big room, turning slowly so that the canvases melded into trails of color, like the wake of a boat along the river. Stepping outside into sunlight, she'd looked up at the now clear sky and paused again. It had to be all right to think it was blue. That was, after all, what it was. Who was she to try to make any more of it than that?

Now, in Ida Lewis's studio, she looked again at the colors the artist's paints had left across the floor. *Cerulean,* she thought, *ultramarine.* The words sounded so rich, they might almost have been forbidden. On the table by the easel, silver tubes of pigment lay scattered. Elsie shifted the water bucket on the floor—positioning it carefully between the overflows of color—and ran her fingers across them all, reading the names on the tubes. Alizarin crimson. Viridian. Scarlet Lake. Olive, cutch, sap green. So much more than pink or green or brown or red.

In the magazine she'd read with her cup of tea that morning, Elsie had paused at the line where the heroine swooned, and wondered, what would that feel like? How would it come? Now, with these thick words pressing in on her and the floor a brilliant spectrum, she thought, *swooning, well then. Yes. There you are.* And she stood for a moment, trying to get her breath.

Outside in the garden, a magpie called. Elsie could see its young one hopping on the grass, worrying for worms. The baby's feathers were grey: Elsie concentrated—*like cinders.* The mother's were darker, and darkened again by the shadows in which she stood.

They were black, thought Elsie carefully, *black like coal*. And for a split second it seemed she could even see tiny sparkles glistening along the bird's wing, like the fuel's secret scintillants. She straightened her shoulders: she'd thought these things; she'd noticed them. There was power, there was poetry in that, and it was hers. Then she set the compact tubes of paint in a long, careful line, ordering them like a rainbow, carried the hot water over to the window ledge, and began to wash it clean.

She knew where she was with this work.

She loved the sight of baby birds—loved the idea of lives beginning. The day she and Clem saw the house they would buy, there'd been a baby crow in the yard. That she never saw it again, she knew, was the reason she and Clem had had no more children. There were messages implicit in these things, even if she rarely put them into words.

It was afternoon before the room was done, and she stood in Ida Lewis's kitchen, wolfing down the cake, and draining a second large glass of water. She brushed the crumbs into her hand and stuffed them into the pocket of her housecoat, loath to put anything messy in the now-emptied bin. Then she picked up the little rectangle of card, and the pen that lay beside it.

Thank you, she wrote in her most careful hand. *I hope the studio will do. And I'll see you in the morning.*

Letting herself out the back door, she saw the two magpies at work on the thick lawn. The mother cried out, a rich round gurgle that sounded exultant and utterly free.

~

"There now." Ida Lewis pulled the wicker chair towards the northeast corner of the room, where two of the huge panes of glass met. "Sit you here and you'll have something to look at while I look at you—there's always something to see in a garden, don't you think?"

Elsie nodded, her hands busy with the handles of her purse; she wasn't sure where she should put it. But she sat in the chair as Ida indicated, placing her bag near her feet, and kicked it a little so it rested behind her legs. Perhaps it would be distracting to a painter—*an artist*—to have a quilted purse in clear view by their subject's toes. *Their model.*

"Oh, don't worry about that," said Ida, arranging the blue scarf—*cerulean, ultramarine*—into rolls and folds around the back of the chair. "I don't see half of it once I've got you in place. Now, don't jump." She leaned forward and placed her hands on Elsie's shoulders. "I know it's a shocking thing to have someone push you around—"

A shocking thing to have a stranger touch you, thought Elsie, trying not to flinch. Ida seemed so very sure.

"—but I just want to make sure we've got everything facing the right way before we start." Ida stepped back and narrowed her eyes. "Could you turn a fraction more towards the window?" Her finger was light against Elsie's chin. "And could you try not to look down so much? Look up, look out. That's it."

Elsie had counted to five before the artist took her finger away.

"And I think we're ready." Ida stood with a palette resting on the wrist, the palm of one hand, a canvas propped up on the easel before her. On the palette, Elsie could make out a stripe of blue, a stripe of red, and a mound of something brownish orange, or orangey brown. It looked for all the world like the substance Elaine would soon be washing out of a baby's nappies: Elsie pushed her lips together, afraid that she might laugh.

"Now then," said Ida Lewis, and raised her brush to the canvas.

Outside the window, the leaves of the trees flickered a little in the breeze, just a shimmer, and the shifting planes of their shapes caught the early morning light. Elsie watched as another cluster of leaves shook with the flurry of movement of a bird, hidden among the green. Clem didn't dislike trees. But they made a yard messy, he always said, and it was a bugger to mow around the trunks. At least he tolerated the poinciana his mum had planted when he and Elsie had bought the house, but he pruned it ferociously each year.

Elsie watched the breeze play across the poinciana in Ida Lewis's garden: she'd never noticed before the way sunlight on leaves could make them look wet, or flare them into a ray of light as bright as might shine from a powerful torch.

"Did you lose your electricity last night?" Ida Lewis asked then, as if the thought of brightness hovered over Elsie's head. "Ours went down for half an hour or so; I thought it was a fuse, but Richard's much more likely to attribute these things to union malcontents."

Sitting stock still, Elsie wondered how much of her would move if she spoke. She was suddenly conscious of a nervous tic she had of raising her hand to her cheek, as if to brush off a fly, whenever she was unsure what to say.

"You'd rather not talk?" Ida said then, stepping back behind the board so that Elsie could only see the strokes of her right arm. "No, that's fine, that's fine."

And Elsie went back to the light and the leaves.

What would Clem say, if she told him tonight? What would Clem say about her sitting as an artist's model? She watched the leaves a little longer and then found that she wasn't watching anything at all, and couldn't have said how long she'd been staring at nothingness.

Ida was crouched down beside her, fussing at the fabric by her feet. "It's hard, I know, but you do need to stay with me a little, if you can."

The artist was so very close; Elsie glanced down and almost touched her fingers to the other woman's soft-looking red-brown hair. Her words sounded like a scrap of conversation you might catch from the other side of an open space. Another blush blazed from Elsie's forehead to her chest.

"Oh, Mrs. Lewis, I'm so sorry—did I—did I fall asleep?"

Back at the easel, and stretching both arms up towards the ceiling, Ida Lewis shook her head. "No, no, but you wandered off somewhere. I always find it's easier to try to catch the shape and the sense of a person at the outset if they can keep their imagination in the same room as I am, but I know that's a lot to ask for a first day. And you're doing very well; we'll have a cup of tea in ten minutes or so. An hour is a long time for a first sitting."

An hour. Elsie swallowed. Through the window, she could see that the sun had inched across the garden, and the movement of the breeze had swung around and busied itself in an altogether new direction. There were clouds too, wide white tufts, in a sky that had been, the last time she looked—*the last time I paid attention*—perfectly clear and blue. An unaccounted-for hour: *what was I thinking?*

Once, when Donny and Lainey were just babies and struggling with a cough, she'd sat by their bassinets through one long, awful night, patting them and soothing them as they needed, changing their soggy nappies, and making sure they drank their milk.

"I don't know how you do it," Clem had said in the morning. "If you'd had a light on or something, you might have read—anything to pass the time. But to sit there, from ten till five, in darkness, with two hacking littlies . . ." He shook his head. "I don't envy you that, love."

That way he had sometimes, she thought now in Ida's studio, of talking about the children as if they had nothing to do with him.

But that night, that night with the twins, there were seven hours for which she could barely account. Sitting with Clem the next morning, watching the way he could eat a fried egg in four mouthfuls, she'd wondered where her mind must have hidden so as not to have noticed so many silent, passing minutes. And now, sitting in Ida's studio, she wondered about it again, and if its lost time linked up somehow to the time she had lost here, this morning.

I was thinking about the light and the leaves. I was thinking about the garden I would plant if Clem didn't have to mow. I was thinking about Clem, mowing, and the way he stands when he's finished, with his head tipped back and more satisfied than at any other moment, pouring a tall bottle of cold beer down his neck as if it could run straight to the center of himself. I was thinking about how loud the sound is when he swallows. I was thinking about how loud Mrs. Lewis's brush sounds against her board. I was thinking about the way Donny snored even when he was a baby, and how adorable that sounded. I was thinking about that look of Elaine's, so blank, like she doesn't even know me. Her voice so cold sometimes. I was thinking I must get on to that last rug for her little one, and about the rugs I knitted for the twins, scratchy brown war wool, but they carried them about with them for years, and brown as good a color as any for two children who were always playing in the garden. I was thinking about the time I thought I'd lost Donny to the swamp, and how pale his little hand looked with the rest of him speckled by its mud. He brought me a bunch of water hyacinths: we set them in the bowl my mother had always used for fruit, and they seemed to light up the kitchen. I can't remember the next time we had cut flowers in the house. I can't remember the flowers I carried at my wedding. I can remember Elaine wanting more flowers in her bouquet and I'd never before thought she was greedy . . .

"I'll see about that kettle," she heard Ida say, and then her own voice, as if from a long way off: "That can't have been ten minutes already."

"More like twenty." Ida rubbed at her hands with a messy cloth—Elsie could smell the turpentine in which it was soaked. "You'll be reporting me to your union." She laughed. "Come on, come and have a cuppa. Come and tell me where you went while I was trying to pin you to my canvas."

Stirring her tea, Elsie heard herself say, "Do you remember very much about your wedding? In there, while I was sitting for you,

I couldn't remember what sort of flowers I carried. You know that feeling, once you're scared you can't remember something; the way it disappears completely from your memory."

Ida prised the lid off a biscuit tin and slid it across the kitchen table towards her guest. "I didn't carry any flowers when we were married. It was a registry office, just the two of us and two witnesses. We'd had to wait for Richard's divorce to come through after the war. I regretted that though—the flowers, I mean, not the divorce. I always said I didn't mind not having the dress and the church and the cake and all the rest of it. But I do wonder that I hadn't thought to pick a posy of flowers as I walked out through the garden to the car. There'd have been roses too, that time of the year—the house we were living in had beds of the most beautiful apricot roses. I can still remember their scent."

"We were married during the war," said Elsie. "I wore the dress I was wearing the first day I met Clem, with a pretty chiffon layer on the skirt. It was green. I don't know the word a painter would have for that color, but it was light, like the new growth on trees. Perhaps I had a rose in my bouquet. I remember Clem's mother making it up for me from the flowers in her garden and she could grow beautiful roses. You're right; I can remember what it smelled like. I sometimes wish I'd had a new dress—but it doesn't matter, does it? As long as you're together in the end."

She'd never before met anyone who'd had anything to do with a divorce; and yet how easily, how flippantly, Ida Lewis had mentioned it, and how easily she had replied. "Your husband's first wife," she went on. "What did she—?"

"She went back to America eventually, although she stayed on a while in Sydney. It was a blessing really, us coming up here. I was always afraid I'd run into her in the grocer's or on a tram and have to think of something polite to say."

From the corner of her eye, Elsie saw a lizard dart across the kitchen floor, a tiny brown thing, half the length of a pencil, and she jumped.

"Oh, it startles me when the outside comes inside," she said, blushing again. "Clem says I'd be no use in a proper jungle, but there were mornings in his mother's house when I'd wake up and find a plant had grown in through the window—I swear it happened overnight."

Ida Lewis laughed, reaching up from the table to a long shelf lined with notebooks. "You want proper jungle?" she asked. "That's where I met Richard, up in New Guinea. I was nursing there. He was an officer, and a good one, his men said. But he would sneak in a bit of fieldwork where he could. His precious flies. He would sit for hours watching creatures coming and going on a single plant— and I'd sit with him, sure I could see the plants growing while I had my cup of tea." She flipped through the pages of one of the books, patting it open on a spread of washes in browns, greens, olive, khaki. "I met a woman up there, an artist—it was her job to paint bits of the war. She got me started, gave me my first notebooks. I got quite creative about interpreting the tones of mud. That was all I painted the first few years, as if that was all the colors in the world. I've never painted so many clear blue skies and so much light as I did when I first came home. Pretty still lifes, with china and flowers, and everything clean and bright."

"And peaceful," said Elsie, shivering. "You must have been scared, Mrs. Lewis. Weren't you scared?"

"Ida, please," said Ida, refilling her cup. "I was never scared, no. I was busy, always busy. But I made my first paintings of some of the men—soldiers, and so forth. Some of them I had to finish from memory when they were dead."

That awful war, thought Elsie. She couldn't—she wouldn't imagine it; had worked so hard to keep it far away from herself, from her children, from her world. And now it was sitting in front of her with this woman, in a quiet sunny room that was so safe. *How had she borne being there, seeing that?* Elsie thought. It didn't feel like a thing she could ask.

"I'd love to see your paintings," she said instead. And she curled her fingers tighter around her teacup, as if to draw in more warmth through her skin.

"Oh, they were just my first attempts—I painted over lots of them." Ida laughed. "Which is good, I think. They're not always the kind of things you want to have around the house. Now, shall we get back to it? Do you need the lavatory?"

Sitting on the toilet with the bright morning light coming up through the cracks in the floorboards and in through the high, slanted louvers, Elsie swung her legs like a little girl and laughed.

7

The family

BEN TOOK a taxi to the airport, thinking *Down the rabbit hole* as the car drove into the tunnel below the river and the rain was immediately cut off. He wondered how old Tom should be before they read about Alice and her adventures.

There was a catalog growing in his head of which books he would read to his son, and this surprised him. He'd never really thought of having children, even as he'd watched his peers race on ahead through prenatal classes and day care and swimming lessons and school runs and affairs. The idea of fatherhood seemed always at some remove, just as family life itself had always been beyond him somehow. He lived in the pinpoint focus of himself and his mum, with a card from his grandma at Christmas—none of the numbers and siblings and noise that he thought a proper family required. The noise and spread of family life: they were nothing to do with his world.

Now here he was, after so many rational and hypothetical discussions with his wife about the two of them and whether there should be any more. Here he was in the thick of it, suddenly remembering things he'd loved about being young—books, games, wonder—and passing them on. These past weeks they'd been making their way through A. A. Milne's poems, which his mum used to read him every night before he slept. He was surprised to find some of the verses about Winnie-the-Pooh so very familiar. He was remembering things about his mother he hadn't thought about for years. He was wondering about things to do with his father—who'd shot through almost as soon as Ben was born—for the first time as well.

Parenthood mushroomed the size of emotions, Ben thought as the cab came back into daylight—and the rain—and took the road that traced the river's curve. It blew out the capacity for observation as well: he noticed every jacaranda tree they passed, recalling Tom's exuberance—"More purple! More! More purple!"—and wondered if there'd ever been so many bloom before.

"You said international?" the driver asked, stilling the windshield wipers as the rain eased off at last.

"International," said Ben. Just for work; just a story; just a long flight across the Pacific to sit in a conference bunker on the other side. He thought these were the perks of his job—the travel, meeting people, wining, dining, and then the tiny pocket of time that had to balance the creation of a story against its deadline. He flexed his shoulders and yawned; he could use the break. Lucy was evangelical when it came to Tom's routine—it made Ben want to mess it up sometimes. Yet she seemed to believe the routine was magic.

"You in a hurry, mate? We're getting every red light here."

"Tons of time," said Ben as the car slowed again. It was his habit to arrive at international airports hours early—he loved to sit near the arrivals gate with a coffee and watch the business of people flying in, flying home, flying on. A multitude of stories.

"And another one," said the driver, slowing for another amber light. He flicked on the radio and the car filled with one of the songs Lucy had been playing over and over at home.

"Ha!" said Ben, before he could stop himself. *There should be more dancing*. It had felt good, twirling on, twirling around the kitchen. A long time since they'd moved together like that.

His fingers tapped the rhythm of the song as he watched people on the footpath—a man jogging on the spot as the lights pulled him to a stop; a woman with an umbrella that had worked itself inside out; another woman with a baby in a stroller and a toddler holding onto its strap. They were crowded around the stalk of the traffic lights, the little boy hitting its pedestrian button again and again and again. Ben imagined the rising pitch of the mother's voice—irritation accelerating from caution to chastisement and on to rage. There was something primal about it, something volcanic. He'd watched Lucy do this, with Tom, over what Ben saw as the tiniest of infringements. It was always a short, sharp blast, like the slam of a yacht's boom as its sail changed tack. Yet in all the years they'd been together he'd never known Lucy to have a temper. He slunk away from it now, squirming at its immediacy and its volume, never quite sure if he should ignore it, or endorse it, or call her on it. And then she righted herself, and went on.

She talked of fear. She talked of catastrophe—she made it sound almost mythological, the ways a mother could divine it. But she never talked about these flares of rage.

He had no memory of his mother being frustrated or angry. Only once that he could remember had she shouted at him, when he'd made a mess of the backyard with the wild idea of launching a rocket with a cache of homemade explosives. Her stern words then had felt pretty justified. He rested his head against the window: the more he saw the way that Lucy sparked off Tom, the more he admired his mother's equanimity.

~

He was twenty-one years and a day old when his mother died: a massive heart attack. He was a year shy of the age she'd been herself when, a new bride and already pregnant, she'd sailed from England to Australia with her husband, Alec. So charming, so gregarious, Alec was the life of any party—although all the flirting he'd done with her before the wedding, before the ship sailed, seemed now perpetually directed at anyone else. She gave their son his name—Alexander—and then Benedict. Never used his first name once that Ben recalled.

"You were three months old when he came home and told me he'd fallen for the woman who brought the tea round at his office," his mother explained. "I told him to go. Well, I'd never been able to make his tea the way he liked it." The only version of the story that she told.

Only once had he heard her speak of being lonely. She was talking to a woman at the butcher's counter while Ben wound around her legs, four or five years old, waiting for the butcher to notice him and hand over the prized treat of a free red frankfurter wrapped in smooth white paper.

"Oh, we get by, we cope—and he's lovely, Ben, he's a lovely little thing. After his father left I let myself have one good afternoon of crying. Took a train over to the south side and sat in a park, somewhere I'd never been before and would never go again. Ben was only a few months old, and sound asleep in the stroller.

"And then this bird came swooping down at me—it swept down and tried to peck my head; I could hear its feathers flapping and its horrid beak clacking. And I howled and howled, and thought, no one likes me in this country—not even a bloody bird, pardon my . . ."

Her hands, belatedly pressed over Ben's ears, stayed there, so that he didn't hear the butcher's usual question—"Tempt you with a frankfurt, Benny my boy?"—and didn't notice the offering, so deliciously smooth skinned and bright, until he saw it being taken up again, and swept back onto the other side of the counter.

"Mum! My frankfurter—the frankfurt."

"Thought you didn't want it," the butcher had said, handing it to him with a wide smile. "Thought you might've grown out of such a treat."

"You could go back, Mum," he'd said over and over, as he grew older. "You could go home." All through the rush of his cadetship, the first rounds he got to cover, the excitement of seeing his own name in print, he'd squirreled away money ahead of the day when he could buy his mother the fastest trip back to England.

And then, twenty-one years and a day through his life, he'd had a call at work in Sydney from his mother's neighbor. The two women had been due to take the bus together into town, and when his mother hadn't shown up, the neighbor had let herself into the house rather than call him right away. "Oh, Ben, I hope you don't mind," she'd said.

"I was about a month away from having the money for her airfare," he'd said to Lucy the first time he told her the story. "Not that she knew. It was going to be a surprise."

And Lucy had taken his hand and kissed it. "Oh, Ben. On your own."

It was a nineteenth-century sort of word, "orphan," but there it was. He shrugged. "I'd already moved to Sydney, got this place in Darlinghurst—I went home to Brisbane, sorted everything out, came back and got on with my job. I did think about finding my dad, telling him what had happened. But I didn't know what I'd say after that." He shrugged again.

The flat in Darlinghurst: more than a decade he'd lived there, with girlfriends coming and going, before this impossibly bright thing with the impossibly pretty name—Lucy Kiss—moved in. Nearly a decade younger than he, and as pretty as her name as well. She wanted to hear all his stories. It took him years to believe in his luck.

Lucy Kiss was the least-orphaned person in the world, with her big, loud family of long-divorced parents and three sisters, already loaded up with husbands and three kids apiece, and everyone with an opinion. Now, he was sure, Lucy liked life beyond their cacophony as much as he did.

It hadn't been bad, moving north again; he even took a certain pride in the idea of Tom coming to know the air, the light in this place as if it was a kind of heritage. And no matter how many people had told him it would be a disaster, what with Tom just a year old, Lucy herself had never balked, laughing at the terrible predictions people made. "Come on, it'll be an adventure."

She always made a game of learning their new places, set herself to revealing special things that made them all feel preordained. His favorite obscure beer in the bottle shop closest to home. A street with a strangely apt name.

This fixation she had with Elsie Gormley, the previous owner of their house; even that made him smile. Trust Lucy to find an uncanny new friend. Everywhere they'd lived, she'd hunted for connections, for something extraordinary. "There's a *reason* we chose this place or it chose us," she'd say. Well, whatever helped her settle in. She went anywhere his job happened to take them and made the place her own, while he hid behind the safety of the same job, just at another desk.

She was braver than he was, he realized, and especially with Tom. She had been from the get-go: doing what she was told through all the hours of labor and standing up against the disappointed comments of her mother, her sisters, when it came to a caesarean in the end.

But this new Lucy, this sometimes enraged Lucy: it was as if some deeper, more subterranean version of her had emerged. Perhaps it happened to every woman who had a baby—he didn't know, and he wasn't sure whom he could ask.

There should be dancing, he thought again. Her fury, her fears: these were not things he knew from before. He knew music. He knew brightness. He missed that.

When Ben was small, his mother sang him songs every night before he slept—"Summertime," "Unforgettable," bits and pieces of the Beatles as the sixties folded into the seventies. He went to sleep for an entire year with "Here Comes the Sun" in his head. It was a talisman, his mother's voice. It was security. He saw Lucy sitting with Tom, singing softly, lulling him to sleep, and he knew the power, the protection of what she was doing. Perhaps she was right. Perhaps there was magic in all these routines. The messy things: perhaps they fell away.

"I think I was ten when I asked my mother to stop singing me to sleep," he'd told her not so long ago. It now seemed a mean thing to have done.

Lucy was leaning back against him in the armchair made by his body against the wall—the last day before their furniture arrived.

"Sing something for me now," he said, his chin resting on the top of her head.

"No," she said. "I'm saving them all for Tom."

"Ha!" said Ben. "He'll never tip like I do." Making light of it, while some part of him wanted to contest his son's new primacy.

They had talked vaguely of children for a decade, all the way out of Lucy's twenties and on, closer and closer to the end of her thirties. Her youth was his excuse to avoid making a decision. It was interesting, Ben thought sometimes, that she never called him on his fears. She listened patiently to his red herrings about their nice life, his own complete lack of any knowledge of fathering, their nice life, his job, his age, her age (increasingly), the nice life the two of them had. Together. It was only when she said one day, her voice an odd combination of sheepishness and elation, that she was pregnant—"I guess even the best safeguards fail"—that he wondered if she'd been as terrified as he was and had hidden behind his anxieties too.

Was it really a failure, he'd asked her once, later, when it was too late to do anything about it, "or did you decide to play the odds?"

"I thought we should give it one shot," she said. "That was all. Here we are."

There they were.

They were lying in the sun when she said this, the sections of the weekend paper spread between them, Lucy's belly breaching like a whale.

"You were probably right not to say," Ben said. "I'd have tried to talk you out of it again."

"I know."

He was holding her hand, not conscious of the tightness of his grip.

"Ben—" She had to use her free hand to loosen his fingers. "You'll be great. And we'll be fine."

"What?" He shook out his hand. "Give us the nine-letter word?"

She passed across the puzzle page, shaking her own fingers light and free.

He glanced at the sheet and shut his eyes. It was his party trick, the speed with which he could rearrange nine muddled letters into a word. He'd done "abhorrent" in an instant, he liked to boast.

"'Entrapment!'" he said almost at once. "Pretty close to the record now." He was trying to make a joke of it, and he knew that she could tell.

Lucy pulled the page towards her as she lay on her side, her belly ballooning and round.

"No," she said. "That's ten. You'd need another *t*." She squinted at the paper, her lips sounding out the letters. She pushed the sheet away and grinned.

"Had to happen, Ben Carter, but it's the first time you've been beaten. It's 'permanent'—look. It must be." She laughed at him, rubbing his arm.

~

As the song began to fade on the radio, Ben heard the taxi's engine rev and felt it pull forward for the green light. Just as the woman with the stroller and the toddler stepped onto the road in its path.

The world slowed. The driver swore. The jogging man reached out to grab the stroller while the woman with the umbrella let it fly off with the wind as she grabbed at the mother, striding forward.

"For fuck's sake!" the driver shouted and swerved. And then the cab was away and there'd been no impact, no collision. "What the fuck was she thinking?" As the car surged on and away, through the next amber light.

"She wasn't," said Ben. "She was shitty with the kid about the button." He'd felt his heart stop, felt the floor of his very being drop away. He strained his neck, trying to look back—were they still there, the jogger, the other woman? Were they saying something smooth, something calm, something that had no expletives?

He couldn't see, and he rubbed at his neck where he'd pulled it, somehow annoyed by its pain.

"Fuck me—I don't need that." The driver took the turn onto the freeway and the car sped up again.

"I reckon she didn't either." If it had been Lucy. If it had been Tom.

If it had been me.

He had felt it for the first time, the terror that Lucy talked about—felt it swell and stretch the middle of himself to pure tautness, and then collapse back into nothingness.

He'd need a double shot of coffee to sort himself out before he flew.

8

The photographs

LUCY WAS standing on a stepladder, rearranging the emptied suitcases on the highest shelves of the linen cupboard, when she heard a noise above her head—a possum? a rat?—and almost lost her balance, bracing herself against the trapdoor that led into the roof above.

The cover shifted, and as she righted herself, she knocked it aside altogether. She poked her head into the roof space for the first time and saw, in the shadows, a single grey box, its lid held down with tape. The air up here was even warmer and thicker than the air outside, as if the house held an extra dose of tropical summer in reserve.

She pulled the little carton towards her, blowing at the dust. The tape gave way at once, as well as one end of the box, and a mosaic of photographs spilled down through the gap. Past the cases and onto the wooden floor below—the thick, matte cardboard of old black-and-whites; the slightly bleached colors of the sixties, the early seventies. There were men, women, and children. There were cars and buses, streets, beaches, parks. And this house, this very house.

Climbing down from the stepladder, Lucy gathered the heap of rectangles and flipped over some to read the words written there. *Mount Nebo. Mount Glorious. Marcoola. Wellington Point.* A ball was going on in Cloudland—there was the back of a woman in a shimmering silver dress. And there were children: one generation, then another.

A woman, often pictured, who might be Elsie herself. Why not? *Nice to meet you.* Lucy smiled, shifting this last picture from side to side, as if some more of this person might appear.

The woman in the picture smiled back.

And you must meet Ben. Lucy let the conversation run on. *He's overseas at the moment. I think you'll like him.* How easy was this daydream of a game.

"Of course we'll be fine on our own," Lucy had said as Ben left for the airport earlier that morning. "You have a lovely time." Now, squaring the photos into a pile, she noticed a heavier silence.

"Tom? What you doing?" she called. "Are you OK?"

He was standing at the front door, pointing, a huge grin on his little face. "Mummy! No rain! Look! No rain!"

She left the photos where they were, racing to harness him into his stroller and get out into the air before the next shower came through. The street was bustling with people taking advantage of the break in the weather—checking letterboxes, dumping garbage, carrying parcels from the car. Somewhere nearby a brushcutter roared into life, working against the lush tropical growth brought up everywhere by all this water.

The vines, the trees, the leaves and branches on every plant in this place: she could almost see them growing while she watched.

On an earlier walk, a few streets from home, she'd seen an old weatherboard house, the same dimensions, probably even the same layout as her own. In its front yard, and all around, the garden's plants had grown up to the gutters and beyond—they passed the roof's apex in some parts and were heading for the sky. They reminded her of the jungle that grew in the boy's bedroom in *Where the Wild Things Are*, and she'd said as much to Tom as they stood and regarded the thicket.

"Look, sweetheart, a jungle, like in Max's room. Do you think there are wild things in there?"

It had looked a sad place—abandoned, she'd thought. Until today, as they came around the corner and she saw that the entire yard had been threshed down to the ground and a path cut from the pavement to the front steps. Did someone live there? she wondered. Had they been in there all the time, unable to leave, waiting for some fit young relative to come with a scythe, a mower, and one of those loud machines with razor-sharp line? Or had the occupant had to fight their way out in the end, pushing through to the shed with inappropriate knives and scissors, whatever came to hand?

The idea of nature's reclamation. The idea of disappearing, being overrun and immersed. No wonder this place made no sense, the shapes, the directions of roads and the river. Perhaps they, too, were constantly being overrun and diverging to find themselves a clear new path.

She saw a laneway to the left and ducked along it, blinking when it delivered her just up from the end of her own street—"A wormhole, Tom!"—as the clouds broke and the rain came down again.

And she ran, the stroller's wheels humming, all the way back to their porch.

"Well, we made the most of that!" Lucy laughed, peeling off Tom's wet things and rubbing at his hair. "Mind Elsie's pictures—they're just there on the floor." Watching him barrel back into the house, his legs wide like a cowboy's, as she fiddled with the hinges on the stroller.

After she'd dried herself, she squared the stacks of photos on her lap and set them gently on Elsie's star-shaped doily, as if some magic might spark between the other woman's objects. Tom drove his little train back and forth across the floor, its wheels making a satisfying clack as they turned. He had rich-brown hair, unlike hers, unlike Ben's. His own mother's hair, Ben had said.

She'd thought more about Ben's mother since they'd moved up north. Perhaps it was to do with being new herself, to this place, and to motherhood.

A single mother. Brisbane. The early 1960s. Had she known people by the time her husband had left? Had there been money sent, support somehow maintained? All the practicalities that Ben had never mentioned—perhaps he'd never thought of them himself.

What would I do?

Mrs. Carter wound up working in the office of the school that Ben went to—the only solution, Lucy saw now, to the necessary demands that he made on her time.

Did you love her enough? she wanted to ask her snoring husband once as she lay awake in the kind of sudden 3 a.m. funk when everything felt hopeless. *Did you thank her for all that she did?*

How had she borne it, this hot strange place, so far from London, and on her own? How had she found the way, the means, of feeling capable, sufficient, by herself?

Lucy wished she could have told Ben's mum that her boy would turn out well. She wished she could have known her. She thought of her own parents in a kind of shorthand as distinct and perfect opposites. She'd never known them together—had always bounced between their separate lives. Ben's mother was a blank canvas that she could imagine and enrich. Sometimes, holding Tom, she wondered what shorthand he'd design for her, for Ben, when he was grown up himself.

She'd been flicking through Elsie's photographs—once; then

again—and now she spread them across the floor, well away from Tom's trains. All these moments, caught on film. Perhaps they'd slot together like a jigsaw. A blue one; another blue one—she reached over as she sorted them, selecting different variations of the same color.

"Look: we can make our own picture," she said at last, perching on the edge of the sofa to admire the collage that she'd made.

And as she angled her phone to take a shot, it buzzed once—a message from her father, checking in on Tom and the rain.

All good here, she tapped back, *and look what we found—Elsie!* Sending through the photo collage in reply.

What a thing to leave behind, thought Lucy, *on top of having to leave here at all.*

"She'll be so thrilled to have them back—" she started to say when another sound came from above and Tom jumped too.

"What do you think? Is that a possum living upstairs?" Lucy spoke quietly, trying to lessen her own heart's thump. She just hoped it wasn't a snake.

There was another bump, and a rustling noise like the sound of rain. And then there was rain—another wall of it. Lucy sighed and leaned her head back, looking up.

"No possums in London," Lucy observed to her son. "And I never had one in Sydney either. Perhaps it's come in from the wet too."

This astonishing place: sit still long enough and the wildlife took such liberties. It was as if there was only a porous border, at best, between what was outside and what was in.

Tom climbed into her lap and they settled themselves on the sofa. The collage lay like a rug across the floor.

All these moments: Lucy glanced across the images. Here were the people she took to be Elsie's family—Elsie herself, as she guessed, her husband, her boy and her girl. Here they were with a steam train. Here they were with a wedding car. Here they were arranged across the front steps of this house. A record of a life now left behind.

"I hope she didn't know," Lucy whispered against the softness of her son's hair, "about the photos or having to leave her own place."

She leaned back again, resting her head on a cushion. The smell of warm rain, swelling and swelling, came in through the window, and the day's grey light touched the surface of a patch on the bathroom door. There was a strange patina on it, broken by glossy streaks.

With Tom on her hip, Lucy crossed the room and brushed its paintwork. An oval of fine white dust clung to her finger.

"Talcum powder," she said, showing it to Tom. The only people she knew who used talcum powder were her two grandmothers, both long dead now.

She dotted the white on her son's forehead, on her own, a tiny brand, and they made faces at each other in the bathroom mirror as the rain ramped up another notch outside and the frogs called louder and louder.

"Here we are," Lucy crooned. "Safe and sound, warm and dry."

"Sing, Mummy. Sing." Tom swept out his arm like a conductor, sending a shelf of bathroom products crashing to the ground and littering the floor with glass and goop.

"Tom—" She heard the quick, sharp fury in her voice and stopped. She counted through five breaths—so much for safe and sound and warm and dry.

And breathed again.

"Let's get all these photos off the floor," she said, leaving the mire, the glass, the disaster behind them as she closed the bathroom door.

They sat together on the sofa again, Lucy gathering the different moments of life into one bundle, while Tom squirmed and slithered around. Perhaps she'd parcel them up while he was asleep and they'd take them to the post office later. She could send them to Elsie's daughter—Elaine, wasn't it?—care of her solicitor. The daughter would know what to do.

"Or I could just wait till she comes over next time." The footsteps on the grass. The noises in still rooms. She smiled to herself. "We could have tea."

"Tea! Mummy, tea!" Tom was piling his train set up on the floor, precarious arrangements of carriages made with his right hand and then batted down with his left.

"I know." Lucy bounced up, scooping him with her. "Bread. Let's make some bread. Lovely fresh bread for your tea."

She hadn't made bread since her twenties, some share-house phase, but it would be fun and Tom could get messy and then it would smell good and then they would eat. She held his little hand steady as they measured the flour into the bowl. And then they mixed and kneaded and set their loaf to rise, Lucy opening the jam and honey in anticipation.

It smelled glorious as it baked, that warm, slightly malty scent of the yeast and the crust. Lucy washed the bowl, the cups, the spoons, staring through the window above the sink without seeing the wet street beyond it.

Here we are. Safe and sound. Warm and dry. She loved these moments of contentment, shored them up against the other times. It was peaceful, Tom was playing, and there'd be fresh bread to eat.

And then she stepped around the doorway and saw the game that he had made, the honey and the jam taken from the table and slathered onto every single frame of Elsie's life.

She pulsed with a hot, fast rage at herself for not paying attention and swept Tom into his crib, where he sat howling at being taken away from his activity.

I have spent my working life fixing up messes, she told herself. *I will stay calm and I will make this go away.* In the living room, under the sound of the rain beating on the roof, Lucy pushed the pictures into one pile and shoveled them into the bin. The sweet slick of the two spreads smelled like spring—she couldn't resist licking her fingers.

Now she had to clean the bathroom before she could clean Tom. She opened the door and stepped straight onto the slimy, glassy puddle. And she felt herself starting to cry.

9

The crow

IT WAS a cawing kind of cry that Clem heard as he sat on the back deck in the warm sun, his eyes closed. *What you see behind your eyelids, it's never really black—black as coal, black as pitch*, he thought, opening his eyes to try to focus on the crow. He'd seen a flash of purple and a soft, round brownness, and now the black bird blurred and shadowed in his gaze. He winced; must be something that eyes weren't supposed to do. Or he was getting old. At forty-three, with his kids grown and his daughter almost a mum now herself, he didn't want to think so much on that.

Years before, back when he and Elsie were looking to buy a place, they'd walked down from Clem's mum's, up on the ridge, to this one—a little box at the end of a row of other similar boxes, and the backyard a mess of mud and clay and paspalum. It was new, and might be theirs, and Elsie liked the view out through the kitchen window towards the swamp and the wide eastern sky.

Picking among the green as they stood on the back step, a baby crow had been following its mother, mouth open, squawking.

"Look at that, Clem," Elsie had said softly. "I've never seen a baby crow before—their feathers glisten, don't they? Such a beautiful thing."

Then she'd wanted to live in the house more than ever, and talked about the crows—how special it had been to see the baby; that it boded well, surely, for two people raising a family of their own. The twins were bigger now, she'd said, and perhaps there might be another child, one day. And she blushed when she said this, the way he liked, a tiny frill of pink rising up from her chest towards her throat, and he kissed her cheek and smiled. He was sure of her, the things she meant to say.

The day the mortgage papers were signed, he could hardly speak for the shock of the amount they owed. And then they shifted down from the rooms they'd had at his mum's since they were married, seven years before, and put the twins' beds in the bigger bedroom, taking the smaller one for themselves. He and a mate had added a deck as the summer came around.

"Look at us, with our very own place," Elsie said, positioning a palm in a pot. "Our tropical paradise."

She washed the floors daily and the windows once a week. This new house, and them the first to live in it: he could see how seriously she took that responsibility, as if it touched on everything she said or thought or did. Laying down a good impression; laying down their family foundations. She had a bigger sense of herself, somehow, with her own house as a backdrop. And no worries about the mortgage size for her—he envied her that.

"My little homemaker," he'd say, hugging her, and then the kids would run up and burrow in as well—Donny like a shot, and Elaine a moment later, as if she knew she ought to—and he'd say something glowing about their mum. That was love, he'd thought in those moments. And she'd nestle against him, telling him again she loved that they were the first family to call this place home.

It fascinated him how much she loved this sense of ownership, this sense of being the entire story the house had had so far. "I mean, that bedsit, on the northside," she'd said to him as if it was a desperate kind of confession, "I never knew how many folk had been there before me. I never knew the number of people who'd already slept in that room."

"People come and people go, Else; like the birds. There'll be other people living here sometime, and none of it our story."

"Oh no, Clem, no. Here's home for us. It's ours."

But she'd never stopped wondering about the crow—"Never saw it again, did we, love? I was so excited to have it to show Lainey and Don, but we never saw it again."

"Must've moved away—maybe crows do that. I don't know."

He'd never mentioned the day he and a mate had brought the bathtub—a day or so before they'd moved in. Straining across the grass, the white enamel blinding him as it caught the sun, Clem had turned at a strange noise and seen a rough brown dog busy with something by the back fence.

"Take a spell," he said, lowering his end of the burden and walking towards the noise. There was the little crow, crumpled and bleating among the sticky paspalum stalks. "Go on with you!" Clem shouted at the dog, his hand flinging out above its head and his voice harsh. He watched it slink into the shadows that filled the swamp beyond.

What now? he'd thought. *What the devil do I do with you now?* But as he crouched down he saw the gash in the bird's body, the way its wing was creased out awkwardly.

With his friend beside him then, Clem had shaken his head. "Young crow—that dog was at it. Poor blighter." And he'd raised his boot and stamped before he could think about it twice. It was only then that he noticed a strange silence, as if every nearby bird had stopped calling.

And then the cries began, a litany of long and wide laments— *every bloody crow in the neighborhood.* He'd plucked some paspalum as if to line his hands before he had to touch the bird. His hands, he saw, were shaking; he knew about crows and their mourning.

"Don't tell Elsie, eh." His voice caught, and he carried the broken bird to the lowest corner of the yard where the dirt was moist. Scrabbling a hole, laying the baby bird's body inside, his shoulders hunched against the swoop and peck he expected from its mother at any moment.

Overhead, the crows' noise built and built, and then at last it dropped away. And Clem, leaning over his brand-new diamond-wire fence, let his head drop as he threw up. It felt as if every piece of food he'd ever eaten was raking itself out of his guts.

"Geez, you're a soft touch," his mate had said. "Put it in the bin, I would've. All that fuss for a crow."

All that fuss for Elsie, thought Clem now, *and for all the crows*. He watched as this new black bird balanced on the railing. He'd never told a soul that crows made him nervous.

Behind him, in the kitchen, his wife was singing, her lovely voice thickening as it dipped towards the song's lowest notes. It was always Elvis at the moment, and he loved to hear her sing. Lainey had better have a little girl, or Elsie would be after her to call it Elvis. And what would Elaine think of that?

They rubbed each other the wrong way, his wife and daughter— that's how he saw it. It had to happen sometimes, like him and his scratchy old dad. And Lainey, there was something rare about her—something special, something different and fine—where Elsie always looked for a carbon copy of herself. Clem sighed. The friction she endured with their girl: he wished she didn't make it all so personal. He didn't; they were good kids, well done, let them be now as they pleased. While Elsie fussed and grabbed and fretted.

He'd always thought it would improve. Now, in the autumn sun, it occurred to him for the first time that it might not. *I might go to the grave with their spat*. He shook his head, as much at imagining the end of his own life as anything else. Surely Elsie would do better than that. Surely one day she'd see how to make it right. Straight and true: you could depend on her for that.

"Time for another cuppa, Clem?" Elsie called, coming onto the deck and pulled up short by the sight of the crow. From the corner of his eye, Clem saw her stop, and in front of him the crow tilted its own head to take her in its sights. "You did give me a fright," she said to the bird, and Clem knew what was coming next. "Do you remember that morning we walked down to see this house? Remember the baby crow after its breakfast in the backyard—I've always wondered where it went. I'd've fed it the scraps, you know, watched it grow up."

"You had the twins," said Clem, and it sounded a little too abrupt. "What more watching did you want?" Because it ate at him, the memory of how frail it had felt under the heel of his boot. It ate at him that he hadn't told her fifteen years ago, and couldn't now, no way. "And what's with these omen things anyway?"

If we'd come down half an hour earlier or later; if we'd come down the day before, we'd never have seen the bloody thing—would she have wanted to buy the house then? Or if I'd come with the tub in the afternoon instead; that dog would've finished it off and probably eaten it as well. She was a practical woman, his Elsie, but she could invest a lot in small, strange things.

He knew perfectly well why crows made him nervous, and it was nothing to do with that tiny death in the sticky grass. He watched Elsie watch the crow as he finished his tea and held out his cup towards her offer.

"Fill this up, love, and I'll tell you a story about crows. From back when I was a kid."

The bird shuffled along the rail, first one way, then the other, as Clem heard the noise of the kettle and the tea canister from inside.

"You can't have a new thing left to tell me," Elsie called, and Clem sensed an accusation in her tone.

"'Course I can," Clem said as she set the tea on the table and leaned towards his words. "I've a secret tale or two."

She was smiling at him, her pretty smile, and he could smell her hair like flowers. It still astonished him sometimes, to be close to her, to know her. *We're still young*, he thought, *even with a grandkid turning up*.

"When I was a boy," he began.

When he was a boy, his dad had taken him shooting, out near Lightning Ridge—he was only six or seven, and he'd spent his days fossicking in dust and gravel, pulling out tiny flecks of opaline stone, their colors fired like rainbows. He was a quiet boy—nervy, his dad said—and wanted nothing to do with the shooting. The sound of the rifle and the way it jumped back against your body when it fired; the way an animal's eyes dulled down to horrible, blank milkiness: these things terrified him.

His dad had dropped a wallaby; the mate had dropped two more; and Clem had inched farther and farther away, busying himself with getting water, or sticks for a fire, or folding swags— anything to avoid the gun's weight, its sudden jerk.

On the last morning, with the mate leading the tally by a couple of points and starting to boast, Clem's dad had looked up from the tea he was stirring and smiled. "There was no warmth in it," Clem said to Elsie, "just something nasty, and hard."

Clem's dad set the billycan on a rock, set the spoon he'd been using alongside it, and reached for his gun. Propping it, adjusting it, he'd pursed his lips into something like a kiss. Then he'd pulled the trigger, shooting a single crow—"a big one, huge"—out of the top of a silvery gum.

"So fast," said Clem, "I didn't have time to cover my ears."

The crow dropped to the ground. Clem could still hear the thud. His very body seemed to shake now, so that Elsie, across the table, reached to take his hand, as if to quiet it.

And there it lay, a tiny pile of darkness against the soil.

"I was seven years old, and I couldn't hear a thing. Thought the bloody gun had deafened me. Then it started, this angry sound. All these crows were flying in, diving and wheeling. They damn near covered the whole tree, and they yelled and they wailed and they howled. Must've been a hundred of them in the end. I remember when I learned the word 'cacophony' at school. I knew what it meant; it was heartbreaking. Most mournful sound I've ever heard."

Crouched by the fire, he'd watched the black shapes swoop and settle, more and more from as far as he could see.

"Then a dingo came too—after the body, you know; Dad hadn't scooped it up the way he did with pigs and kangaroos and all the stuff he called 'real game.' And blow me down if these crows didn't go after the dingo, swooping it and pecking until it slunk off and left them to their funeral." "Ululate": another word he'd learned at school. The wailing of mourning women, his teacher said. *And crows*, he'd thought. And crows.

In front of Clem, now, the crow started and took flight as a truck clattered around the corner, its tray laden with ironwork and scrap metal.

"The pigs, they were one thing, even the 'roos—and Dad would never shoot one with a joey. But a crow; they're magnificent. I dunno why he did it. It seemed so mean, so unnecessary." He sat a while saying nothing, staring into the middle distance of the yard.

"My dad drove home without a break—petrol here and there, I suppose. I can't even remember whose truck we were in, but I was glad of its noise. Didn't want to have to say anything. Didn't know what to tell Mum either. But I was terrified of being taken on another shoot after that." He'd even wished his dad dead, so he wouldn't have to go again.

"Then I was eight years old, and he did die—pneumonia in the middle of winter. It was just me and Mum, and then it was boarders, and people's mending coming in, and the typing she did for one of the university blokes, me going to sleep to the clicking of that ruddy machine. Still," he rubbed Elsie's hand in his, "she made me a good life, and she gave us a good home till we got sorted here. Never told her about the crow, neither. But I always wondered if it'd marked Dad somehow—"

Clem cut himself off, pulled his hand away. It was an enormous thing to think, an enormous thing to say. He drank the fresh tea and watched a kookaburra balance on the garden wall. He'd always wondered if it was his wishing his dad gone that had done that too, the pneumonia. But that was even less sayable.

They sat in silence, each with their cup. Across the table, Elsie set hers down and clasped her fingers together as if in prayer.

"Oh, Clem," she said at last. "Oh, love." So soft.

He drew in a breath and blew it out. "Anyway—" while she reached out and patted his hand.

He couldn't remember his mum and dad just sitting together like this. He couldn't remember their laughter or their jokes or their smiles. They were two tall and silent people in his childhood, and then one of them was gone. When he met Elsie, when he set his cap at her, as his mother joked, he determined to make her talk and make her laugh.

"There's no one like you for blarney, Clement Gormley," Elsie had said to him at the quiet end of one of their first long days together.

"I've got years of stories to tell you," he'd replied. More than twenty years of talking he'd done now.

"Does he still work over there, that professor your mum used to type for? Did you ever think to find him over there?"

If her tangent surprised him then his own next words surprised him too. "I used to wonder if he was sweet on her—he'd bring her chocolates sometimes, and a card once for her birthday: that made her blush."

A different life, he thought suddenly, *if your dad was one for learning.* Maybe Clem would have gone to the university instead of just polishing its floors and fixing its window sashes.

He shook his head and stood up, passing the empty cup back to his wife as she reached for her own. *And done what?* He was never able, really, to see things other than the way they were, he believed, and he took some pride in that.

"I'm off then, up the hill. Shouldn't be late tonight, if you want to wander up and meet me." He liked it, cutting through the cemetery as he walked down over Highgate Hill, seeing her there among the trees, her brown hair lighter than the foreshore's shadows. They'd head home together, the river turning and lapping alongside them.

"I'll do that then." Elsie smiled. "And something nice for tea—a bit of lamb, or some steak, if you like." She paused in the doorway, watching as he stretched. "Maybe he was showing off, your dad. Maybe he thought it'd impress you, taking a great bird like that when it could just as easily have risen up and flown away."

"It was never me he wanted to impress," said Clem, shrugging his arms into his coat. "Just his mates, always his mates. Might've been different if I'd been older and he'd thought I could shoot things myself. But I don't think he really minded what I thought about him—don't think it occurred to him I thought anything. I never saw my mum cry when he died, you know," he said, checking his pocket for his wallet and starting down the stairs. He'd sometimes wondered if his mum had wished his dad dead too.

As the ferry headed for its wharf, Clem wedged himself against its railing. He loved the river, its twists and curves, and the quietness of it. If he wanted anything, he thought, it was a little boat— get himself over to work faster, and he could go rowing on the weekends, too, maybe throw in a line. *Wonder what Else'd think of that?* Probably pack up a picnic and want to come too.

Him and Elsie: twenty-three years now, he figured. He could

remember the first time he saw her, the day war was declared in 1939. He was stomping through Brisbane trying to feel like a grown-up and wondering if he should enlist. A tram slowed on Adelaide Street and she'd swung out before it fully stopped, bright and young in her pale green dress. The sun caught her hair, the wind caught her skirt, and she'd looked so impossibly pretty that Clem had paused and without thinking put out his hand to help her down. That was that. At twenty, he'd just scraped under the age for the militia call-up, and then he found work with the city's electricity department.

"Safe and sound," as he told Elsie. "Out of harm's way."

They were married in 1940, and she'd worn that same green dress prettied up with some kind of lace. His mum had loved her—thrifty enough to make do with a frock she had, and alive enough to stop Clem from hankering for the war.

They'd had good times, the three of them—and then the five of them, with the twins—in the old house on Highgate Hill. He still missed it, and his mum; he used to call in for a cup of tea with her on his way to work. She'd been dead now for a decade.

The boy threw a rope out to the jetty, and Clem braced again as it tightened and held—he liked to feel the decking shift as everyone else rushed off before him. His first job today, he knew, was in the Physics Building, a dodgy door on one of the lavatories—shouldn't take more than half an hour, and if he got to it while there was a lecture on, he shouldn't inconvenience anyone about the convenience. He smiled at his play on words and set off for the caretaker's house, where he gathered his tools. Cutting into the Great Court, the morning sun against its sandstone dazzled him.

Scoping the halls of the Physics Building, he saw students hurrying towards a class and stood a moment in the foyer, his eyes adjusting to the low light as the crush passed.

"Mr. Gormley, is that you?" Clem recognized the quiet voice

of one of the physics lecturers, and nodded. "You're here about the lavatory? Because when you've dealt with that, I'd appreciate your having a look at my office door as well—I'm teaching now, but you'll see it's left open, down the hall. If you could pop by, when you've got a moment. I would like to make it secure."

Clem turned in the direction the man indicated, and turned back to see him disappearing into the lecture hall. "All right, all right," he heard the man bark—such a different tone from his polite request to Clem—as he carried his kit to the bathroom.

They were always cold, these buildings. Clem shivered as the men's room door swung behind him—the smooth cold floor, the tiled walls, the stall doors that clattered. He saw the problem, re-screwed the hinge, and was done in ten minutes, washing his hands at one of the basins and smiling as the hot water came through.

The physicist's room, and then he'd get into the sun.

He pushed at the office door, feeling the way it sagged from the weakness of its upper hinge. Clem pressed at the rectangle of metal, feeling in his back pocket for his screwdriver.

He glanced at the desk behind him, taking in the papers, squared with each other and the desk's edge, the pot of pencils, the half-drunk cup of tea set neatly on a mat. There was a typewriter too, pushed to one side—no women tapping away for this man—and at the front of the desk, a dome of glass on a varnished wooden stand.

Inside was a funnel full of black stuff—tar, thought Clem, or maybe pitch. When Clem was a boy his uncle had built a boat, and Clem had spent weekends by the river, smoothing over the joins in the little craft's hull, proud to be involved with something that sounded as grand as *caulking*.

Uncle Perce: he hadn't thought of him for years—and then what? The boat finished, the man had kissed his sister—Clem's mum—goodbye, and prepared to set off, across Moreton Bay, and on towards New Zealand.

"But how do you know how to sail her, Uncle Perce?" Clem, pleading, desperate to be taken for a turn. "Oughtn't you to take her out for a run before you try for the whole horizon?"

"It's in my bones, Clem, the wind and the water—ask your mum about growing up on the shoreline with such a bad influence for a brother. Once I go, I don't turn back." He'd named the boat for Clem's mum too: the *Pearl*.

"She sounds like a pirate ship," whispered the boy.

There might have been a Christmas card from New Zealand that first year, Clem thought now, but nothing after that, and he'd never asked his mum where Uncle Perce had gone, or why. How funny, he thought, that his uncle had been so disposable: *if Donny upped and moved to another country*, he thought, and then smiled. Elsie would never let her children get away. She'd know where they were, and what they were doing, until the last life left her body.

"My babies," she still called them sometimes, though they were twenty-one, the pair of them. She swore it was accidental.

Maybe he would see about buying a little boat—call it the *Pearl II*. Clem bent down to gather his tools. Straightening up, his leg knocked the desk and something moved. He turned towards the glass jar and saw the pitch that had been dangling down into the funnel, thick and heavy, snap so that the new drop lay in the beaker below.

No, no. Clem stared at it—had he done this? Had he damaged this thing? All the possibility he'd felt—the lovely idea of a boat, a day on the river—shattered and dissipated. *Just get out*: he grabbed his bag and reached for the door, fumbling in his haste. The physicist was standing outside, his own hand reaching for the knob.

"All done? Grand, thank you. I've just come for my book—" He stepped around Clem, stopping as he saw the jar. "Well," he said quietly. "Well, well."

"I don't know how it happened," Clem stammered then. "I was rescrewing the hinge and when I turned, it was . . ."

"So you didn't see it?" The man was holding his arm now, and leaning in quite close. "You were in the very room, and you didn't see it?"

Clem blinked, swallowed—this was worse than being hauled up and asked to spell *cacophony* in school. He took a guess at the right answer.

"No—no, sir, I didn't."

The physicist laughed and inched the jar towards the window. "Eight years since the last drop—and it was only the fourth since Parnell began the experiment. And you know the mad thing? No one's ever seen it happen. Ever. I've had it here on my desk for a year now, waiting. And the blessed thing waits till I'm talking to a bunch of students—and waits until your back's turned and you're busy with the wretched door. Then off it goes. An historical moment. Unseen by anyone—pah!"

He grabbed at a book, so fast that Clem jumped aside. "Shut the door on your way out, would you?" the physicist called, rushing back to his class.

"But should I wait? If it's going to happen again, I could wait and watch for that? If it matters that I missed it this time?"

From deep in the hallway, Clem heard the man laugh. "Come back in seven or eight years," he said. "When the next drop is ready to taunt me." And he disappeared into the gloom.

Outside, in the elegant loggia of the Great Court, Clem stopped a moment, visualizing the pitch's drop again. Maybe he'd tell Elsie as they walked home together. Maybe he'd tell her as they had their tea. Or maybe it'd take him as long to tell her about the silly pitch as it had to say something about his dad and the crow. There was something sweet about a story you kept to yourself.

But the physicist was standing behind him on the ferry back across the river that evening, and Clem overheard him talking to a colleague—in his polite hallway tone, not the rousing bark for students. "And blow me down if it didn't go today—I was giving a lecture. Parnell's pitch gave way, and there wasn't a blessed soul there to see it."

Alone at the handrail, Clem saw his knuckles grip to whiteness. *No*, he wanted to call out a correction. And: *Hang on! There was a blessed soul—and he did see it.* But the man had gone into the next part of his conversation, and Clem knew he'd missed his moment to say a thing.

He let go of the rail and shook his head, seeing himself as the physicist might—a plain man with ginger hair and stubble, pushing through his forties; worked a bit too hard and living a bit too little.

All these moments, he thought as the boat eased away from the riverbank. They added up to something, but he could never quite see what.

10

The river

ON THE path down to the river, Elsie paused to watch a heron pick along the grass. It was so pretty here, with lush gardens planted by the water she still thought of as a creek—but then, she couldn't really remember what it had looked like before.

"It's a drain, Mum, a stormwater drain," Elaine had said when they'd walked its length together the day before during a brief patch of sunshine. "Gerald says it will flood with all this rain."

Nicer to walk here alone. On her own, she didn't have to take such care of what she said—no one was going to mind if she thought it was Friday or Sunday, 2010 or 1962. It seemed likely all these things were true.

The knob of her walking stick—that good idea of Donny's—felt as certain as the world against the palm of her hand as she paused to watch the bird take flight. It was an impossibly elegant creature, and although it looked too long and lanky to be able to manage liftoff, up it surged, folding itself into a thin, fine line, like the line of a drawing, and heading west towards the river.

Sweet little one, her Donny, and now he was grown up himself and it was his boy—no, his grandson—with the loud guitar and the fancy word for echoes. She shook her head. You never knew how things would go.

It was a nice walk, but it felt like a long one—wasn't this the path that Gloria used to run in five minutes? Elsie felt she'd been walking for days.

Once, when Gloria was tiny and having trouble settling to sleep, Elsie had taken her and Elaine in for the night, closing the door between mother and daughter and taking the baby out to walk through the predawn light. At four thirty in the morning, all the pathways by the river had been thick with pedestrians making the most of the cooler air before the summer's day came on. It was like a whole world, a whole network of intersections and exchanges, that most of the city's population, fast asleep, knew nothing of.

"Our secret," Elsie had whispered to the baby, lying back in her pushchair, her eyes wide at the blue sky and the soft trees. It had been hard, watching Elaine struggle—watching her hate her own mother whenever Elsie took the little one and settled her in a moment.

"I'm clearly not cut out for this," Elaine would hiss against Elsie's protests that any baby settled for anyone who hadn't been trying to do it for an hour. "I don't know why I even try."

Which words sounded almost like a foreign language, thought Elsie, because who didn't want a baby of their own to hold and comfort? Who didn't think that motherhood was the thing they might do best?

The artist, she remembered, and it stopped her in her tracks. The memory of Ida Lewis in her messy room, the way the light came in through all the windows. Ida Lewis had once asked if Elsie regretted having her kids.

What an awful thing to say.

All the days she'd taken Gloria for Elaine—"to give you a break, love," she'd said at first, and then: "to give you some time." And while Lainey traipsed into town and had her hair done, or met a friend in one of the tearooms, Elsie read with Gloria and played with Gloria and taught Gloria how to hold a crayon and hold a fork and pour her own milk from the bottle to the cup and tie up her shoelaces.

"She'll grow into it," she'd whispered to Clem, on the edge of sleep, after Elaine had collected the little girl and taken her home.

And Clem would shake his head and say, "She's a good girl, our Elaine; let her work it all out for herself."

But she never had, as far as Elsie could see, and she'd had no more children either. It was Carol who'd turned out to have such a knack for mothering.

Things never work out quite the way you expect.

She shook her head and made herself keep walking. Behind her, in the new apartment (Elaine used this grand word all the time, but Elsie preferred to say "flat"), everything had been unpacked, and no more boxes or belongings were to come from home. There was no doubt she'd arrived.

The new place was so very spartan, all its surfaces white—walls, cupboards, ceilings, bench tops, drapes—and a sort of caramel carpet at her feet. Too bare, too spare, too silent. At home, she'd had the tonnage of conversations and decisions, all that laughter, living, life. She had only to sit there quietly to hear it, to remember. The new place was a clear and empty space.

"This place isn't friendly," she'd whispered to her daughter-in-law as she came and went with deliveries.

"Ah, Mum, just give it some time." Carol had held her hand, patting it before she let it go.

Her daughter-in-law and her daughter. The girls, as Elsie still thought of them. She couldn't believe they were getting close to seventy, especially as they bustled to and fro with things for her. She was blessed, she thought, to have help to make this nasty, brutal move. Well, if Elaine could quite ever be helpful.

"I wonder, were we ever friends?"

Elsie had been sure she'd only thought these words but when her daughter stopped and turned from the box she was unpacking, she realized she'd said them aloud.

"You're my mother," Elaine said. She leaned back over the box, her head down, fussing with its contents. And then: "This carpet's much more practical than your bright green stuff," nodding her approval at the thick caramel pile as if nothing else had been said. "I don't know why you chose that color in the first place. And I'd've gone mad with all that wallpaper. You could hang some nice paintings in here."

Clem's wallpapers: he'd taken pride in the job every time he did it, carefully matching patterns across the strips. He'd papered every two or three years through the fifties, the sixties—"freshen the place up, Else; make it nice and new"—so that she'd been secretly relieved that it had been changed only once more after he'd died. Donny had done it after the flood. She'd never heard him swear as much as he did at all that hanging—"sorry, Mum," after every expletive. But he'd done it—a different pattern in every room, just as Clem would have chosen, and lining up the pictures across the joins.

"You could have a bit of wallpaper if you wanted," Carol had whispered. "I'm sure Don's recovered enough from the last time to give it a go—it's nearly thirty-seven years now, after all."

Carol had been busy with a delivery of rugs—a green one she'd chosen specially—and plants, some of Elsie's cushions, and a raft of family photos in matching frames.

"I still think of your photographs lost in the flood," Carol had said as she fiddled with who would hang where. "I still remember Don coming home to tell me they were gone."

"And there was a painting too." Elsie frowned. "I don't know how I'd find it now." All of it, washing away.

"A painting?" Carol shook her head. "I don't remember. I can ask Don, if you like?"

The flood; that terrible flood. The risk of a house around here. She'd thought of moving elsewhere after it happened. But it was her place—and Clem's, more importantly. He had just passed away when it happened. If she'd moved, how would he have known where she was? In the week after he'd died, she'd slept in every room except the bathroom, trying to find a place where his going made more sense. She never did, but the shock of opening her eyes somewhere slightly unexpected offset for a second or two the shock of mourning him. And that had made her strange sleeps seem worthwhile.

Losing Clem was the strangest part of the sadness of these weeks, nearly forty years later. She watched the sun sparkle on the creek's surface and wiped at the edge of a tear. How on earth would he track her down now? She could remember the disproportionate grief she'd felt over the photos when she'd lost Clem to pneumonia just before. It had felt like losing everything at once.

On the path, Elsie stepped aside to let a cyclist whoosh by. She thought of how lovely it was to have Carol call her "Mum"—and how little she liked it when Elaine's Gerald did the same. Yet Clem had liked him. Clem had said he was a good man, and Elsie supposed he was. They hadn't much in common, which seemed a queer thing to say about your son-in-law. They had Elaine in common.

Gerald could have made right whatever it was that Elaine had always deemed was wrong, Elsie thought then, strangely adamant. The problem she'd never resolved.

"Elaine's all right, Mum," was all Gerald said the only time she'd broached it. "You're just such different people—that's all."

As if she should just make her peace with that.

She was by the river now, the round sound of casuarinas high above her and the water rushing by towards the bend. They'd built a bridge over to the university—Clem would have loved that; off to work and home again in no time—and Elsie gazed at its tall pylons. They looked like the magical spires from a fairy tale. She'd like to cross that bridge one day; Don said they let no cars on it, which seemed odd, but that you could walk or take a bicycle or a bus.

Perhaps the latter; in the old days, she'd have set off on foot before breakfast, but it looked a way off now.

She'd marked her life by the tides of this river from the first time she'd seen it, walking down from the train she'd caught into Roma Street and standing on the North Quay to watch it pass. She loved its tempers, its twists and turns. She kept pace with the way the tides moved through each twenty-four hours, high and low, pulling forward by about half an hour each time. A constant and a change.

The water had been clearer back in the old days, but she quite liked the khaki it wore now. It looked durable, workmanlike. And its watercourse defined the landscape; there was no doubt about that.

The sunlight moved and the surface of the water changed again.

Olive. Cutch. Sap green—what were these words? The random nonsense of too many crossword clues, thought Elsie. She tipped her head one way and then the other, as if to dislodge them. She thought of brown carpet. Stripes of color. Waiting for Elaine. Something more.

She shook her head. The sun was too hot and the shadows had all but folded into noon. Who knew how long the walk back might take? She crossed the road, her stick-spiked footsteps steady on the path.

Until she reached the point where the concrete pathways branched—the southern arm heading towards her new flat, the northern arm towards the hill, beyond which her old home sat. What was happening there? Donny said the family had a little one.

Middle of the day—there'd be lunchtime, and some quiet time, and a sleep. She smiled. The rhythms of the beginning of life; she'd loved their order and their certainty.

She set her feet south, and headed back to the new apartment. In the five minutes Gloria's running legs took to cover this path, Elsie felt she'd barely moved at all. The heat thickened the air into something like molasses, and her feet dragged.

Glory. Maybe she'd be home for Christmas. Elsie must ask Elaine if there was any news. And as if on cue, a car drove fast along the road that edged the parkland, a Christmas carol—something about joy? something faithful?—blaring as it went.

"This is why we walked out in the evenings," she said to Clem. She often talked to Clem; he didn't mind. Perhaps she and Clem could walk home together later tonight when the day cooled.

She closed her eyes and saw herself in her kitchen, turning a pot of tea to steep in the first quiet moments of her children's sleep. Elaine always asleep faster and for longer than her brother. Donny always somehow heartbroken when he woke—those hopeless cries.

Clem had cried like that a little, at the end, in his sleep. He'd cried a little then, beyond her comfort.

"But how lucky we were, Clem." With her eyes closed, he was there, just by her side. "I was taking a tram on through Adelaide Street, and I stepped down, and there you were."

It still frightened her, the idea that it might not have happened—if she had caught a later tram; if she had used another stop; if she had been the second, third, or fourth to disembark.

"It's all right," she heard Clem say. "I'm here."

She held the sound of his voice at the center of herself and kept walking towards her new place.

11

The intruder

ON A silvery summer morning when a fine film of cloud turned the sun's light to glare, Lucy and Tom set off for the city, whose spires gleamed like a mirage at the end of their street. Santa was in the shops, and Lucy wanted Tom to have his picture taken. When she was little, she'd begged her mother every year to be taken to tell Santa what she'd like for Christmas. There was a direct correlation, she'd believed, between the fact that she was never taken and the fact that Santa never delivered the right thing. Lucy could see now what a wrangle it would have been for her mother, on her own, with four girls and a full working week. But when she got the Holly Hobbie doll instead of the Strawberry Shortcake (like her friend Astrid's), and the bike with training wheels instead of the one with the white basket (like her friend Astrid's), she felt that not seeing Santa was somehow to blame.

Then, when Lucy was seven, Astrid's mother, Linnea, took the two of them into a department store and sat one on each of Santa's knees.

"My girls," she said to the lady behind the camera. "Aren't they just adorable?" Lucy beamed at the deception; Astrid frowned.

"When I grow up and have kids," Lucy had said to Linnea on the way home, "I'm taking them to see Santa every single year." She'd shown off the photo to her sisters, gleeful at their envy. Now, she half expected to see some shadow of her own small self in the picture with her son.

In his stroller, Tom leaned forward a little, one arm reaching out so that Lucy, pushing behind, saw its starburst of waving fingers. "Santa," he called towards his own shadow. "Going Santa."

And after Christmas, she should maybe try to find a job in this new place, she thought vaguely as she set her shoulders to push the stroller up another hill. She missed work sometimes—the work that wasn't Tom; she missed its focus and its purpose, the sense of finishing something. But then there was the question of another child, and she never quite managed to think about that, let alone have a conversation about it with Ben. She pulled her shoulders back a little more and began the climb. *Maybe take another calculated chance.*

The topography of this place still amazed her, the way it rose and fell so abruptly. Lucy had walked for hours, intrigued by its constant crescendos and falls. She'd walked pathways and roadways that cupped the edge of the river and she'd pushed the stroller around their curves, trying to decipher its calligraphy and understand its ever-changing direction. Where she grew up, north of Sydney, the coast ran obediently north to south; you stood on its shore and looked directly east, out across the ocean. You knew where you were. Her sisters still lived on that coastline, suspicious of any place that had a river, not a beach. In their new house—*Elsie's house*—the back door faced almost due east and Lucy loved that. One sure point in a floating world.

Here were rises and ridges, dips and hollows, climbs so steep that stairways had been cut into hills and seemed to push straight to the sky. There were crests and corners that seemed sometimes to consume sound and sometimes to amplify it: the river could pass the sirens of its ferries—its CityCats —along to her house, although she was well away from it, upstream.

As they came in from the river at the old Customs House, she found herself on Queen Street at its famous corner, the MacArthur corner. Well, famous to Lucy, who'd read about the World War II general and almost expected to see him dashing into the handsome sandstone building for a meeting that would surely win the war. Standing behind Tom, she nudged the stroller back and forward as she nattered on to him.

"Who else has been here, I wonder," she said as the cars passed. "Who else has waited on this corner? Maybe Dad's mum? Maybe Dad when he was small? Maybe Elsie, with her twins?"

This habit of calling up Elsie. She hardly noticed anymore that she did it—it had become automatic. She'd stood in Elsie's kitchen conjuring conversations with the older woman. *Of course, in your day the world had fewer things to worry you.* And: *It must have been simpler then.* To which Elsie would reply with observations about clothes dryers or the boon of vaccines.

It felt a friendly and comforting thing—"an imaginary friend," said Ben, and Lucy smiled. That was how she'd thought of Tom before his birth. Now it made her feel a little more at home.

"I don't even know if there were traffic lights," said Lucy to her small son. "Isn't that funny? I can imagine trams, and ladies in nice dresses and hats. But I don't know how they crossed the road." She balked at how little she knew of how this place had been before— who was here; where they lived.

She felt her elbow bounce as someone nudged it, and imagined— horrific—the stroller, rolling forward. But as she steadied herself and watched the man run on through the mall, she was sure it was Ben rushing by.

"Hey!" she called before she could stop herself. "What are you doing here?" A quick pulse of shock and desire. But the man turned back, once, to look at her, and he was somebody altogether different. Of course he ran on and Lucy watched the sole of his left sneaker flap. *Ben would never wear those.*

Still, she stood for several minutes in the Santa queue before her heartbeat settled down.

~

She was coming out of Tom's bedroom that evening when she noticed the back door open wide and swinging at the other end of the house. It squeaked as she walked towards it, and when she leaned out to pull it to, there was a cold edge to the summer darkness. *I mustn't have clicked it shut,* she thought blankly. Although she knew, of course, that she had.

It was eight or so at night. Tom had been asleep an hour already, and in America, Ben would not yet be awake. A few more hours, she thought, before he would call home, and she pottered about with the dishes and a broom, starting at the sudden crash of empty bottles from somewhere along the street. She needed to take out their bin.

She pushed open the back door, flicked on the outside light and went down the stairs, looking for her gumboots. Through the first months of Tom's life, Lucy had felt a gnawing anxiety if she went outside when he was inside, patting her pocket for keys and propping the door with a plant, a shoe, a brick. Now, in the yard, pushing her feet into her boots, she looked up at the stars. Of course Tom was all right inside; what was nicer to think about was how much he would love being out here, looking at the night sky.

Overhead, Venus was bright, and Orion pulsed out its cartoon-saucepan shape. As she walked the length of the yard, she felt the slip of the rain-sodden grass under her boots. She pulled the big container to the curb. From down here, the house looked like a facade in a movie set—a little weatherboard thing propped up at the back of a stage, picture-book blue, with a pretty white trim.

"Sky," Tom had said earlier that day, pointing to the color of its walls. And he was right. It was the perfect shade to designate sky. She still couldn't quite believe it was theirs—or the bank's—but she loved it, loved the garden, loved the promise of the trees they were planting, and the coziness of its small nest of rooms.

Heading back across the grass, she saw the tracks her feet had made, and as she kicked off her gumboots and went up the stairs two at a time, she thought of those little footprints in the grass the week they'd moved into this house. Elsie, popping back to check on them: it felt like a benediction.

The destruction of the photos still made her blush. She hadn't been able to tell anyone and she swallowed now to think of it, a deep and awful shame. The collage shot she'd taken on her phone—maybe she should send that on to Elsie, to make good. Maybe there were tiny bits of detail that could be blown up and reconstituted. She'd have a look. She'd see what she could do.

It took her just a few seconds to realize her phone was not where she'd left it in the kitchen.

I must have plugged it in to charge, she thought, heading into the bedroom, where she knew she'd find its power cord hanging limp and disconnected.

I must have left it in my bag—remembering, as she shook the satchel and felt its emptiness, that she had checked her phone twice, maybe three times, while Tom ate his dinner, just in case Ben was awake at some strange time of his night, checking in. She knew then that she had put it out of her own reach, behind her, just there, on the bench.

And then she remembered the swinging back door, and her body lurched as though she'd missed a step.

Tom—and she was through the house and into his room. Where he lay asleep, of course, curled up with his hand beneath his cheek.

The kind of sweet pose Lucy might have tried to capture with her smart new phone. Her father had insisted that she buy it. "Text me everything—*everything*—my grandson does," he'd said when the move north came about. "I don't want to miss a moment of it by not living close by."

She reached for the house phone and called the police.

"Is the intruder still in the house?" the policewoman asked.

"Of course not, no." Her own certainty sounded reassuring, but she darted into the different rooms, suddenly not so sure. "I'm here with my little boy—my husband's away. We were in the lounge room, reading books. We were in the bathroom; he had a bath. Someone must have opened the door and just walked in." Her stomach flipped.

"You didn't have the door locked?"

She heard it as an accusation, and she bit. "Do you always lock yourself into your house?"

"Yes, I do," said the policewoman. "You can never be too careful." And Lucy saw herself from above, walking away from the gaping house to wheel out her rubbish, leaving Tom fast asleep and unprotected inside.

I have taken great risks, she thought. *I have placed my child in great peril.*

"Well, I'll make sure I'm more careful now."

"Is there anyone you know who might have done this; anyone else who has access to the house?"

"My husband's away," Lucy said again, faltering a little. "I'm here with our little boy. There's no one—there's no one who'd come . . ."

"And I see your property backs onto a park," said the woman. "You know it's school holidays at the moment. This is probably a kid, probably a dare. There's always a spike in thefts around the holidays. We'll send someone in the morning—but don't get your hopes up. Take down this number; you'll need it if you have insurance you want to claim."

"I see," said Lucy, uncapping a pen and trying to sound competent and unfazed.

She took down the number, repeating it calmly—although as she spoke, she was picturing footprints in wet grass, and Elsie, and all the pleasant things she'd imagined about the house's former owner twisted towards something more sinister. And hadn't she told Ben that Elsie would have a key?

"Was there anything else, ma'am?" The policewoman's voice was crisp.

"It's just—when we bought this house, the old lady . . ." But Lucy swallowed. It would sound ludicrous. "I'm sorry; no. Can I just check that number again?"

When she'd hung up, she flicked the back door's handle twice, three times, to make sure that it was locked. And then, coming back, she noticed the linen cupboard door was ajar, and the most paranoid part of her wondered if the intruder was still in the house, and was hiding there, folded in with the towels and sheets and quilt covers, or up higher still, with the bags, below the trapdoor—or higher, in the roof.

Of course not.

Still, she wedged the door shut with the laundry basket, and jammed a wooden spoon behind the door handles.

I'm going mad, she thought. *I should ring the insurance. I should ring Ben.*

But instead she sat at the kitchen table with one of Ben's favorite CDs playing too loudly, as if that might make him manifest back on her side of the world. Staring through the locked screen door into the flat nothingness of nighttime, her head ran through a loop of images—sitting with Tom on the sofa; in the bathroom while Tom had his bath; sitting with Tom in his bedroom, singing softly. And somewhere in this, somewhere while these quiet, gentle things were happening, some person—*some kid*, she reeled back—was coming up her stairs and chancing a dash across her kitchen.

She stared at the darkness. Nothing stared back, although it occurred to her, for the first time, that anyone might have been standing on the outer edge of the balcony, leaning against the sky-blue rail, staring straight back at her in her safe, wide puddle of light.

And she would never have seen them.

She poured herself a glass of wine and drank it too fast. Here was another loop of images: all the things that might have happened. *If I'd been standing in the kitchen when they came in. If I'd walked out of the living room to get Tom's milk. If I'd come from the bathroom to pick up my phone. If I'd been carrying Tom through to his cot. If I'd seen them—if I'd seen them.* She closed her eyes: she could remember Ben's number—maybe her dad's. Everyone else's she'd trusted to her phone.

"They'd have had some bullshit story about someone they were looking for," said Ben, when she'd finished another glass of wine and dialed his number. "It's a shit, Lu, but it's done now. It's not going to happen again."

"But remember those footprints? All my jokes about Elsie coming back? I thought that was such a nice thing. What if it is her—or someone else *casing the joint?*" She was almost whispering, crouched down in the doorway to Tom's room where she could hear his every murmur.

"What if all the Lucy Kisses had their phones nicked on the one night? A serial *vardøger* theft." Ben was looking for a joke to take her mind off it, she knew that. But she hated him for trying it just then.

"This isn't helping." Her words sounded like a hiss.

"Come on, Lu." He sounded too far away and the connection crackled badly. "*None* of this is helping. I'm sorry it happened, but it's over; it's done. It's not Elsie—it never was. And I'm on the other side of the Pacific. Ring the insurance; have a shower; try to get some sleep—I know you won't, and I wish I was there. But it's some kid who wanted the latest phone. And our place happened to be the place he tried tonight."

Our place happened to be the place. Lying in bed, in a room bathed with the light and the music she couldn't bring herself to turn off, Lucy played out in her mind the choices she'd made that might have changed this story—as if by going over them, she might find one with a secret catch that would rewind time to a place where the door wasn't unlocked, or the phone wasn't on the bench, or Ben wasn't overseas, or she hadn't bought a smart new phone, or they hadn't bought this house. But she balked at that one, and pulled herself up, literally, leaning back against the wall and looking around her bedroom.

This house was the place that chose them.

She felt as if she was just a kid again herself, and she wanted to stamp and cry and say that she wanted her mum. Her busy, competent, exacting, certain mother. Well, maybe she wouldn't be so soothing. *Whatever you do, you'll be fine.*

She felt quite a long way from fine.

It had been a great relief to Lucy when she realized she wasn't anything like her mother. She admired her incredibly; she knew her work was amazing. She'd watched her sisters make their own ways into medicine—a nurse, a GP, a pathologist—and then realized that she didn't have to do that. She was eighteen then, and she and her mother stopped fighting. They went along quite nicely after that. There was the odd rankle about a point of difference, but mostly each left the other alone.

She'd fought with her mother twice while she was pregnant. The first time, exhausted by morning sickness that didn't let up, she'd stopped work early. "It's archaic," said her mother, "giving up your job to be supported by your husband."

The second time, she'd objected to being manhandled towards an obstetrician when she wanted to stay with midwives. "I just think that at your age, Lucy," her mother's growl was even more pronounced, "you'd not want to take any risks."

"If anything goes wrong, the midwives send me to a doctor. Honestly, Mum, I thought you'd be on my side, the great GP for women. You didn't have a problem when my sisters all did this."

"Your sisters were a damn sight younger than you are," said her mother. "I just want this to be all right."

"Fine." Lucy heard the snap in her own voice. "And I want it to be all right too. And to be right for me I want nothing to do with obstetricians—they make me think of men playing golf. I want to do it this way, and this is how I'll do it."

Such a long silence then; she thought her mother might have hung up. Then she heard a long intake of breath.

"I will say this once," her mother said. "You can put your foot down about this. You can have your tantrum. But get used to the fact that you're going to be a mother—and no matter how much you've been in control of all the other parts of your life, you're about to enter into a thing that you can never control entirely. Ever."

"Hypocrite," said Lucy, and hung up.

Although she saw, now, that her mother was right.

Outside, a herd of curlews shrieked and called, and a possum seemed to reply. Two frogs passed the percussion of their noise between themselves, and a car took a corner too quickly, skidding a little, and revving its engine as it sped off.

"Fuck you," said Lucy, louder than she'd intended, but she didn't know if she meant the too-fast driver or the kid sitting somewhere wiping all her photos, her little films, her screens of messages. There was a knock on the other side of the wall as Tom rolled and hit the side of his cot, and for a moment Lucy thought the sound had come from the linen cupboard, and she froze.

I said, "Fuck you," she thought, her innards shaking. She'd always pegged herself as someone who'd drown if they saw a shark—"no fight, all flight."

"But if Tom was there," Ben would say, "you'd be formidable. If Tom was there, you'd take on all comers."

The curlews called again, so melancholy, and from way off down the river, Lucy heard the chime of the last CityCat, ready to slip from its wharf.

Take me, she thought suddenly. *Take me somewhere else.*

12

The astronaut

IN A window seat of the fifty-ninth row of a jumbo jet heading westward on the overnight trans-Pacific haul, Ben closed the book he kept trying to read and stuffed it into the pocket in front of him. He should know better than to think he could concentrate. All the white noise of the engines: there was no space for your mind to stretch out. He pushed up the window blind and looked at the darkness around him. *As above, so below*: a quote from somewhere but he couldn't place the source. There were stars too, and closer than usual, or so it felt. A trick of the light or a misplaced reflection, and it looked like they surrounded the plane.

He hated red-eye flights: fourteen hours from Los Angeles to Brisbane. You lost an entire day crossing that line that kinked between a hundred and sixty and a hundred and eighty degrees east: the spectacularly arbitrary thing that made sense of time everywhere. It felt like magic—"*pff,*" as Tom would say when his mother threw a towel over one of his toys and made it disappear.

Pff, thought Ben.

He leaned his head against the window's thick thermoplastic and looked at the stars again—*as above, so below.* Lucy would remember where that quote came from. She did their remembering—although he was better now at remembering to snap pictures. Tom on a swing. Tom on a slide. Tom fast asleep.

"And who is remembering me?" Lucy had asked once, scanning through the photos on his phone.

"I've got you safe and sound right here, Lu." Tapping his head. "Best and brightest version there is."

In front of him, the map on the screen showed his slow progress across the vast ocean—what he wanted, he realized, was a map that showed him where the plane was in relation to the constellations. This was probably the closest he'd get to outer space, more than five miles above the ground—which wasn't even out of the troposphere. He gazed at the blackness: there were satellites out there, always. No shuttles now until next year. But somewhere was the International Space Station, whizzing around the planet sixteen times a day.

When he was a boy, he'd wanted to be an astronaut. He'd wanted to shoot away from Earth and into outer space where he could see the stars, all the time, and all around. His mother had given him a book about the universe one Christmas when he was five or six, and he'd pored over its pictures—the rainbows made by the spectral images of stars; the time-lapse pictures that turned them into lines of light; the spooky darkness of the sun in an eclipse.

He still had the book—it was almost fifty years old, a milestone he was rushing towards himself. Not that he felt it. He thought of himself and Lucy as the same age rather than ten years apart. He was always genuinely surprised to realize that his memories pre-dated hers and the soundtrack of their childhoods diverged.

Tom loved looking at the old book's pictures while Ben tried to explain how much more was known about the universe now, and how much more of the universe there was.

"You see, Tom, this book thought the cosmos had a radius of

thirteen billion light years; and now they reckon it's something like forty-five billion light years."

"Million billion," Tom would repeat with a grin as if it was part of a tongue twister.

Ben was seven years old when Neil Armstrong stepped onto the moon. He had watched it, like everyone else he knew, through the crackling static of a big old cathode-ray television set, black and white, of course, so that for years, without realizing, he had believed that the only color that existed in the universe must exist on Earth, and that anything that might exist anywhere else was a kind of monochromatic fuzz.

"It has a stark beauty all its own," Armstrong had said. "It's different, but it's very pretty out here."

Well, thought Ben, *of course there was no color.* Because color meant life—humans, or animals, or plants, with their different petals, their changeable leaves, the way their chlorophyll pulsed bright and vital with the warmth of the sun. "Photosynthesis": that had been his second favorite word when he was seven. His favorite: "luminescent." Even if they both had more than nine letters.

His mother was suspicious of big words—she thought them pretentious; a bit fancy.

He was born on the twentieth of February 1962, as John Glenn's *Friendship 7* passed over Australia's east coast. For years, his mother had told him the story as he waited to sleep.

"When he crossed over Perth, everyone turned on their lights—it must have looked so beautiful from all the way up there." She let him sleep with the blinds open, so he could look out to the stars. "After John Glenn had crossed Australia, he headed out across the Pacific. He thought he was flying through a field of fireflies—thousands of them, he said, streaming towards his spaceship. Imagine, Ben, imagine how beautiful that would have been. 'I am in a big mass of some very small particles,' he said. 'They're brilliantly lit up like they're luminescent. I never saw anything like it.'" And she'd pause a little, stroking Ben's hair, smoothing his quilt.

"And you know what he said then? 'They look like little stars. A whole shower of them coming by.' I'd never heard anything like that. There you were, this tiny person I had to take care of, and I was hearing these things that some man had said, way up in space."

Ben had known, from the youngest age, that she had found this wonderful.

Now, remembering her words, he felt he could have reached out to touch her happiness—so bright, it always felt precious. "That line in Shakespeare, you know: 'there was a star danced, and under that was I born,'" she'd once told him. "That's the only Shakespeare I remember from school. And that's why I put Benedict for your middle name, love—Beatrix, I planned, if you were a girl. And there you were, my little one; there you were."

Alexander Benedict Carter: his own ABC. She'd called him Ben from the moment his father left them, she always said, and even now, almost fifty years later, Ben smiled when he saw his own byline—*by Ben Carter*—to think his father wouldn't know that this was him. He'd be looking for an Alex, if he looked at all.

How could you do that? The idea of not seeing Tom. It was beyond him.

He'd looked forward to this trip, his assignment. Technology; science; the future and how it might change: it was still as exciting to him as it had been when he was a kid and he looked forward to writing these new stories. His was a dream job, he reckoned, but being away this time had been hard. Being away from Lucy and Tom—and then there was the mess with Lucy's phone. It had seemed wrong to be so far from home.

This was the longest he'd been gone since Tom was born, and for a split second he thought the boy mightn't remember him. People came. People went. His own father: well, he'd gone without a trace.

"Better off without him." That's what his mother always said. And he'd believed her, young enough to take her at her word. It was only since he'd spent time watching Tom that he felt angry with his dad—and here they were, living back in Brisbane, where the man had disappeared. Sometimes he stopped in the middle of a crowded street, scanning its faces. He wouldn't know his dad if he walked by, and he quite liked the safety of that.

Safety. It felt different now there was Tom. Lucy had set great store on how safe their new home felt. Now that her phone had been taken, he wondered how she'd feel.

The police had come and dusted the bench, the door handle, the stair rail for prints. And Lucy had fixed a new latch to the screen, to fasten it from the inside. But she woke, she'd told him, every night at every sound.

"You'll be right, Lu." The cheerfulness he mustered up from so far away. "There might be a rat in the roof." That was what she'd do if Tom was worried. She'd tamp it down, defuse it, make him feel things were all right.

~

Lucy and Tom stood on the porch as Ben's cab pulled up outside the house. "You see, Tom? It's all right now. Daddy's here."

Ben shivered. Yes. She was reminding Tom who he was.

But then he scooped them in, the two of them, and relaxed. It was so warm, so easy. Here they were. All together. He was home.

That night, Ben propped his head up at the kitchen table, trying to stave off his jet lag a little while longer. He swallowed a yawn, flicking through a magazine to keep himself awake and wishing he was tucked into bed like Tom.

"Did you see this, Lu—how did I miss this?" Spinning the pages towards her as she came into the room. "The Iranians say they launched a rat, a turtle, and some *worms* into space . . ." He scanned the story. "Last *February*? I can't believe I didn't know. What was that dog's name, the first one in space?"

"Laika—there was that film."

"Swedish. We went to see it. One of our first dates."

"I loved that film."

They smiled at the memory shared and Ben turned the page. "I wonder how the turtle fared in orbit." If he could stay awake an hour or so longer, he'd have a better chance of sleeping through the night.

Lucy filled the sink with hot water, squeezing the detergent in such a rush that a cloud of the smallest bubbles rose up towards her. "Imagine being married to one of those astronauts. Those guys on *Apollo 13*, or your guy, Glenn, cramped into a tin-can spaceship, honestly not knowing if they'd make it back or not. My imagination would run riot if you went and did something like that—and I say that now, when things are run by proper computers and not a handful of batteries and some toggle switches." She dropped the dinner plates into the sink so that the water surged onto the floor, soaking her sneakers. "Shit!" Banging the side of the sink. "Shit."

From the table, Ben watched her shoulders heave: it seemed an enormous reaction to an insignificant thing. "Lu? Are you OK?"

"I just . . ." She was sobbing; she was actually sobbing. He stood up, pulled her away from the sink and cradled her head against his shoulder as she would have cradled their son's. "And I think I cracked a plate."

"What is this? What's going on?" Trying to look at her, smiling and frowning at the same time. "I'm never going to get fired into orbit. I go to work and sit at a desk, doing nothing more challenging than making up sentences. I even cross at pedestrian crossings. *And* with the lights—" He saw the woman step out with her stroller, and gulped: not a story to share. "I live the safest life in the world . . . what are you worried about?"

She shook her head, leaning against him. "I'm just tired—that's all—worrying—and the stupid phone, you know? And I *missed* you," as he kissed the top of her head. But he could feel tremors through her body, and she wouldn't meet his eyes. "Of course your mum wanted you to be an accountant," she said at last. "No one wants their child to be blown up into space."

Ben kissed her again. "She did help me build a great spaceship out of cardboard boxes one summer holiday. Then I wrecked it by trying to launch it in the backyard. Nearly blew the place to bits."

"You tried to *what?*"

"I made this gunpowder mix with stuff you could get from the chemist—the seventies; you could buy just about anything. I went into town to buy it—it was seventy-four, just after Brisbane's big flood. We had an extra week of school holidays because of all the water and Mum let me go into town on my own. Not that I told her what I was buying. Well, the cardboard, the duct tape: she knew about that."

He'd spent the summer holidays modifying his design, and on the first sunny day in late January, he'd caught the train to the edge of the city, and walked around to the address she'd given him—an art supplies shop—and the chemist just down the road. Saltpeter. Sulfur. Charcoal. It was the first time he'd gone into the city alone and he could still remember the tightness he'd felt in his chest and how much longer it had seemed to take to walk anywhere—from home to the train; from the train to the shops—without his mum. As if he might never arrive.

The way his voice had cracked as he asked for the cardboard. He was glad he'd bought that first. He'd cleared his throat and pulled his shoulders back before he asked for the stuff from the chemist's—they measured it out for him without a second glance. And he carried it carefully home.

"I packed the powder, buried it, and ran a fuse line along to my rocket. Probably lucky I didn't blast myself to pieces. I didn't know how hard you had to tamp it, see, so it never would have worked. But the smoke smelled terrible."

He could see Lucy's face reflected in the kitchen window, the frown marks burrowing deep between her eyebrows.

"What will I do if Tom's like that? I wouldn't know what to say—what did your mother say?"

"Gave me the hardest slap I'd ever had and told me how much I'd frightened her." He squeezed his wife's shoulders and smiled. But she was right: what would they do if Tom did a thing like that? Today's was a different world. No kid got to do those things anymore—not even the trip into town on their own.

"Here's a thing," Ben went on. "When I got into the city, I met this girl. We were both looking for the art shop. It was her first trip to town too. She was buying blotting paper. Her grandmother's photos had been inundated in the flood. And the weird thing was, where I was, on the hill, on the north side, I didn't even know the place was flooding. I mustn't have seen a newspaper, or the telly. This girl told me about it—her grandmother's house had gone up to its windows, and whole suburbs were under water. It was like she'd come from another planet." He laughed. "I wanted to invite her to see the launch of my rocket, but I was too shy."

He could see the girl so clearly. They'd stood and talked—it felt like hours. She'd had the darkest rich red hair—he'd never realized before that that was Lucy's color too. He might just keep that part to himself. He kissed his wife's forehead.

"What was her name?" Lucy leaned her head against his shoulder again.

But Ben shrugged. "You know, I can't remember. I spent ages on the lookout for her, any time I was anywhere new. But I never ran into her again." All these years; he'd never told the story until now. "Come on, let's finish this stuff."

He flicked at the dishes with a tea towel and they shuddered in the rack.

"I see people I think I know without even looking for them," she said at last, as if she had a story to match his. "When we first moved up here, I saw people from our old life everywhere. Except none of them were really here." She shook a handful of cutlery so that it rattled under the water, and the metallic sound echoed and amplified. "I saw you in the mall the other day, while you were supposed to be off in America. You were running; you didn't see me. You just ran by."

"I would always see you, Lucy Kiss—you know that." He smiled. "Do your other people see you, or do they run by too?"

"They run by—the guy from that juice bar we used to go to. A couple of old friends . . ." She laughed, then shook her head. "They're always a bit messier, a bit less like themselves—like they've swerved away from who they really meant to be."

He was drying his hands, squaring the magazine up on the table. Her words echoed in the room like sirens.

"Is that what it feels like, coming here? Like a crazy decision that took you away and made you some lesser version of yourself?"

And Lucy was still then, and silent, for what felt to Ben like a moment too long.

"Of course not, that's not what I meant," she said, her head still turned away. "You know I love being anywhere new. I just think it's funny the way my brain tries to make sense of strange places by imagining its people are all familiar." She didn't turn. She didn't stop sorting the knives from the forks.

"Anyway," she went on, "I think having Tom—well, I don't mean that was a crazy decision. But it'd make everything feel different, or new, wherever we were. Don't you think?"

From his bedroom, Tom let out a single cry, as if to punctuate his mother's words, and Ben watched as Lucy froze, holding the cutlery in one hand.

The house was quiet. A second passed, and another. Tom was still asleep, and Ben saw Lucy realize this, saw the tension drop away from her shoulders, saw her drop the last handful of spoons into the right place in the drawer.

She was living on this level of alert.

Make her laugh, he thought. "When you were pregnant, you never ate anything half as strange as I was hoping for."

"I did eat peanut butter and hard-boiled egg sandwiches," Lucy said, "but secretly, so you wouldn't know." She glanced up and he caught her eye in the window's reflection and he smiled as she poked her tongue out at him. "Three in the morning."

"Did you tell your midwife that?"

"You should hear some of the things other people ate . . ."

"I was dying to be sent out in the middle of the night to get Coco Pops with lime cordial and grated carrot. The modern man's equivalent of a knightly quest."

"Did you just think of that combination then, or is it some secret breakfast fantasy of yours?"

Ben smoothed the pages in front of him. From the corner of his eye, he could see Lucy wiping the sink with the same meticulous pattern of strokes and squeezes she performed every time she washed up—and every time he did too, for that matter, going back after him just to finish things off. The rhythm, the ritual of her—*and now she will fill the kettle*, Ben thought, as she did. He loved the certainty of these actions, as if he could predict her future.

"I wonder what Tom dreams about," Lucy said, flicking the kettle's switch, "when he cries out, just once, like that. I wonder what you dream about when you're so small, and most things must seem wonderful and new."

The low whirr of the water, of the element: it made a warm and comfortable spiral of sound.

"Some girl once read me a poem," Ben said after a while, as the kettle sang, "about all the things we can remember from all the other lives we've had, for forty days after we're born. 'Some great forty-day daydream,'" he pulled the line from the crevasses of his memory, and he wasn't sure how, "'before we bury the maps.' Maybe it's not forty days; maybe it's all your dreams in childhood, bits of memory you can't decipher because they belong to a person you no longer are . . . What?"

Lucy had turned from the kitchen window. Her arms were tight across her chest; her face was grim.

"What do you mean, 'some girl read me a poem'?" She was glowering. "That was me, Ben Carter. That was me, on one of our first dates. That is a poem by Michael Ondaatje. We were talking about dreams—don't you remember? We were talking about dreaming, which you said you never did, and I had that book of poems in my bag. We were sitting on the floor of your place, and I pulled it out, and I read it to you:

> For his first forty days a child
> is given dreams of previous lives.
> Journeys, winding paths,
> a hundred small lessons
> and then the past is erased.

"I used to recite it for Tom when I was rocking him to sleep— for six weeks after he was born."

"But the girl with that poem—that wasn't you. I went out with her for a few weeks; that was all." The pounding of his heart inside his head was loud. It was as if he were watching a character talking in some bad film—and it was so bad that Ben himself was thinking, *Why are you saying this? Mate, this isn't going to help.*

But the night and its sounds were blurring around him; perhaps he was already asleep. As Lucy pulled a book down from the bookshelves, he felt the room sway, and he grabbed the table.

She set the volume in front of him—a slim paperback, well thumbed. "Open it," she said, nudging it forward. "He signed it for me. I carried it with me for months, like treasure. Even though you laughed." Her voice was cold and she leaned against the doorjamb, as if to keep her distance.

Ben felt a lump in his throat as he folded back the cover and saw the minimal inscription, *To Lucy*, and the signature: a flourish, then a long line, straight, like a horizon. He would have sworn he could remember everything to do with Lucy Kiss, everything to do with the time he'd known her. So how had it happened, this one memory slipping and recasting itself—and landing him, floundering, here? Because he could hear it, now, the poem in her voice; he could remember her reading it, her voice younger, the room lighter, the two of them not much more than forty days together.

"Oh, Lu," he began, swallowing the bad taste. "How could I forget?"

"I depend on you." Her voice was quiet, ferocious. "I depend on you to remember who I am. How we are—or were."

He blinked at her, a band of pain tightening around his head. "Would you read it for me now?" he said, clutching at some kind of reparation. "I miss the way you used to read; I miss the way you used to sing." *In for a penny*, he thought. "And of course I remember." He could see that she didn't believe him. "Of course I remember that afternoon."

She glared again. "I'm going to have a shower." She closed her eyes as another cry, short and sharp, came from Tom's room. But instead of moving towards it, she turned away and went into the bathroom. "And if he wakes up and wants something, you deal with it. It's your turn now that you're home."

She slammed the door. Tom cried out, and Ben waited, so tired that time seemed to stretch.

There was a lull.

Go to sleep, Tom, he thought. *Please. Just go to sleep.*

He opened the book of poems wherever the pages fell, his eyes catching lines here and there. He just wanted to be asleep himself, the weight of his lost day suddenly tripling the weight he felt himself to be. Another cry—awake and sustained. Ben let the book drop and walked into his son's room.

"You're all right, sweetheart," he said, the way he knew Lucy said it. "You're all right, I'm here."

But the child cried longer and louder, his eyes screwed tight against seeing where he was or who was there.

"She's in the shower, Tom." Ben's exasperation was immediate and total. "Come on, come on, come here." Picking him up, which Lucy always said he shouldn't do. "It's all right, Tom. Come here." Nestling the boy's head against his shoulder and rocking him gently.

"Mumma?" said Tom then, once, and noncommittal.

"She's in the shower, sweetheart. You're all right. I'm here."

Maybe there was magic in it, parenthood. Maybe there were words that worked like spells or incantations—said the right way at the right time. He stood and rocked Tom quietly back and forth, and he felt his son's weight thicken as the boy slid into sleep. Whatever the spell was, he'd got it right this time.

"There," he said again, and repeated it a few times. He laid the little boy back in the cot, smoothing the covers around him.

What do *you dream?* he wondered. *What do you see, that you can't describe? And how could I not remember it was your mother who read me that bloody poem?*

The small boy snuffled a little as he turned onto his side. In the dim nightlight that Lucy kept on for him, his rich brown hair glistened and shone.

That girl after the flood: what was her name?

Ben let his hand rest gently on his son's body, then he crept out of Tom's room and slid the book of poetry back into its place on the shelf. Lucy was right, of course. She was always right. He'd misplaced something essential. There was work to be done but he couldn't see what, when, or how. And with the next yawn, he felt his mouth open so wide that his skin seemed to stretch too far.

From behind the bathroom door came the noise of the water dropping and gurgling. Before now, before there was Tom, he would have opened the door, walked into the steam, stripped himself off and climbed in with his wife, holding her, caressing her, trying to make things at least better, if not right. The water dripped and trickled. Lucy used to sing in the shower, but she didn't anymore. And as Ben listened to her silence, he realized he hadn't even noticed when she'd stopped. He heard a louder splash and another, and guessed that she was cupping the water in her hands and splashing it onto her face. She was as routine in a shower as she was with the dishes, and if she was up to this cupping and washing, she had less than a minute to go.

"Hardly worth it," he said aloud, turning away. And found he couldn't remember the last time he'd stood with her under a jet of warm water, washing away everything else in the world.

Collecting his magazine from the kitchen table, he walked into the spare room where his laptop sat, its screen black and inert. He loved the way he had only to jiggle the mouse with the tiniest movement for the whole extraordinary machine to come to life.

Iranian space mission, he typed, and *animals*, and he sat for the instant it took the complex mess of circuitry and processes to trek through the infinity of cyberspace and find him the exact thing he wanted to know. The Iranian government planned to launch a vessel with a monkey in the new year, and there were snide comments about those earlier astronautical worms.

What happened to the turtle? He idled through other pages about astronomy, about rockets, about Mars.

I have no model for marriage, he thought in the expansive way he had when something had gone wrong and he felt he was somehow responsible. *It's no wonder I break it.* As if all things were now on the brink of collapse.

"It's an argument I'd make for Tom having siblings," Lucy had said once, early in Tom's life. "You only children, you've no idea how to fight without it feeling like the end of the world."

In the bathroom, the water stopped, and Ben listened to the noise of the rail as Lucy pulled down her towel. He'd lost count of the number of times she'd mentioned that one of them should tighten it.

From outside, in the darkness, he heard two curlews with their strange, discordant cry. The sound came again, and once more, and then the noise of rain beginning. This summer, it seemed never to stop.

"Can't believe you don't know there's been a flood." The art-shop girl had laughed at him—he'd liked that. "Twenty-seven inches of rain on the weekend, my dad said. As if you can't know about that!"

He looked up the recent rainfall: they'd had half that this past month.

At the front of the house, Tom cried one more time, so short that Ben hardly registered it before the house was quiet again. Then he clicked through to John Glenn's description of the cloud of "fireflies" swirling around his spacecraft. He could have recited it by heart. Brisbane. February 1962. When a manned spaceship first passed over this place.

On the other side of the wall, Lucy was cleaning her teeth—he heard the tap of her brush against the sink, the spit of water as she rinsed her mouth. If he hurried, he could be in bed with his eyes shut before she came out. Then nothing would need to be said, or done—or thought—before the morning.

He pushed his arms up towards the ceiling as far as they would go. *What kind of a coward are you?* And knew the answer as he heard his son call out, once again, and felt himself curse. No: he'd wait; he'd make the tea Lucy had started making. He'd think of something to say. He'd kiss her.

He'd make it all right, no matter how his body ached. He'd put them together again.

Somewhere outside, a car door slammed and the engine burst into life. The sound seemed larger in the night, and dangerous.

Ben listened, careful, but Tom, the curlews, and the car were silent—the only sound now was rain and more rain. And when he glanced up at the screen, it had dimmed itself down to pure blackness, so that all he could see was his own pale reflection.

13

The portrait

ON THE train into town, Elsie watched her reflection in the window. It surprised her sometimes, the way she looked—if she caught herself unawares, she always thought she looked like she was frowning. And yet Clem always assured her, reassured her, she was such a happy thing. Which face would Ida Lewis catch? Which mood would she see? Elsie watched her smile stretch and spread in the window's mirror, and blushed when she saw another passenger watching her.

How you looked, who you were, how the world saw you. You must look your truest self when you were happiest, she thought, and she thought of the scene she'd described for the artist—swinging down from a tram in Adelaide Street, and Clem reaching up for her hand.

Such a thing of chance; it still took her breath away.

The moments when I'm most myself. She stepped off the train at Central and made her way down to the shops. At home, in the quiet, at the end of the day, with a fresh pot of tea before bed—that was happiness, even if it was only Clem who slept under her watch now; Elaine and Don in their own marriages, their own new beds and homes.

That was happiness—that, and dancing. They should go to Cloudland again soon.

She pushed open the door to the haberdasher's, taking in its bolts of luxury. There it was: the clouded silver silk. She'd take a sample.

"A ballgown, dear?" the woman asked from behind the counter, her great heavy scissors making a satisfactorily loud chop across the grain of the fabric.

"I don't know," said Elsie slowly. "It's just so beautiful—it reminded me of moonlight. What sort of a dress could you cut from the night?" The strangeness of the words. These sessions with Ida, they were doing something to her soul. Fancy words and fancy notions. The sooner she was dancing with Clem on that sprung floor, the sooner she'd be anchored in her world.

The woman laughed, sliding the swatch across the counter. "Whatever you make, this color will look lovely on you—bring out the pretty color in your hair, among the grey. Make you look a bright young thing again. It's always nice to see a lady make the most of what she still has."

Holding the fabric tight in her right hand, Elsie coughed, her other hand brushing her cheek. "And how much did you say it was, per yard?" The woman's impertinence, making her feel decrepit when she was only forty-one. Even if she was almost a grandmother. The silk bunched between her fingers, its magical promise gone, she barely paid attention to the woman's answer before she walked out of the shop. There was an older lady who worked in the fabric shop on Saturday mornings; Elsie would buy the length from her instead.

But back at home, sitting with her sandwich in the full sun of her deck, she pulled out the little square again and watched its color change under the light. Here was her reflection again, in the window beside her, and she liked the way its imperfect mirror smoothed the lines from her face and lit up in her hair.

"Radiant" Clem had called it when they were younger—and still would now, if he came and found her sitting in the sunshine, her hair out and drying. It was one of the nicest things he ever said.

Would her hair shine in the painting? Could Ida Lewis make it look like that?

Elsie brought the silk up towards her mouth as if to kiss it, but rested it instead in the dint that shaped the top of her lips and ran up towards her nose. Soft things felt softer rubbed there—she'd learned that with her children's skin, when they were little. It was the one way she could soothe their crying, to rub something gently—a silk-edged bunny rug; a furry bear—against the smoothness of their own young skin. She'd remember to tell Lainey that.

And on Tuesday, she'd be back in Ida Lewis's studio for the next session of painting. She watched her reflection chew hard on the day-old bread of her sandwich. How quickly something new became habitual—*and now I pose weekly for an artist*, she thought, feeling grand. When the picture was finished, she'd take Clem around to see it. She'd wear the new dress made from her shantung.

In the meantime, these sessions. There was something exciting about them, as if anything might happen. *Imagine me.* She'd never much imagined anything. And here she was making conversation with an artist while she sat there. And was regarded. And was re-made—a whole new version of herself.

～

On the fourth Tuesday sitting for her portrait, it rained and rained. Inside the glass studio, her body molded to precisely the right pose by the regular sittings, Elsie watched as the garden was washed clean. The clouds were quite high and light—*silver*, she thought, *like my dress*—but the rain fell solidly, changing the layered leaves to their brightest green.

"I love a rainy day," Ida Lewis said, squeezing another line of blue across her palette. "There's nothing nicer than being inside when it's wet and miserable outside. I hated that during the war: whenever it rained—in Moresby and in the jungle too—you felt that it might never stop. Nowhere felt warm or dry or safe. The first time it rained when I came home, I crawled into bed and stayed there, just crying." She flicked the crumpled paint tube back into its box with all the others, and settled her palette on her arm. "Do you cry much, Elsie? Are you a weeper? Or more stoic? You know, I never saw my mother cry. I don't think she knew how. One of my sisters was the most lachrymose person I ever met, until her sweetheart was killed in the war. She never cried then, just got on with it and went out and found herself another soldier. My other sister, she was like my mum, but sunnier. No tears, but no tempers either. Me, I'm a jumble of everything, and there's nothing like a good cry sometimes. I always wanted to paint someone in the middle of a weep—nothing howling and tragic, just a washout. If I'd have thought of it earlier, I could've tried it with you."

On the other side of the easel, Elsie let the artist's words wash over her like the ocean. *One more after today*, Ida had said as she rearranged the fabric that served as Elsie's backdrop. *One more, and I'll leave you alone.*

Elsie wasn't a crier, never had been. But she'd been surprised by how much she'd cried when Clem's mum passed on, and by how much she'd cried when she'd held Elaine's baby, little Gloria, just last week, the day after the baby was born. A new life—and a new life for her.

"I'm your grandmother, sweetheart," she'd whispered, scooping up the tiny mewling thing when Lainey went out to the loo. "You and me, well, we're going to get along fine."

"The nurse says not to hold them when they're crying," Elaine said when she was back on the bed, and she nodded at the empty bassinet.

"Ah, one cuddle, just while I'm here," said Elsie, cuddling the small baby close.

"Of course you'd think that you know best," said Elaine.

Elsie remembered that as she looked out into Ida Lewis's garden, and she did want to cry. She wanted to cry out as much water as the rain, and then some more. Because she'd antagonized her own girl yet again. And because she didn't want this new thing now to end. She loved sitting here, listening to the painter—whether she was talking or humming; even if the only sound was the busy rustle of her brushes, the occasional clatter of something set down or taken up again. She loved listening to whatever the artist had to say—always something a little more, a little larger than Elsie expected. She loved sitting here, sitting still, being herself. And she loved the sense of Ida Lewis's gaze, and the alchemy that converted whatever Ida saw into the image Ida made. Ida Lewis saw her in a way that no one ever had; Elsie was sure of it. And the very idea made her shake.

"I won't look until it's done," Elsie had said at the end of the first sitting. "I want it to be a surprise, finding out what it is you see."

Ida had laughed. "You've a lot of faith in me," she said. "What if I get the shape of you, and not the features? What if I paint a version of you that no one sees but me?"

The danger of it, the frisson: the only thing that had ever come close was when Clem pushed the door open while Elsie was in the bath, came in, and washed her, very slowly and carefully, and went away, all without saying a word. Twice or three times he'd done that in all the years they were married. Elsie cherished it.

"But then I suppose mothers can't cry," Ida Lewis said now, her words narrowed by the tapered brush she'd poked in the corner of her mouth like a cigarillo. "Spend all their time trying to shush their children, don't they? It was one of the reasons I didn't want children—they seem so upset for the first few years, and then you send them off to school. And Richard was older, of course. What about you? Did you ever regret having yours?"

A single drop of water detached from the window's top frame onto the glass, and traced a perfectly straight line down to the bottom. Elsie watched it the whole way, her eyes tensing to follow it.

"People like me," she said as the drip pooled along the window-sill, "I don't think we decide to have children. It was all I ever wanted—to get married, have a family. No one had me cut out for anything else. All I wanted was a baby of my own. Me and Clem, we never talked about it. We got married; we had the twins. I did wish there were more, but I was blessed with the two of them. And now we've a granddaughter and it starts all over again."

But for the first time, in the sound of those words, Elsie felt a great rush of exhaustion. If this new baby, Gloria, had her own child when she was twenty or twenty-one, Elsie would be a great-grandmother before she knew it. And you could fit another generation after that, if you were quick. Great-great-grandmother Elsie, up around eighty years old: the length of her life lived again.

And she did cry then; not the kind of crying she'd done before, snotty and sobbing and gulping, the way it was in the most dramatic of movies. This was quiet and profound, the tears running as simply and directly down her face as the rain ran down the window's glass. It was a minute, maybe more, before Ida noticed, and set down her brushes and her palette to cross the room, a man's handkerchief in her hand.

"Here, it's clean—I am sorry. I didn't mean to upset you."

But Elsie, silent, shook her head and let the tears wash out of her. She felt the handkerchief's softness on her cheeks, the artist's hand warm on her shoulder.

"What's the matter, Elsie?" she heard Ida Lewis ask after a while. She could feel the artist's hand rubbing small circles on the skin at the top of her spine. "What's all this about?"

Outside in the garden, the rain was easing—Elsie caught the delicious smell of new wetness. Perhaps things weren't so bad after all; perhaps life wasn't such a short loop, played over and over.

"I'm doing this because I wanted a dress—a beautiful one, made of silvery material. That's what I want to use the money for." The pragmatism of her answer bruised against all the nuance in the question. "And it's lovely, you know, just sitting here, *being*. I could sit here forever, in this lovely room, with you. It's the loveliest thing I've ever done. And you—" A deep breath. "And now it's almost done, and I'll go back to all the things I did before. Maybe nothing will be like this again."

She caught Ida's hand and brought it up to her lips, kissing the painter's fingers before she had time to stop herself, or to think. And then she let go the painter's hand and closed her eyes.

Somewhere outside, someone was trying to start a truck, its engine gagging and choking. Somewhere outside, someone was calling instructions—something about three pints of milk and some bread. Somewhere outside, the rain had eased off and the birds were beginning to sing. But here, in this glass room, Elsie Gormley sat still and alone in a wicker chair with her eyes shut, wondering what would happen when she opened them, and who, in that moment, she might be.

She opened her eyes. Ida Lewis was standing again behind her canvas, the high rectangle obscuring anything her model might have seen of her face.

"Your silver dress," Ida said, her painting arm busy again. "It sounds quite like starlight—I should have painted you in that for this new age. Those spacemen, whizzing by: I stood in the garden, looking for the *Friendship*. Well, I couldn't see a thing. You know they crashed a spaceship on the moon the other day—it was supposed to send back photographs, but something went wrong. It's some world, isn't it, where we send men and great big cameras into space. I can't say I thought I'd hear of that. But—" Ida stepped out from behind the easel for just a moment, and smiled. "Well, anything's possible, I guess."

Then silence, as she went back to her painting and her arm moved up and down. Sitting quietly, Elsie wanted to say something about surprises, about the unexpected—or about the size of the sky, beyond this world. But nothing she thought of seemed right. The sleeve of her dress itched at her skin, and she tried to scratch it with an imperceptible gesture, barely moving a muscle.

As the sun began to shine at last, Elsie heard a clock strike midday—it must have been in the house next door. She'd never heard it in this house before.

"That's time then," Ida said, putting down her brushes and smiling at her subject. "I'll put the kettle on and we can have a cup before you go—I'll see if Richard might like one too. That's his dreadful clock; I'm sorry if it startled you. It's always so peaceful when he's traveling and has taken it with him." She set her brushes down and went into the kitchen.

And from somewhere in the center of herself, Elsie felt a new sensation—mortification, and a swirl of embarrassment that she hadn't felt since she was a schoolgirl. Squirming, she realized she wanted to use the lavatory, and badly, but she could hardly walk through the house if she might run into Ida's husband on the way. And who knew what he'd seen going on?

"I won't stay," she called towards the kitchen. "I don't think I told you but my daughter's had her baby—a little girl. Gloria. Most gorgeous dark red hair—like my Clem's, before it faded down to ginger. If I get on now I can manage a visit and be home again by teatime. They're so precious when they're tiny."

Crouching down for her bag, she saw Ida, standing in the doorway, watching her.

"Don't worry about it, Elsie," she said gently. "It happens sometimes. It takes some getting used to, having someone stare at you. If you're sure you won't have tea, that's fine—go off to your little grandkiddy. But stay for lunch next week, and see the picture."

As Elsie reached for the handle to let herself out, Ida caught her hand and held it, firmly, for a moment. And then she let her go.

Walking fast to the bus stop, Elsie felt more tears' wetness on her cheeks. This time, these days; the baby and the painting. Everything was a jumble of big things to care about, and Elsie was tired. She paid her bus fare and settled herself in a seat, looking out through the window and determined not to be surprised by anything she might see. The bus pulled away from the curb, and she leaned her head against the window frame. She was asleep before it had reached the next stop.

On the morning of her last sitting for Ida Lewis, Elsie slipped her new silver frock from its pretty hanger and stroked the fine material. It did look like moonlight; it did make her hair shine. Behind her, she heard Clem come into the bedroom and give a small gasp at the sight of her holding the new dress in front of her, with her hair scooped up onto her head.

"Should take you out in that, love," he said, rummaging in his lowboy for a handful of pennies. "That's a classy dress."

"It does look like a dress for a celebration," she said, turning a little in front of the mirror. "Maybe I can wear it for Gloria's christening."

"Christening be blowed," said Clem, coming close behind her to kiss her neck. "That's a dress for Cloudland. What are you up to today?"

"I've been doing some work for Ida Lewis," said Elsie, as carelessly as she could, loving the way the secret strangeness of it burrowed in at the center of her body. All week, she'd turned back to the sensation of those tears, the sensation of that kiss, the warmth of one held hand—reminding herself that it was hers. A tiny, secret thing. Who knew what might come after that? Another portrait, Ida might say, or *Would you care to accompany me to*—what? *Accompany me to this gallery? Come round sometime for tea? Just sit here and hold my hand?*

"Nearly done, I reckon," she heard herself say; as if her work for Ida Lewis was nothing out of the ordinary. "Do you want me to tell her about the mangle? How are you going with that?"

Clem patted at the dress just as he'd patted at his granddaughter, respecting it as treasure, something rare. "Oh, I took that round for her a couple of weeks ago—she showed me that picture she was painting. Very nicely done, I thought. Fancy my wife ending up in a por*trait*—" He broke the word awkwardly, making its second syllable too long and too hard. "And keeping it all so quiet too."

Spinning away, Elsie stuffed the dress into the wardrobe. Its heavy panels rattled as she slammed the door.

"What? What did I say?" Clem looked up from counting coins in his palm as she pulled on her old housecoat.

"It's just—the painting—well, I wanted it to be a surprise. I was going to take you up when it was done, and show it to you then. I didn't know you'd have a sneaky peek when you'd lugged your stupid mangle up the hill."

Clem laughed, hugging one arm around her shoulders. "You know me and surprises," he said. "Ruin them any way I can, and usually without meaning to. Off you go then and finish your modeling. I'm proud as punch of you, Else. And you looked—well, you look gorgeous. Tell Mrs. Lewis to call me if that mangle needs adjusting." He kissed her neck again, and was gone off into his day, the coins jangling as he ran down the back steps, two at a time.

In the dimness of the bedroom, its blinds and curtains drawn against the brightness outside, Elsie peeled away her housecoat and stood before the mirror: bra, panties, stockings, flesh. She peered at herself, piece by piece: her head, her torso, arms, legs, and belly. What did Clem see in this shape—what had she seen, her whole life? She pulled her shoulders back and dropped her chin: she was a film star in a magazine—Doris Day; no, Marilyn Monroe. Imagine that; imagine having such bright and brilliant hair. She let her body sag: she was a grandmother who'd have been better off taking in ironing. And her brown hair was turning quite grey.

She kissed her own hand and felt a fool. She heard the theme for the news on the radio—top of the hour—and sighed. She hadn't meant to be late.

Coming up to Ida's gate, Elsie paused to catch her breath. She had a jar of lime pickle in her bag as a present, although it seemed a slight and inappropriate gift now that she was on the brink of giving it.

I could go home. I could say I had a headache. I could leave it as it is, unfinished and undone. But then Ida might finish it without her, and that seemed worse. Her hand moved towards the latch and she was across the lawn and knocking on the door.

"I brought you this." Thrusting the jar at the artist as soon as she answered. "It seemed rude not to bring you something." Elsie didn't know the etiquette for such a moment—had never seen a note about it in the advice page of the paper.

"I hope you'll like the painting," said Ida, stepping back to let Elsie pass, and following her into the studio. "You might bring Mr. Gormley up on the weekend if he'd like to see it when it's finished—he was very complimentary when he came. Richard will be here; we'll make a party."

It would be too much, thought Elsie, the four of them staring at this new version of her. She needed it to be private and small—kept apart. Her body settled immediately into its pose, so easy, and her eyes fixed on the spot in the garden outside that she most liked to look at. The bushes had grown in the six weeks of her sittings and the fence behind them had all but disappeared.

"Surely it's been a nicer job than cleaning," Ida said after a while, "although perhaps you can come back and do that when I next need to deal with the dust."

So it was over. So that was its end. *A char*, thought Elsie, and resolved that she wouldn't cry again.

"Where do they go, pictures like this?" she asked at last, realizing for the first time that other people might see the painting, apart from Ida, apart from her professor, apart from Clem.

"I've got this one in mind for a competition," said Ida, pausing with her brush. "I'm terrible at names though—you couldn't think of one for me, could you?"

"You could just call it after me," suggested Elsie, her voice as shy as a child's. It would be something to have her own name attached to this painting—as if anyone she knew might walk into a room where it was hanging, and recognize her, and think, *well*.

"That's what I usually do," said Ida, busy again, while Elsie wondered how many other women had sat under the painter's gaze and felt themselves remade by her concentration. Or how many men.

"Clem asked if the mangle was going all right," she said then. "He said he can pop up and adjust it if you need him to."

"Very thoughtful, your husband, but I think it's working fine. I have a lady who comes to do the washing once a week, and she hasn't made any complaints."

And Elsie saw it, this traffic of people doing for this woman who stood still at her boards in the center of it all, catching bits of their busyness and their being.

"Well," she said, "you just let me know about the cleaning. I'm bound to be busy now with the baby, but it's no trouble to run up the hill with a duster." Thinking, *So much for this.*

When the professor's clock chimed twelve, Ida stepped back

from the easel and declared the work done. "Have a look, Elsie, do—I'll leave you with it while I wash my hands. I bought prawns—do you like prawns? There should be something like a celebration. It's always worth a fuss, seeing something to its end." And Elsie heard the bathroom door and the running water before she was brave enough to get out of the chair and cross the room and look, for the first time, at what was there.

And there she was. Elsie, but not herself, and so still, so quiet, so calm. The eyes were hers, she could see that, and the mouth was set quite straight and firm, with no sense that it ever smiled, or even spoke. The hair was redder than her own fading chestnut brown—more like Ida's, she thought. And where was the evidence of all the thinking she'd done: the staring and the puzzling; the wondering and the remembering? Where was all the time she'd sat, patiently, as if she was inventing herself so this other woman might invent a picture? And the kiss—that magic kiss; where was that hiding in this tidy, formal canvas?

This has made me want more. The thought was so emphatic that she wondered if she'd said it aloud, and felt herself gulp. At the top of the painting and around the shape her figure made, the background shone with a thick, regal blue, so rich that Elsie thought it must be infusing the air. *If I can keep that color by me,* she thought, reaching out to touch it as gingerly as if it were a snake, *I might hold this other me.*

She raised her other hand to her cheek, patting it to make sure she still felt somehow like herself and hadn't been entirely transposed into this other guise. Behind her, Ida Lewis was busy in the kitchen—plates, flatware, the fridge—and Elsie wondered, for a moment, about slipping out the side door. There was nothing to say now; it was done and made as she, the artist, had wanted. This was the version of Elsie that the world would see—Ida Lewis's imagining of her, rather than Elsie herself.

"I was just saying I could take a photograph of it, if you like—if you wanted to show your daughter or something." Ida was standing in the doorway, a tomato in one hand and a knife in the other. "You know, I think I've made you look a bit like me." She pointed the knife at her own head, at the reddish hair of Elsie done in oils. "Must have been the sunlight on your hair. I've shelled the prawns, and I was going to suggest a glass of something cold—but I don't think I've made you brave enough for that in the middle of a bright, warm Tuesday." She crossed the room and peered at her own work.

She's flirting with me, thought Elsie. "The prawns are treat enough, really."

Standing beside each other, they both stared at the painting.

"What do you think?" Ida asked at last. "I'm pleased with it—and these colors have come up so wonderfully."

Which was nothing to do with Elsie.

"I thought it would be more like a mirror," Elsie said after a moment's hesitation. "But then I thought it would be more like a painting too—like something I didn't quite understand, I mean, or something I didn't know how to look at." And she told Ida the story of standing in the gallery—"years ago now, when Elaine and Donny had just started school"—and not knowing what to say to the man about the painting by a woman, of a woman, called *Care*.

"But do you like this?" Ida asked. "Is it all right? Is it all right with you?"

And Elsie nodded. There were things that it was possible to ask for, or to say—she felt her way towards what they might be.

"I want to ask two things," she said slowly. "Can I take a tube of . . ." she braced herself for the unusual word, ". . . of cerulean with me when I go? And can you never mention . . . ?" Her words trailed off, and she waved at Ida's hand.

"Here." The painter caught Elsie's hand, pressing the small silver tube into her palm. "You must remember there are other words for blue. And a color like that is as good as a kiss anyway—you can have that from me."

Elsie blushed, and wished she could bear to say thank you, not sure if she wanted the other woman to say it was something, or nothing, and never mind.

"Come on, then, let's get at these prawns before the flies have a field day," said Ida instead, heading back into the kitchen and leaving Elsie alone with herself.

She stepped forward then and let her fingers rest again on the brilliant blue that surrounded the shape of her body—the sky, or the sea, or just a pure breath of that magically named blue. She shouldn't wear silver; she could see it now. Her skin, her hair—it was a deep, rich blue that set them off, that brought them to life.

The weft and warp of the canvas beneath the pads of her fingers were coarser than she'd imagined, and she felt no trace of the paint, the beautiful color, that formed the barrier between its fabric and her skin. Bringing her fingers up to her face, she looked again for a stained smudge of blue—and if they had been marked, she'd have rubbed the color hard on her cheeks, above her eyes, like some fierce old war paint.

I want this thing to mark me.

As for Clem seeing the portrait, she wasn't sure it mattered. What she needed, she knew, was him—she needed him to trace out her body and make her feel it was hers again. His was the gaze that defined her; she'd just lost sight of that for a while.

So she sat at the wide green kitchen table, and she ate the luxurious prawns, and the fresh sweet tomato, and the thick slices of bread. And she let the size of the artist's words wash over her one last time—let them soak into all the chinks and crevices of herself she hadn't known before this work began. She heard Ida Lewis suggest that she come and clean the house once a month—"so I can keep you in new yards of fabric," Ida said, smiling, and pushed the last of her payment across the table to her—and heard herself reply that she would find someone else to come.

"As you wish," said the artist, and that was all.

When the professor's clock struck one, she helped Ida stack the plates in the kitchen, and she went away, after shaking hands as businessmen did in the movies at the end of a transaction. Then she walked down the hill and unlocked her own front door. It was quiet and dim inside, and she moved quickly, pushing back the curtains and pulling up the blinds so that the house filled with light.

"Here I am," she called to the empty rooms. "I'm home."

Then she drew a long, hot bath, even though it was only early in the afternoon, and let herself lie there a while, at home and at ease.

She was clean and fresh, powdered and perfumed, zipped into her new silver frock when Clem came home around dusk to find her sitting there, waiting.

14

The flood

NO MATTER how much Lucy wiped the kitchen bench, the door, the handrail on the stairs, she couldn't quite remove the small puffs of fingerprint powder the friendlier policeman had dusted about as he looked for nonexistent prints. It lay like a shadow, dulling the different surfaces.

"Our house has a layer of frost," Ben joked. "Perhaps that's what's on the bathroom door as well."

"How many robberies do you think have happened here?" Lucy was appalled.

"Well, now, I don't know. Is this a robbery?" He was serving Christmas dinner as the rain drummed on outside. "Maybe it's just a fact of modern life—the loss of an expensive phone."

"Well, I don't like it." Lucy pushed the wet cloth once more along the laminate, frowning at the powder that it caught. She thought: *tarnished*. She thought: *residue*. She thought: *pall*. Her safe new house: she couldn't bear this breach.

"My kind of festive," Ben said, setting out the food. The three of them together at the table. On their own.

Lucy brushed imaginary dust from her hands. "It's certainly one of the calmest we've had."

"Calm, wet, and not too hot. I told you it was best to work through." Ben was scooping potatoes onto his plate. "We can take a holiday when the sun shines, hey, little man? And these duchess potatoes, Lu—you've made them just like Mum's."

Tom was moving his potatoes with a spoon, separating them into discrete and fluffy lumps. "Clouds!"

His father smiled.

"Remember that Christmas we had in Helsinki?" Ben poured a little gravy for his son and leaned close to scoop the food onto his fork.

"Of course I remember," said Lucy in a flat voice. She watched her husband's sudden discomfort at a clinical remove.

"I said I was sorry, Lu. I was so bloody tired, you're lucky I could remember who I was, let alone anyone else."

She had laid it out for him like this: his forgetting that it was Lucy who read him the poem was as if she'd forgotten the first time they met.

At which he'd shrugged and said, "You know, I think it's not that big a deal."

"Like the phone?" she'd batted back.

"Yes. Like the phone."

And it had festered from there.

~

On New Year's Eve, they popped a bottle of champagne at nine o'clock, the city's early fireworks croaking like thunder in the distance. It was a clear night—the first, it felt, in forever. They sat on their back deck, their feet on its rail as if they were on a plush ocean liner, steaming south. They'd played at making resolutions, played at saying they were fine. But still it niggled. Lucy felt a jag in her throat every so often, somewhere between disappointment and a threat.

"I love you," she said out of nowhere. "But I'm going to bed." It was barely ten o'clock.

"First year we'll have missed it." Ben grabbed at her hand, trying to keep her by his side.

She shook her head. "Don't care; too tired. I'm ready for my new year, Mr. DeMille." The in-joke from their earliest days, when everything had felt as glorious as a production number.

Are we such a long way from that now? Lucy wondered as she waited to fall asleep. She'd fix it in the morning; she was done.

It was hours later when she woke, startled, listening to new noises in the night.

A bang. Another bang. Like something rapping on a door. And then again.

She sat up. Possums? Robbers? Elsie? Sliding out of bed, she looked across Ben—fast asleep—at the clock. It was just after three. Then another knock. It was the laundry door downstairs, blowing in the wind. She wedged the back door as she went down, still cautious of being locked out.

The sky was dry and vast—it felt like a long time since she'd seen that. Standing on the concrete underneath the deck, Lucy looked out and saw tiny patches of starry brilliance between scuttling clouds. New year. Dry year. She'd take that. And something moving overhead—a satellite, not a shooting star, but she may as well wish on it, she thought.

The arbitrary promise of a new year: she pushed her hair back and stepped onto the grass, the lingering dampness rising up around her feet.

Here we are, safe and sound. Just like she'd say to Tom. It was as simple as that.

Yes. Here they were: they had a house—and they had never owned a house. They had a kid—and they had never had a kid. And life went on. This place was good. This place was safe. And there was Elsie. She was guidance, or guardianship. A little daydream, nothing more.

It was easy to tell herself that.

Inside, in bed, Lucy went straight back to sleep, dreaming only of sun and of newness.

Then, in the morning, a grey-day pall—she woke as tired as if she hadn't slept at all. The rain started. Stopped. Started. Stopped. An erratic punctuation throughout the month's first days, until the balance tipped from dry to wet entirely and beyond to saturation. There was more rain than sunshine, then no sunshine at all. The sinkholes in the park filled with water and stayed full, their surfaces thick with mosquito larvae and their edges busy with frogs. There were no breaks in which Tom could go out to play, and the house shrank with his containment. Suddenly, it was always raining, and when it began to feel as if the rain couldn't possibly get any heavier, any thicker, it did. It was like someone playing with the volume of a stereo, nudging it up, and then nudging it higher.

Lucy stood on the deck under a Christopher Robin umbrella, holding Tom high. The park had a deep layer of water across its car park now and a curtain of water obscured its grass.

"What do you think, Tom? Will Dad have to sail to work in an umbrella, like Winnie-the-Pooh?"

Tom chuckled and squirmed and Lucy squeezed him before she set him down.

"Should we worry?" she asked Ben as he arrived under the canopy of his own umbrella. She nodded at the heavy sheet of rain.

"You can't worry about everything, Lu. All the warnings are for flash floods, and that's nothing to do with us here."

"Then what is?"

He shrugged again. "A river flood, I guess."

"Like seventy-four?"

"Like seventy-four."

"And will that happen again this time?"

"I don't know. They're releasing water upstream, so I don't think so. I'll make some calls when I get to work—" flicking his watch around on his wrist "—where I should be heading now." He kissed the top of her head, their umbrellas butting and showering spray. "You don't want something else to worry about, do you?"

"What do you think?"

He smiled then, and rubbed his hand across her back. "Come on, Lu. It's fine. It's all fine." Kissing her head again. "I might be late tonight—there's a bloke out from England that they want me to write about. He's doing a talk at the uni; I'll call you on the way."

"Home by eight?"

He nodded.

"Say bye to Dad, Tom—he won't be home till you're asleep tonight."

Tom nodded.

"Then I'll see you both tonight," said Ben, fastening his bag.

He was halfway down the stairs when Lucy called, leaning down towards him, "Can you let me know earlier next time, if you're going to be late? It's fine, I mean, of course it's fine. But I wouldn't mind a bit more warning of a bad day, when one's coming."

"A bad day?"

"I just feel sort of storm-stayed." She waved her hand at the grey wall of water dumping on their yard. "And it's nice when you come home, you know, at the end of a long day with Tom."

"I won't be that late," he called back. "OK? Can we talk about all this tonight?"

She nodded as a smash came from the kitchen, and she wheeled around and went back through the door, calling for Tom—who stood, smiling brightly among bright shards of his mother's mug that were scattered on the floor around his feet.

"Crash, Mummy, crash!" he said happily, and Lucy, bending to pick the pieces out of the puddle of cold liquid, heard Ben call out from below, "You right, Lu? I've got to get the train. I'll ring you on the way."

"Big noise, Mummy," said Tom above her. "Bi-i-ig noise." While she sat, very still, on the floor.

Happy new year, she thought. *At least it wasn't Elsie's cup.*

She rang her mum. She rang her sisters. She rang her dad. No one picked up.

Maybe I'm no longer real.

And the rain surged hard again.

~

It was days before the flood came, creeping across the lowest reach of their backyard and stopping there, while all around them other buildings became islands, marooned by waterlines that breached their battened skirts, their floorboards, their windowsills. Some were fully immersed, their roofs invisible under thick brown fetid water. And it was quiet, so quiet, with no cars, no power, no ordinary, everyday life. As if the world had gone away.

In the quietness of their torchlit house, Lucy felt gratefully, inexplicably spared. Elsie's house had gone under in the last big flood, in 1974: they'd heard the story when they bought the house, taking the neighbors' tales of rising water as of historical interest only and nothing to do with them.

"We need to tell her," Lucy said as this new flood peaked. "We need to let Elsie know her house is fine."

"*Our* house," said Ben. "I'm sure someone she knows has come by to check—or would you have her coming across the park in a boat?" He tousled his hand in her hair, trying for a joke. But Lucy didn't smile.

And if it was shocking that the flood came, it was also shocking how quickly it went, under a sky of hot and sudden sunshine.

It left a thick, rich smell, organic and alive. It left households to decide what might be salvaged from everything that had been immersed—from the garage stuff of Christmas decorations and drill bits and screwdrivers to the entire contents of a family home. And it mobilized an army of people, ready to stand and scrub and hose and sort.

Lucy volunteered too, almost embarrassed by her own dry good fortune. She went, in gumboots, shorts, and an old T-shirt, on the first day that Ben was home. Tom offered her his little plastic beach bucket as she left.

"She might need something a bit bigger, mate," said Ben as he unhooked his son's fingers from the handle and made them wave goodbye. "Ta-ta, Mum," he said for him.

"Ta-ta, Mum," said Tom.

She only had to turn two corners to find a house that needed help.

The smell was ghastly, and the mud was everywhere—the husband muttering about lawsuits and hydrology reports. "It came twenty-four hours earlier than we expected," he said to Lucy as she came through the gate. "We should have been more prepared."

His wife looked at everything she was shown and asked that it be put in the middle of the yard, in the zone that she'd designated for items she'd think about later.

"Can I get you some tea?" Lucy asked her after an hour or so. "Do you have a way to boil this kettle?" Her own mother's approach to shock: hot, sweet tea, given often—"and tell them a doctor said they should."

But as the woman shook her head, Lucy realized that the sounds of ripping and moving she could hear were those of the innards of the house being stripped and cleared above and thrown onto a pile of rubbish at the front.

"He said it would come on Wednesday," she said. "He thought

we had another day. I didn't even have time to clear the kids' rooms." She stared at the muddy plastic container of photo albums she held in her hands—someone had wiped a cursory streak across the grime on one side, through which Lucy could see the same woman in the tight white shine of a wedding gown.

"Throw them away," the woman said. "I don't want to remember. In fact, throw it all away. Why would I try to save stuff?"

She waved her hand at the growing pile on the muddy grass— the yard, its trimmed lawn, its landscaped pool, its topiaried figs: all of the colors that these things should hold had been reset to shades of brown, like a sepia photograph from some battlefield in World War I. A group of surly-looking teenagers stood by the fence, painstakingly rinsing a boxful of little plastic building blocks. Two women in bright gym clothes carried boxes of glasses down from the kitchen to their car, to take away and wash in their own blemish-free kitchens.

"I kept a clean home," the woman of the house was saying. "I kept it spotless. We were in the local paper once for a story on design. And now look—how could this happen?" She stared at Lucy. "I don't even know who you are."

An old Valiant turned into the street, honking its horn. On the rear driver-side window was a sign—*Free beer, one per worker*—and Lucy ran towards the car. Maybe beer instead of tea; she counted the people around her.

"My back's buggered and I'm not good for much," said the elderly man at the wheel, "but I thought youse could all do with a cold one." It was XXXX and she knew that this particular can of it would taste better than any she'd ever drunk before.

"There are eight of us here," Lucy said to his granddaughter, who was dispensing the beers from the boot. "And thanks."

The girl smiled. "Have the army been round yet? I've been waiting to see some soldiers."

Lucy shook her head, and the girl shut the boot with a slam, rapping it twice: drive on.

Walking up the stairs to find the woman, Lucy could hear the two owners shouting at each other—about a rug, in the first place, and then the whole awful shambles of it next. She opened one of the beers, wincing at the force of their words. They were into grievances that were decades old, still so ripe for the picking, and the noise boomed, amplified by their emptying world.

"Do you think they'll be all right?" she whispered, describing the scene to Ben at the other end of the day as Tom wound through her legs to welcome her home.

Ben shrugged. "It'll take a while to get through all that mess," he said.

"Not their stuff; I mean them. She was so angry about it all."

"She could have moved things herself if she thought he was wrong."

"And he could have paid more attention." Lucy bent down to pull her gumboots off, tickling Tom as he passed. "What would we have done? What would we have taken? We thought we were fine—we were lucky. How would we have known when it was time to go?"

Ben shrugged again, scooping Tom onto his shoulders to carry him up towards his dinner. "It didn't come, Lu. We were safe. In seventy-four, Mum and I were on the north side, up a hill. I hardly knew it was happening."

She stood awhile gazing at the grass of their back lawn. It looked like a color wheel, changing from thickly green at the top of the rise near the house to the encroaching brown of mud at its boundary.

Then, setting her shoulders, she pulled up the garage door and scanned the stacks of boxes and containers that would have been lost if the house had been a little lower, a little closer to the river's reach. It was so gloomy down here in the unlit dusk that these stashed possessions looked like they were already fading out of being.

It was easy to picture herself in the angry woman's place—everything coated and gummed up by this foul-smelling mud, and the horrible process of having to decide what to throw out, what to wash, what to salvage.

As she reached for a box of her own and imagined it mucky, destroyed, Lucy blew out a breath, remembering—again—the ruin of Elsie's photos.

I should have tried to clean them. Now that she knew how much of the mud could be washed away, she thought she might have been able to clean off a little jam.

Out of habit, she flicked the light switch, then remembered the power was off and reached for a lantern. Standing in the middle of the puddle of light and the wide stash of storage, she took stock of what she hadn't even realized was at stake. There were bulky things about which she had no opinion—bikes and the lawn mower, and stray pieces of furniture for which there was no room upstairs. There were the desultory artifacts of their arrival—tins of paint, boxes of tools, offcuts of wood. There were boxes of documents—the receipts and justifications of old tax returns, programs for concerts and gigs spanning more than two decades, the glossy squares from the years when people still printed photographs. And then there were the boxes of letters and postcards.

She lifted the lid from one of these and saw a postcard of the Sydney Harbour Bridge half-built, one arm of its arch reaching up into space and a man perched, precarious, in the box of its end. She'd seen it in an exhibition with her mum, who'd sent the card a week or so later, saying how lovely the morning had been. It was a long time since they'd done something together like that, and that seemed suddenly sad.

A generic beach shot, complete with scalloped edge, slipped

from the pile and Lucy sat back on her haunches. It was a postcard from her old friend Astrid.

> Lucy, you won't believe this! I'm working in a café by the beach. This woman walks in—I swear it's you, but you in twenty years. Red hair—still crazy curly red—and bright red glasses; your eyes are going, love. She's wearing a pink shirt you'd like—nice Chinese collar. I had to make the owner take her order—didn't know what I'd say. And what if she'd ordered soy? Don't you take up soy in twenty years. You looked great, though. You looked happy. I like your glasses. You looked well.

And then a scrawl and lots of kisses. As if Astrid had seen her future. She checked the postmark: Sydney, 4 February 1991.

Almost twenty years ago.

And in a café by a beach: somewhere in the world, she hoped that's where one of her *vardøger* was.

She slid the postcard back among the rest and sighed. She hadn't been in touch with Astrid for years, although a Christmas card from Astrid's mother, Linnea, always found her, no matter where she was.

Crouched beside the box, Lucy read through messages at random—so many moments, her own and other people's—until Ben came down to tell her Tom was ready for bed.

She heaped handfuls of letters and postcards into her lap and sat there, cradling them. There was something mesmerizing about these rectangles of life: something mesmerizing about how easily they might have been lost; something mesmerizing about their recovery.

"How could I have let all this go?"

Ben pulled her to her feet and into a hug. "You didn't. We lugged them with us everywhere we went. Here they are. Safe and dry." He clicked the lid onto one of the containers. "Come upstairs, Lu; you've had a long day. Probably not the greatest time to open Pandora's box. Come on, put it away. Tom's waiting for you. Come up and I'll get you a drink."

Leaning against the stack of boxes, Lucy looked out at the clear night sky. "It looks as if it had never rained at all," she said. "What are they going to do now, all those people?"

"Find out if they have insurance. Go and stay with friends. Wait for builders." Ben shrugged. "I'll tell Tom you're coming," he said as he turned towards the door.

An aeroplane tracked north across the sky, heading for the airport with its lights flashing. "One house I went to already had loads of people helping," Lucy said. Through the open garage door she watched the plane's descent. "The guy had all the notes from his PhD spread out across the lawn like a carpet. I saw him again when I was walking home. He was bundling them up and stuffing them in the bin."

Ben was waiting, his hand out. "If it were me, I'd chuck the lot," he said. "Some things you just can't save—like that woman said about her wedding photos."

Which wasn't quite how Lucy had heard it.

She pulled a sheet of paper from the closest box, glanced at the messy writing and smiled. Ferdi Klim—the bloke she'd left before she met Ben. She scanned the first few lines. Hang on: who'd left whom? She shook her head: it didn't matter. He always liked to have the last word.

She laid the sheet on the floor and began to fold it—in half, and then two wings, and then some shaping: a crude paper plane. "Ferdi Klim," she said aloud, aiming the plane through the wide open door and sending it soaring. It caught an impossible draft and sailed on towards the street.

Off you go, then; off you go. Still, he did have the best name—

151

they'd joked that they should be a double act, Kiss and Klim. It had been a bit too much circus.

Then: *one giant leap*, thought Lucy, and she'd leapt free. On her own in the world; out late in pubs with ice cubes to keep herself cool.

She smiled, restacking the boxes then pulling the garage door and taking the stairs two at a time. She could trace a direct line from that leap to here—and to Tom in his cot, ready to be cuddled and sung to.

Only he'd already gone to sleep.

She leaned forward, resting her hand on his tummy. *Here we are. Safe and dry. Just us three.* The words came automatically—but *safe and dry*? Perhaps that was just an accident of luck.

Waiting for catastrophes was exhausting. She dipped her head and kissed her sleeping boy.

In the bathroom, she washed her face in the tepid temperature of no hot water system. She'd send a card to Elsie's daughter. She'd confess about the photos; she'd let Elsie know that her house was OK.

The real Elsie, she thought, stretching her tired arms above her head and flexing her shoulders. Not the one she liked to think came by.

"All those places, all those yards," she said to Ben as they ate their candlelit dinner. "I kept imagining they were ours, strangers walking in and helping us."

Reaching across the table, Ben cupped his hands around Lucy's, as if to spring their pressure. "I worked it out—those holes drilled into the floorboards? Water in; water out. They must have drained the house in seventy-four."

That would be Elsie, thought Lucy. *Always prepared.*

"I heard more about Elsie today." She wiped her last piece of bread around her dish. "One of the other volunteers lived round here for years—she said Elsie's husband died before the last flood. She'd lived alone here all that time—decades—her kids all grown up too. I imagined family here, all the time, but it was really Elsie on her own."

"My investigative reporter." Ben laughed. "Does it make you feel better to know?"

"Better?" Lucy frowned. "I don't know. I never thought of her being alone."

Later, under a lukewarm shower with the plug in and water pooling around her feet, Lucy scrubbed at her fingernails, pretending the shower's water was sweet, fresh rain. She felt the puddle rising up and over her feet, around her ankles, her shins, and up towards her knees. *I would have stood here and watched it come. I would have stood in my house and felt it rise.* She ran the scrubbing brush back and forward across her fingernails. *Tom's things, we'd have kept those safe. And documents, important things. Everything else, it's just stuff.* Imagining the bath overflowing, the bathroom filling like a giant aquarium—toothbrushes and makeup tubes floating across the surface; toilet rolls and cotton wool thickening and sinking.

The preempted catastrophe. So close, and then it hadn't come. *Which should make me feel better.*

It didn't, somehow.

The house would have held; it had before. Fibro walls and hardwood fittings. They could have washed it, dried it, and gone on. Compared to the swollen sludge of chipboard, plasterboard, fiberboard she'd seen in other houses, they really could have come home, safe and dry.

But it was clear, pristine water she pictured, nothing like the brown sludge she'd tipped from mugs, shaken from ornaments, tried to sponge from tubs, boxes, and bikes.

She closed her eyes and saw the water running through her

house as if it were possessing the body of a large, sinking ship. She saw it easing clothes from their hangers in wardrobes, easing plastic containers from their cupboards in the kitchen. She saw a silver mosaic of CDs, their smooth surfaces sparkling.

She opened her eyes when Ben leaned in to turn off the water and pass her a towel.

"Come to bed," he said, and he held her close as the house dropped into the next layer of silence and sleep. Lucy, her head against the solid warmth of Ben's shoulder, dreamed—slightly sea-sick—about her whole house filling with tides of people as it rushed on down the river to the sea.

15

The doilies

ELSIE FOUND the key between the leather and the lining of her
handbag when she was rummaging for a hanky. It was a big chunky
thing that Gloria had always said looked like the key to a castle.

"Here's this," she said to her son. "But where are the rest of
them?" They were sitting together in his kitchen, finishing lunch.

He'd brought her home to his house when the creek below the
units broke its banks. The river beyond had surged to fill street after
street, and the power was still out, days later. In Don and Carol's
house, there was power, and sunshine, and a water-free view. As if
all was still right with the world.

And now this key: all things returned to rights.

She cradled it in her palm. *Such a solid thing*, she thought, *like
the good old house itself.*

"The rest of what?"

"The keys—to the house. How else am I going to get in?"

He took the bag from her and set it on the ground. "You know,
Mum," he said gently. "You know we gave the keys to the new
people—when you sold the house; when you went to live in the new
place. They need the keys now. They need the keys to get in." He let

his hand rest on hers, as if its weight might somehow help what he was saying sink in.

"The new people—" she said carefully, as if she was practicing a foreign language. "You told me they've painted the door."

"Yes," said Don. "Red. It looks wonderful—and imagine it when all your hippeastrums are out next spring. I'll take a picture for you; it will make the whole house look magnificent."

"The whole house was magnificent," said Elsie, turning the key end on end in her lap. "The whole house is." She frowned. "Such a bother to have to change it when I get home."

"Mum—"

She looked up, passing the key to her son and smiling brightly. "I know, Donny, I know." *Play along.* "Maybe you should give them this one too—whoever they are."

Don smiled and dropped the key back into her bag. "I told you, Mum—a nice new family, a little boy. Nice to have all that busyness back in the house—that's what Carol said. She drove past when they first moved in and saw them planting things in the garden. Even trees—Dad'd be horrified. But look, I'm sure you can keep this one. I know we gave them a key to that door. You keep this; you have this memento."

Trees: Elsie smiled, leaning down to grab the key again and holding it tight. "I'd like to make sure it's OK," she said.

Donny paused. "Are you worried about the house in the flood? I told you it was fine—and Carol checked."

"Of course I'm worried—not to be there. Not to see it. Not to know." Elsie blushed. She never raised her voice at children; that was wrong. And here she was—shouting, at Don, of all people. "I'm sorry, love." And she patted his hand in turn. "I'd like to see the trees."

"All right." He nodded. "The weekend. How about I take you then? We'll go by and have a look, maybe see the river too. And all the cleanup—just like in seventy-four."

"I wonder who'll do the papering this time."

Don picked up her hand and touched it to his lips. "It didn't flood, Mum. Nothing happened. Not this time."

"You should go and punch the holes out in the floor. They won't know they need to do that."

She watched him blink, her lovely boy, and nod his head again.

~~~~

It was strange to watch her own house from the street. It was so cool inside Don's car. She watched a woman in the garden, in a thin-strapped frock and a broad-brimmed hat, wipe sweat from her arms.

"Do you want to meet her?" Don leaned to open the window.

"No. No. Heavens. She doesn't look a bit like me."

Don laughed, nudged the car forward, around the corner, and away. "Why would she, Mum?" He drove on down to the river then, its flow still thicker and faster than usual and the streets between busy with piles of the flood's muddy wreckage and detritus. They stopped in the park by the cemetery and Elsie watched the water rushing by.

"I miss your father," she said after a while. "I never quite know who I am when he's not here."

"I miss him too, Mum, but it's more than thirty years now," Don said. "You know, it's rising thirty-eight."

Elsie nodded. "I know, love. I do know that. But coming home now—well, I hoped . . ."

He rubbed at his forehead the very way Clem would, creasing down the skin around his eyes. "You hoped he might be there."

"I thought he might be." She took his hand, the way she had to cross the roads when he was small. "Isn't it lovely, Donny, to let yourself dream he might be?" Her son's skin still felt so soft to her. "Thanks for bringing me. And I did like the new red front door." Thinking, *You'll know. You'll know about this when she's gone.*

They watched the water, watched it fold around the rocks below the path, breaking into crystal shapes and foam.

"Do you want to see Dad's headstone in the graveyard? I can drive in quite close to the plot."

"It's not the same, but thanks, love." Elsie patted her son's arm. "The house was a better idea."

"Then let's go back now—I'll drive home the same way."

She leaned into the comfortable seat, her hands flat against her trousers. She could feel the heavy door key in her pocket.

"Slow down!" she cried as the car came into her street. "Slow down, Don!"

Along the new fence, she could see a row of roses, and her doilies were all hanging on the line. She closed her eyes and leafed through her memories of them like the samples in wallpaper books that Clem used to consult when his spring-cleaning moods hit. Plain white; lacy trim; embroidered forget-me-nots; embroidered roses; embroidered violets; a hexagon with a filet crochet edge; a whole sheaf of broderie anglaise. They'd have that crisp, fresh smell—clean fabric, infused with all that sun and air. If she could take one, she would set it on the little table by her bed in that new place, under the orchid that Gloria had sent.

She could still describe her favorite—a pretty thing with twists of pink and red roses and tiny cutwork shapes. Her grandmother had taught her the pattern: her grandmother in a tall armchair, and Elsie on a stool at her feet. She'd only have been six or seven years old. Remember the importance of the neatness, her grandmother said again and again; the importance of a smooth stitch and a tidy pattern. The importance of paying as much attention to the back of your work as the front.

"And here's how you make the rose, see? Just a little shape, Elsie, a couple of stitches, and it suddenly looks like a flower."

So pretty, so delicate, that Elsie could almost smell the roses too.

There was a cream she used to wear, or a perfume. Something to do with roses. Attar. Attar of Roses. Such a pretty phrase.

And you always said the weather was too humid to grow them here, Clem. For all the projects he'd kept up around the place, he drew the line at flowerbeds and trees. She'd planted a single rosebush—a pink one—after he died, but it had died after two or three years.

If I could just take a rose for my room. She should say this; perhaps there were still pruning shears hanging in the place Clem had made for them in her laundry—drawing around them in thick black ink to mark their spot. But something like nervousness kept her quiet. She was afraid to meet these people, make them real.

The breeze picked up, and the doilies danced and jumped as the line spun around. *And at least they've washed them*, thought Elsie, *which is more than I've managed in I can't think how long.* Their patches of white were brilliant in the sun. She wanted to watch them forever.

"Come on, Mum. I'm sure we can come by again." Donny was starting the car as he said this, and Elsie wondered just how much she'd said aloud.

The car purred and Elsie let the window down a little, leaning out towards this landscape that she knew. It was lovely. It was precious. It was home.

In the garden, the woman in the hat had straightened up at the sound of the engine, cupping her hand to extend the shade of the brim. She raised her other hand—the beginning of a greeting, and in the car, Elsie raised her own hand in response.

Welcome, she thought, seeing her whole life clearly in that moment. *I should send flowers. I should send something.* It was lovely to see them taking such good care of the place.

She smiled at the thought. She'd ask Carol to send some flowers, a big, rich bunch of something special, to welcome them into her home.

"Lucy?"

Elsie heard the man's voice through the chink of open window.

"Lucy? Are you coming? Where are you?"

The woman smiled and waved again, and Elsie went on, around the corner and away, her hand still up and waving, like a pic-ture-postcard image of a queen. A second or two longer and she'd have seen the man who spoke. *Clem?* She thought the name so hard, it hurt.

"Let's go home," her son said quietly.

"Back to your place?"

"Back to your place," Donny said, quieter still again. "It's ready now. Power on. Car parks cleaned. Mud all gone. Good as new."

Elsie nodded. She supposed she didn't mind it after all.

"Just make sure to tell your father where I am," she said, leaning back in the seat and closing her eyes.

She knew. Of course she knew. But still.

16

The kiss

LUCY WATCHED the car drive slowly around the corner, and waved once more as it went out of view. She closed her eyes and saw the postcard from Astrid, the day she'd seen the future Lucy at the beach. The woman in that car: she looked familiar. *I'll come back to this place when I am old.*

"Lu? Are you out there? Are you coming?"

Behind her, Ben pushed the garage door open from inside. She let her hand drop.

He called, "Anyone we know?"

And she smiled, pushing her hat off her head and walking into the garage's shade.

"It felt a bit—" She rubbed at the air with her fingers, hunting for the word. "—Like déjà vu, but backwards. You, wordsmith: do you have a better phrase?"

Ben shook his head. "All these cards, all these letters. What's the plan?"

There were piles and piles of them, rising like little skyscrapers from the concrete floor—blue ones made of airmail letters; stiffer ones made of postcards; careful stacks of folded foolscap; a spectrum of colored envelopes graded purple through blue, green, yellow to red. She hadn't realized she'd unpacked quite so much.

Lucy crouched beside one tower, steadying it. On the top was a note that Ben had sent—early days, away on a story, thinking of her.

"From the time when the world was still huge," she said, skimming through his words. "Now, you can always phone home."

"You want to keep them?" he asked, still standing high above her. "And when on earth did you unpack all this?"

"Nights," she said. Her voice was sharp, as if he should know. "Not sleeping."

He shook his head again. "You should have told me."

She shrugged. "So you could—what?"

She let her fingers rest on one pile of papers, as if she was feeling for a pulse. "It's like Elsie's doilies," she said, tilting her head towards the yard. "They've got a worth. They've got a value. And then—" She clicked her fingers, once. "And then it's gone."

"Nostalgic Lucy." Ben sat down beside her and took up her hands.

"Not nostalgic. Fractured. Transient. Nine letters. I don't know." She shook her hands free and rubbed at her eyes. "It was lovely to get all this back. I'd forgotten all the people whose lives are down here. And I feel like the flood brought them in."

He smiled at her, nudging her shoulder. "You've got to stop making things huge."

She let his words hang and they sat there side by side, Ben scuffing his feet against her archive.

"*The Life of Lucy Kiss. A Correspondence*," he said at last.

Lucy blushed, pushing out a postcard here, some sheets of paper there, and glancing at their words. She sighed and tapped another pile to neatness. From the quiet rooms upstairs, she heard Tom wake and cry.

"Can you get him?" she said to Ben. Her fingers grazed against the concrete as she brushed the piles out of their neat stacks and spread them again on the floor.

"Just need to finish this off—" He headed behind her, quick to be immersed in his own stuff.

"Fine, fine, don't worry," she said, pushing herself up off her haunches and making her way to the stairs. The new phone in her pocket beeped—a message—and she glanced at the screen to see her sister's name, the first three lines of text. Some surprise, some visit: something. She'd read it when she'd fed and watered Tom.

From the top of the stairs, the brightness of Elsie's doilies caught her eye and she paused. The star-shaped mat danced wildly beneath the fixed points of its pegs, its fingers flexing, busy in the breeze. It looked as if someone was waving from down there.

Going inside, she dropped the phone into a kitchen drawer—safe and sound—and went on through the house.

~

Lucy lay on the bed in the hot still air of early afternoon. The way this heat hit the planes and crevices of her body, making them all shine and sweat: she felt as though she'd been gilded.

She had her headphones on and Tom was fast asleep. The CD she'd been listening to—the songs that had made her remember dancing those weeks, those months before—pounded into the middle of her brain, and she tapped their rhythms onto the mattress like a drum. She'd sung the first of them, loud, defiant, in the shower that morning, and it had felt good to let out the noise.

"Let's go to Paris," she'd said to Ben at breakfast. Before Tom, before the three of them, they'd had this game: if you could wake up tomorrow morning and go anywhere in the world, where would it be?

Iceland, Ben mostly said, or, once, Perth. "You know it's the most remote city in the world?"

"I'd rather Iceland," she'd said. More exotic; somewhere new.

Last night, she'd slept quite soundly. And when she woke in the morning, she was awake—for the first time in a long while—before Tom. She opened her eyes and made her own way back into the world.

Beside her, Ben stirred a little and she leaned across to kiss him. "Good morning over there," she said. "How are you?"

He stretched. He blinked. He flexed his shoulders and his neck. "And good morning over there. I haven't had that wakeup for a while."

"That's because I'm usually woken by that small, noisy alarm Tom." She smiled. He smiled.

Here they were: they were all right.

Then: "Where would you fly to tomorrow? Where would you like us to be?"

"Well," said Ben after a moment. "I've got a new one. Tristan da Cunha, at the southern end of the Atlantic. But no airport—we'd have to go by ship. Sounds nice and quiet, though; you'd sleep well there." He turned to face her, inching his head closer to hers. "And you? Still Paris for you?"

"Let's go to Paris."

She'd done it once, a couple of years back now, when they'd lived in London. Paris on a whim while Ben was at work. It felt like the best reason for living in the wintry, bleak northern hemisphere, and there'd been more sun as soon as the train emerged on the French side of the tunnel.

She'd eaten a lot of cheese. She'd bought some tacky tourist pictures by the Seine. She'd visited the Musée d'Orsay, the Museum of Arts and Crafts, the Louvre. She carried spotlit moments from that day: a painting of a girl with a red balloon; an aeroplane designed like a bat; a pendulum that showed the movement of the Earth. She remembered watching the pendulum for the longest time, soothed—almost hypnotized—by its graceful regularity. And walking through the gardens towards the Louvre's big glassy pyramids, even now she could recall how warm the sun had felt, and how she'd smiled as she'd watched a bunch of children run and skip. She'd been suffused with the most extraordinary sense of well-being, as if, for those two or three minutes, she was certain that everything was going to be all right—not that she knew what "everything" was, and not that she'd thought there was anything particularly wrong in the first place. But for those moments, on that afternoon, in that elegant public place in that famous city, something contented and complete hummed through her body.

She'd caught the train back home to London and thrown away her contraceptive pills.

"Let's go to Paris," she'd said again this morning. "Let's fly there."

"You and me," said Ben, lacing his fingers through hers.

"You and me and Tom."

And they lay there, saying nothing, until Tom woke with a cry.

"I like the pre-Tom-wakeup Lucy," said Ben as she pulled herself up out of bed.

She stood there for a moment while Tom's cry surged. "Don't we all," she said.

Now, stretched out like a starfish, she realized that the last song had finished and she was listening to the afternoon's silence. She listened to the round nothingness that the headphones pressed against her ears, and then a floorboard creaked somewhere in the bedroom near her head, and she turned to acknowledge its noise.

Expansion, she thought. *Contraction. The house is breathing.*

That's all it was.

She closed her eyes and pictured herself in Paris. She'd buy Tom ice cream at Berthillon. She'd show him the bat-shaped aeroplane. She'd watch him run through the gardens at the Tuileries.

It was all right. Of course it was all right.

He was asleep. Then he'd be awake. Then they would walk down to the river and explore. So many houses still stood empty after the flood; it felt like walking through a ghost town or a film set. She liked their game creating stories for the disarrayed buildings—aliens having a party; bears on some wild spree.

Something creaked again. And then the phone rang and she leapt up, reaching for it.

"Hello?"

"Well, hello."

She knew the voice, but couldn't place it. A man's voice, deep, familiar. She held the phone out from her ear—it showed no number that she knew.

"Sorry. Who is this?"

"It's your deep and distant past."

"I don't—I'm sorry—" as Tom cried out. Lucy took a breath, felt her heart race. "I'll have to go—my son's just woken up."

"I'll ring back later."

"I'd rather you didn't."

"But it's me. It's Ferdi." As if it were the most normal thing in the world.

"Ferdi? Ferdi Klim?"

"The one and only." The man was laughing at the other end of the line, and now Lucy was laughing too.

"Hang on," she said. "Hang on—I've got to get my boy." And she lifted Tom out of his cot, shushing him and holding him, her phone wedged between her shoulder and her ear.

"He's got your lungs then?" said Ferdi Klim.

"You know," said Lucy, "I never thought of it that way." She set Tom down on the living room floor, scooting blocks and trucks towards him. Here was the paper aeroplane she'd folded from Ferdi's letter, swooping high across her memory, and far. "So, Ferdi Klim," she said. "Where did you spring from?"

"I ran into one of your sisters on a train the other day, in Sydney—what are the odds? I'm home for a bit, and I thought it was you. She's dyeing her hair red. It's very confusing. Anyway, she said you'd moved up north, and then work said, Fly north, young man, so I've come up and—"

"Hang on—you're where? You're here? From where?" Was this the text message from her sister that she'd never gone back to read?

"What? No—I'm just up here for work. Be nice to see you."

She thought of dancing in her lounge room; she thought of dancing on her own those years before. She remembered how she'd felt, so young and free. After him.

"I was thinking of that summer we broke up," she said after a moment. "All the bands I went to see then, on my own. You sure you're real?"

"I'm pretty sure."

"Then come over," she said quickly, before she could change her mind. "Come for dinner. Come tonight."

He laughed. "I can't come for dinner—I've got to meet a colleague—but I could come and see you now, if you like."

"Where are you?" Lucy looked around the room with its jumble and clutter of toys, books, clean clothes. "Do you know where we are?"

"I'm at the station: your sister said it wasn't far away."

"What? My sister gave you the address?"

"Well, just the suburb," he said. "She said she thought you could use an old friend. So, where do I go?"

"I guess . . . well, I'd love to see you."

And she gave him the address, talking as he walked down from the station—crossing, turning, like the blue dot that moved with her on the street maps on her phone.

She was rushing through the house, kicking at piles of Duplo, pushing a basket of unfolded washing under her bed. "So, the house is a bit of a mess," she said as she went.

"And of course that's all I care about," said Ferdi. "Is that you? The blue house? The bright red front door?"

"Yes. It is." Lucy opened the door. "And there you are. You're here."

There he was. He held out his arms and Tom, alert to any chance of a hug, ran past his mother and arrived, blinking at this unknown man, his arms out in return.

"You must be Tom. It's good to meet you." Ferdi crouched down, and his face grimaced as if at a sudden stiffness. He held out his hand and inclined his head—his hair more of a faded, greying blond than Lucy remembered—towards Tom's. "You shake, like this." He demonstrated, right hand to right hand, and Tom held out his left hand to give it its fair turn.

Lucy scooped up the little boy, and stepped onto the porch towards Ferdi as he straightened, one hand propping his hip while the other arm reached around her in a hug. "You're getting old, then." She laughed. "And if we'd known you were coming—"

"Well, here I am." He held her for a while. "I think I've shrunk—or have you grown?"

"Me?" Lucy shook her head. "Utterly average, as always. My sisters grew two centimeters each after they'd had their kids. Me, perfectly static. One-sixty-two on the dot." She pushed back from Ferdi, looking him up and down. "A bit more creaky," she said at last, "but you look just like you—I'd have known you anywhere." Not saying a thing about his hair.

"You look just like your sister, which was confusing when I saw her the other day. 'Lucy!' Bounding over like an idiot. 'No,' she said. 'That happens all the time.'"

"Really?" Lucy smiled a measured smile. "She never tells me about it. I wonder who else she's confused. Come on; come in. And mind the Duplo. How long are you around?"

"Flying visit—overnight. I'm based in the US these days. Still working with money. Always money. It'll send me grey one day." He waved away the question she was about to ask. "Brokerage: that's all you need to know. What are you doing—apart from this one? Whose university are you sorting out now?"

Ferdi sat straight down with Tom on the floor and was picking out pieces of Duplo and clicking them together in a long, unstable line. "Light saber?" he said, offering the drooping stick to the small boy.

"He doesn't know about light sabers yet," said Lucy, watching from above. "We're more into Dr. Seuss around here. I'm currently kept busy by the University of Duplo, as you can see."

"Flamingo," said Tom with certainty. It was his current favorite word.

"Well, yes, I can see that," said Ferdi seriously. "I see that now. Let's make some legs then." Clicking wider orange pieces to its base.

"Yay!" said Tom. "Flamingo!"

"Now you make one," said Ferdi, leaning back. "Yes, brokerage. Chicago, Illinois. And you've just moved here? It's for—sorry, I forget your husband's name."

"Ben; we moved here just after Tom turned one."

Ferdi nodded. "And Brisbane. You like it?"

Lucy laughed. "I'm fine as long as I've got a map—I still can't quite work out where I am. Ben's writing for one of the papers. He's very good at what he does." She blushed. "I mean, I'm very proud."

"Of course you are—did I meet Ben?" Ferdi had begun to build another Duplo shape.

"Maybe at a party?" If certain moments were essential, she thought she'd have held on to that one.

"The nine-letter-word guy? The writer?"

Lucy nodded.

"I did meet him. I tried to trip him up with 'astrocyte,'" said Ferdi. "Don't even know how I knew the word. He had it in a flash."

He bowed his head, flattened his palms towards the floor. "I con-ceded immediate defeat—although 'brokerage,' I could try that one now."

"We've been together ten years. And he's only getting better at those puzzles," Lucy said with a laugh. "You'd have no chance now."

"No chance indeed." Ferdi admired his own construction. "You have quality Duplo, Lucy Kiss—I should never have left you."

"I believe I left you." Lucy pulled the toy box a little closer. "And I don't think Duplo would have helped."

Ferdi smiled. "You may be right. But come on, we both ended up in the right place."

"No hard feelings." She turned to go into the kitchen. "Now. What. Tea. Coffee. Beer. That's all we've got."

Ferdi laid a mat of blue plastic pieces in front of Tom, then stood up to stretch, to follow her. "There's a lake for your flamingos, my small friend." He smiled at Lucy. "Tea? Do you drink tea now? Well, this is new."

She was talking as she filled the kettle with water. "I blame this house. I even held off in London, and then we came here, bought this place, and that was it. I blame Elsie."

"Elsie?"

"The lady we bought the house from. I found a teacup and I thought how nice it would be to have a cup of tea with Elsie. I liked to imagine her just dropping in. I think it all started from there."

Ferdi leaned against the doorframe; he was still smiling. "I should say something about wonders never ceasing. Tea! My mother won't believe that."

"Is it such a big deal?"

"You always made it one before."

"Did I?" Lucy felt strangely defensive: she wouldn't have cared about such a small thing, would she? She wasn't sure. All those other Lucys lost in other pasts.

She'd liked Ferdi's mother more than she'd liked Ferdi a lot of the time—a woman with generously sized wineglasses and a scathing opinion of most men, particularly the ones she was related to. "Your mum's OK?"

"Mum and Dad, both mainly fine." Ferdi had pulled a phone from his pocket and was flicking through for photos. "Here—my birthday dinner, the other day."

"Happy birthday," said Lucy, peering at the screen and then at Ferdi. "Your mum looks exactly the same. And you're looking more like your dad. Although he—" She paused. The older man looked old.

"He's not had the best year," said Ferdi. "Old age. The usual." He bent closer and swiped the photos on. "So—here: my lot. Three girls—nine; six; three." A separate image for each one.

"They're in Chicago?"

"The youngest in Chicago. The middle one in New York. And the eldest one in Maine." He took a deep breath. "You know I always liked to leap from thing to thing."

Three girls; three wives? What a life. Lucy poured the boiling water onto the tea leaves and turned the teapot to steep.

"You really have embraced the whole tea ceremony." Ferdi nodded to the teapot.

"I know; I told you—Elsie. All the pots she must have made; I think it must be something in the air."

"The ghost of teapots past?"

"She didn't die here." Lucy looked aghast. "She just moved out, and then we bought the place. I like to think that she sort of pops around."

He was smiling as he shook his head at her—she'd forgotten the warmth of that smile. "You're just the same; you haven't changed at all. Your sister made it sound like things were grim."

Lucy blushed a little. "We all have our moments," she murmured, reaching for her cup.

There was a clatter from the other room and Tom appeared beside Ferdi. "Fall down, Mummy," he said cheerfully. "Flamingo all fall down."

"Never mind," said Ferdi, picking him up as if he was the creature who'd fallen. "Let's see if we can build them again." And he went into the lounge room with the small boy curled against his chest.

Lucy leaned against the edge of the kitchen table, an idea flashing through her head. *If I had married Ferdi Klim, I'd have three girls. Or I'd be divorced. Or I'd have this moment daily—him, and Tom, and tea.* As unthinkable a thing as it was inevitable to think it.

She poured the tea, calling to check that Ferdi took his the way she remembered—"just a touch of sugar at the end?"

She'd had such energy when she'd left him, a full, rich certainty that had made her feel alive. Best thing she'd ever done. Then she'd met Ben. And then—and then came everything that had carried her from there to here. The best things. Still, it was lovely to see an old friend.

"Just a touch of sugar at the end," Ferdi called back from the next room. She could hear him talking to Tom. She could hear Tom's one-, two-word replies as she tipped biscuits onto a plate. And then she stirred the lightly sugared tea and balanced the two cups in one hand, the biscuits in the other.

"It's good to see you, Ferdi," she said, walking into the living room. It was empty. Ferdi and Tom were gone.

Lucy set the tea things down, and blinked.

If I count to five, I will know what to do.

She counted: nothing.

There's nothing wrong. There is an explanation. I'll stand here. I'll call out. This is all all right.

She could call the police. She could ring Ben. She should remember to breathe.

As she breathed, she found her voice. "Tom? Love?" she called, and heard a hinge, a doorknob rattle. And there was Tom leading Ferdi by the hand, coming out of the bathroom.

"What the—"

"He said he needed to do a wee, and I asked him if he minded me taking him, and he said no." Ferdi sat back down on the floor and crossed his legs. Which was where Tom settled himself. "I shut the door—sorry, force of habit."

"He what?"

"Needed to do a wee, and didn't mind me taking him," repeated Ferdi. "Toilet training a bonus service—for you, there'll be no extra charge."

"I thought—I—" And as she spun around, she knocked Elsie's cup, the plate of biscuits, and sent them crashing to the floor. "It doesn't matter. He's never asked—he's never been before. I'll get—"

And she went back to the kitchen, where the tap turned on faster than she expected when she went to wet the sponge, and the water spurted across her body.

"Shit!"

"Well, maybe I'm some sort of kid whisperer," Ferdi called from the other room. "Are you all right out there?"

"I'm fine." She went back in and crouched down beside her visitor and her son, dipping her head. Her face was burning; she could hear her own pulse, loud, inside her head. She mopped up the tea, the crumbs, the tiny flecks of china—Elsie's cup had broken clear in two and she took it into the kitchen, where she paused a moment, very still, easing its halves gently together.

We can fix you. We can fix this up.

"That wasn't the magic cup, was it?" Ferdi called, and she ignored him.

She boiled the kettle, let the leaves steep, made the same two drinks again—in fresh, new cups. Carried all these items, one by one.

"Tea—half a sugar. Biscuits too." She felt like crying, and if she started she wasn't sure she'd stop.

But they sat a while, and talked of bits and pieces. Ferdi had done a better job of staying in touch with people, and Lucy could listen to the roll call of old friends without having to offer a thing. *And now he'll add me to the story—"I saw Lucy. Up in Brisbane. With her kid."*

There was a lull in their words then, and Lucy heard the double thump of small feet in the roof.

"Ben thinks it's a possum," she said as Ferdi looked up. "And Ben lived here when he was a boy—I mean in Brisbane."

"These children," said Ferdi as if she hadn't spoken. "They're a crazy roller coaster of a ride." He dipped a biscuit into his tea and offered half of it to Tom. "Is he allowed?"

An afterthought; Tom had already gulped it down.

"When my first girl was born, my first wife struggled—I made every wrong decision in the book. Never there. Not much use. Fairly clueless. We were over within the first year. Second wife; second child. Much the same. My mum was furious. Said she'd raised me to do better than that. I cried off about how busy I was—how hard it was for me. The only time I've heard my mother swear. Third wife; third child—we're doing better. It's pretty sad it's taken me this long."

He reached across, took Lucy by the hand. "I meant what I said—this stuff suits you. You look really good in all this."

She stared at their hands, linked together; the gold of her wedding band was bright in the gap between two of Ferdi's fingers. *What did it feel like when you left your wives, both times?* Some part of her wanted to know.

"I'm no better at it than anyone," she said at last. "And I don't think anyone always knows what to do."

"Tom's hand—Tom's hand." Her son was wriggling between them, wanting in.

"Yes," said Lucy. "I'll hold Tom's hand." And she let go of Ferdi, pulling Tom onto her lap and knitting her fingers with his. Beyond the porch, she could see the sky dimming to a dark grey; the start of rain smelled heavy in the air.

"Where do you need to get to for this dinner?" she said to Ferdi. "We might have to call you a cab. You bring an umbrella?"

He reached behind him for his satchel, spilling notebooks, a T-shirt and a small umbrella across the floor as it tipped upside down. "Things that I know about Brisbane," he said. "Beware of the afternoon rain."

"You can set your watch by it," said Lucy with a smile.

He stood up and stepped towards the doorway, and part of Lucy wanted to say, *No, please; don't go.*

"I didn't mean that you had to rush off."

"No, I should, Lu—do you still object to people calling you that?" He reached down and pulled her up while she held Tom.

"Nope." She laughed. "These days, it's open slather. I'll answer to anything now."

"Did you change your name when you got married? Do I need to turn you into . . ." He paused, obviously trying to remember. "Lucy Something-Else?"

"Lucy Carter? Nope," she said again. "I'm still the one and only Lucy Kiss."

"I did know that." He was settling his satchel, the umbrella unfurled. "I googled you, when that got going. Same with me: the one and only Ferdi Klim."

"You googled me? That's a little bit creepy, you know."

He shrugged. "Just a different kind of conjuring—think of it like that. But no, I only searched for you once. There was a story about somewhere you were working. In London, I think. It had one of those counters: 'three people are reading this now.' Me and your mum and your dad, I decided. Sitting at home, reading about you, being proud."

"Perhaps it was two of my *vardøger*—the other mes out there all living other lives. It doesn't matter." She waved away his puzzlement and hugged Tom close as Ferdi leaned across to kiss her cheek.

"So I guess I'll be passing by this way again in ten years' time or so," he said, smiling at them both. "I'll come and see what Tom's constructing then."

"Do that." She stepped forward to kiss his cheek in return. "You're right, you have shrunk. Another decade. I'll expect to see you then."

She went back into the house and saw his T-shirt on the floor where it had fallen from his bag. She set Tom down and reached for it, threading it through to right way out.

Force of habit.

There was a fragrance she didn't know she remembered. She pulled her arms clear of the sleeves—it was as if she was trying him on.

"Here." Tossing the scrunched-up ball of fabric out across the garden towards Ferdi as he stood there in the rain. "We don't need more stuff around here. You take care of yourself and all your families, you disaster."

"Ferdi kiss," called Tom. "Ferdi kiss."

"No, Tom: it's Ferdi Klim."

"Ferdi kiss," said Tom, pressing his fingers against his lips and flinging them out like a firework.

"Got it." Ferdi made another show of catching. "I'll see you when you're eleven, little man. My best to Elsie too, when she comes by."

Tom waved so hard his fingers blurred.

They were standing on the porch, watching Ferdi walk off through the rain, along the path that cut through the park. And as he disappeared behind the largest of the great fig trees, they saw another man, another umbrella, coming the other way.

"Daddy! Daddy! Daddy! Daddy!" Tom was down the stairs and out across the grass.

Ben caught him with a flourish. "You two out looking for me in this weather?" he called to Lucy when he was close.

"Something like that," said Lucy. "How was your day?"

"Not too bad." Ben shook the rain from his umbrella as he stepped onto the porch. "I finished early; thought I'd make the most of it."

Lucy smiled and reached up to kiss his mouth. "Come on then, let's go inside."

"Elsie come over?" Ben joked, pointing at the two cups sitting on the floor.

"Ferdi kiss," said Tom distinctly. "Ferdi kiss."

Ben took the cups through to the kitchen. "What'd you say?"

"Ferdi Klim—remember, the bloke with the cool name?" Lucy rinsed the cups, turning the tap on slowly and letting the water run warm. "The one I left before I met you. He's here for work."

"Ferdi Klim? Here? In the kitchen?"

"Well, in the lounge room—he was building things with Tom." And she told him about her sister, Ferdi's visit, her voice bright throughout it all.

"Isn't that a little creepy?" Ben asked as she paused.

"Creepy? No." But she paused again before she added, "It was lovely to see someone who knew me before."

"Before what?"

"Ferdi kiss!" Tom bounced around his father's kneecaps.

"Why does he keep saying that?" Ben picked Tom up and held him at arm's length as if he was an obstacle that needed to be moved.

"What?" Lucy turned from the sink, her bright voice dull now. "What do you think he means? He was blowing Ferdi kisses when he went—you must have walked right by him in the park."

"Right," said Ben, planting Tom back on the floor among his toys. "Whatever."

He pulled his newspaper from his bag and spread it out across the table, smoothing down a page. It would be a story he'd written, Lucy knew. He always read his own stories first. Which, Lucy realized, could seem a bit conceited.

Ben stood a while, apparently intent on the page. "Did I ever meet him?" he asked at last.

"He said you did—at a party. He said he gave you a nine-letter word. 'Astrocyte.'"

"And did I get it? I can't remember." He didn't even look up from the page.

"Yes, Ben," said Lucy after a moment. "Of course you did."

17

The little blue bird

CLEM WAS reading the paper when he heard a man say, "Hello?" and a knock on the door. As he crossed the room, he tried to make the sound match his adult son's voice. It was a rare thing that Elsie was out—with their daughter, and to hear a band, of all things, that Elaine had so wanted to hear. Who else but Donny would knock on a Monday evening?

"You right?" Clem said, flicking on the porch light, one hand on the screen door's handle.

The visitor was a tall older man with a broad-brimmed hat pulled low. He nodded a greeting.

"Found this bird down in the gutter—isn't it a beauty? Pale-headed rosella, I think—gorgeous little thing. Must've run into something, and I wondered, would you have a box I could put it in? It might just have stunned itself. Might be right to go again in a bit. A shoebox? Or a carton? Would you have a thing like that?"

Pushing the door open, Clem stepped onto the porch and peered at the bundle of feathers in the man's hands. Birds were so light and frail, and this one was quivering. The movement shook the colors of its feathers towards a greater luminosity.

"Come with me and I'll have a look," Clem said. He led the way down the stairs and around to the garage door underneath the house. "I usually keep things like that, in case they come in handy." He found a pile of small cartons and selected one with a lid. "Like this?"

"Like that. There you are, little one." The man went to set the bird down and paused. "What about a towel? Or a bit of fabric?"

"Yes, of course," said Clem, reaching for a tea towel that Elsie had demoted to an under-house rag. "This'll have it feeling better in an instant," he said with a smile. The tea towel was printed with bright pictures of birds—lorikeets and parrots and big white cockatoos. He watched his visitor settle the little thing in its small soft nest.

"D'you live around here?" Clem asked then, wondering that the man didn't have his own garage or shed from which to source a container.

"I used to, up in the next street. Moved away a few months ago; came back to see the old place." The man shifted his hat a little, and Clem saw that it was the artist's husband, the professor. What had Elsie said, something about their divorce, and the two of them moving away? Clem frowned, trying to think of something appropriate to say.

"I recognize you—you're at the university; something to do with flies? My wife knew your wife I think." He wasn't sure if he should refer to the portrait, as if it might be illicit or suspect. That was how he felt about it, he realized, as though it was some liberty taken; some intimacy assumed. He cleared his throat. "I was sorry to hear—" But that sounded too much like someone had died.

"I've failed twice at marriage," the professor said bluntly, two fingers cocked as if they wanted a cigarette. "Not a thing of which I'm proud. I don't fail at much as a rule."

Clem scuffed his feet, uneasy about these words. Pass and fail were things to do with school, not marriage. This man had his box; he should go.

But the professor had stepped forward, resting the box on the bench that held Clem's vice and lathe. Beyond the bench was Clem's billiards table.

"You know," said the professor, nodding towards its wide green surface, "I haven't played for years. In the war, in New Guinea, we came across a coffee grower's house, near Sangara. Beautiful place, and exactly what we'd all been yearning for: big verandas, comfortable beds, books and glassware and views across the foothills. And this billiards table, a huge great thing with the most impeccable cloth. We only had two nights—a little respite from the mud and blood and noise. But we had a championship going, twenty-four hours, as if we knew to make the most of it. I never played so well as I played in that place—to be honest, I don't think I've ever played since."

Clem cleared his throat: here was his quiet night, at home on his own. And the world had offered up a companion for billiards. It was all he could do not to smile.

"If you don't mind my racking the balls, Professor, I could stand you a game." Clem flicked on the bar of light that hung directly over the table, gesturing towards the cues at the side, and the professor dipped his hat and rubbed his hands, briskly, glancing at the bird.

"Rack them up, then, rack them up," he said, giving the bird's feathers a gentle pat. "I'd have been here years ago if I'd known that I'd a billiards fiend for a neighbor."

It was the one extravagant thing Clem Gormley owned, inappropriately ostentatious. A mate had told him of a hall closing in the city, all the tables priced to clear, he said, and Clem had found himself carried along to the auction, hardly keen or interested, and going home with fifty square feet of souvenir, wondering how to explain it to Elsie.

"Your wife won't mind?" The professor was chalking his cue, and Clem shook his head.

"Out with the daughter," he said. "That show that's on; those Beatles."

The professor laughed. "World gone mad," he said. "I read in the paper about some woman passing a sick child over to those young layabouts, as if they were saints or shamans. You want to be careful of your wife getting caught up in something like that. Music." He sighed. "I don't see the point."

Clem shrugged, this time defensive. "She likes her music, Elsie, lovely singing voice. When my daughter said she wanted to go, well . . ." Elsie, zipping herself into that special silver dress, the one he liked, and dusting at her cheeks with a flat pad of rouge. He'd have gone with her if she'd asked, whatever he thought of it. But Elsie had tickets for herself and Elaine, treating them as if they were invested with the power of reconciliation.

Elaine: her teachers had always said she was a bright one—"a head for learning," one had said—and Clem wondered sometimes if they'd done enough with that. But she'd never said, his daughter. She'd never said a word about such things. She grew up and got married and had a baby, exactly as Elsie had hoped she would. And she hated it; Clem could see that. She'd hated it from the get-go, and still did.

It flummoxed Elsie; Clem could sense it at night, when she lay staring at the ceiling, doubtless winding back through every moment and permutation she could think of to try to explain to herself her daughter's inexplicable behavior. He could feel the way her fingers played across the texture of the chenille bedspread as if she was trying to trace a path towards some exquisite point where a different thing might have been said, or done, or initiated, and Elaine would emerge, blissful and content and reconstructed in the present. Then Elsie would sigh, and worry at her pillow, and whisper, "Sorry, Clem," and, finally, sleep.

It would have been easier, Clem thought, if his daughter had moved away altogether. Except for Elsie fretting at not seeing the little one, Gloria. She was some sort of blessing.

But it ate at him, the way Elsie threw herself at any tiny enthusiasm Elaine might want to share—*like a dog after scraps*, he'd thought once, not proud of the analogy. And he knew Elsie would've paid for the tickets, although Elaine's smart young husband, Gerald, was high up in mining. *Not that you ever saw his hands dirty*, thought Clem.

He blinked at the sound of the professor's cue against a ball and the triangle exploded across the smooth green surface.

"There's nothing like it, is there?" the professor said quietly, and Clem saw the same look of satisfaction that he felt on his own face.

"Could you use a beer with it?" he asked, setting out two yellow cardboard coasters etched with Mr Fourex, and turning for the stairs.

"Again," said the professor, taking one of the two glasses Clem brought down from the kitchen, "I must now rue that we're no longer neighbors." And he clinked his glass against his host's. "To perfect breaks," he said. His throat made a strange glugging noise as he swallowed—it reminded Clem of water running out of a bath.

They played four games—three–one to the professor—and drank four glasses each, and all the while the little bird lay in its box, each man standing by it as he waited for the other's shot. But as the professor potted the last ball, Clem caught the edge of a different movement in the rosella's feathers, and he touched his finger lightly to its breast.

"Professor?" he said gently. "I think it's gone." The bird's head had slumped, its eyes vacant. Clem flexed his finger slightly against its body.

Coming around to the bench, the professor picked the bird out of its makeshift refuge and held it to his cheek. "Yes," he said, "yes.

We saw it all the time, around the corner—Ida's studio had glass on three sides, and the poor birds used to try to take a shortcut. That terrible thump, and then a tiny bundle of feathers on the grass. Sometimes they were just stunned—but mostly . . ."

Clem looked up, and saw the other man wipe at a tear.

"It's birds, you know, something moves me about birds." The professor pulled a handkerchief from his pocket and blew his nose, hard. "I always hoped to study birds, but I landed with flies—fruit flies, diptera, all those other things with wings. I still miss my birds—their colors, and their songs. I've stared a long time at a lot of diptera and I don't find much of beauty compared to these splendid things."

Instinctively, Clem swatted an imaginary bug.

"Now that's what I should have studied, of course," said the professor, laughing. "The time it takes between the first mention of a bug in a conversation to the instant someone's convinced they're being dive-bombed. It works with fleas too—and lice, I expect. The power of suggestion: it's some thing, the human mind."

Clem slapped again. "What about your bird, Professor?" he asked, scratching at the side of his head. "What shall we do with your bird?" The man still had its body nestled up against his cheek.

"I had a hummingbird in the house once," he said at last. "I was visiting a colleague in America, and I dozed off at his place one afternoon. Woke up to the strangest sound in the room—I could tell it was a struggle, but it was so delicate. And there it was, this exquisite hummingbird, flying from one picture rail to another. It must have come in through the window and not known how to get out. I caught it, you know, and I held it for a second. An amazing thing: it was like holding beauty, or life—an abstract thing made real. And then I sent it back into the world."

"Can you change what you do? Can you change to be a bird-man?" Clem almost blushed. It seemed a presumptuous thing to ask, but here was this man, in his garage, drinking his beer, shooting his billiards, and holding a bird against his cheek like a kiss.

The professor laughed. "In a lot of ways," he said, "that bird brought me nothing but trouble." He laid the rosella's body back in the box, and his fingers rested on its feathers. "My American colleague, he had a daughter. She came in while I was holding the hummingbird, and we stood there, the two of us, in that moment. It felt like the most significant piece of time I'd ever experienced. We were married before my sabbatical was up." He shook his head. "Brought her back here—to Sydney. It was the thirties, and she hated it. We found a little place in Newtown; I had a job at the university. And I loved Newtown. I set out a garden for her, all the flowers blue—it looked lovely in the twilight—and I built a little aviary for a couple of birds, two blue-faced parrot finches. Gorgeous. There was the most splendid gum tree in the yard too, and a tall rangy camphor laurel—they're useless things, block off any chance of anything else having a foothold. But she loved it—the shiny deep green leaves that looked the way leaves were supposed to look, she said. Not like a eucalyptus.

"I told her it'd have to go, because it'd starve out the rest of our garden. I told her I'd wait a year, so she could enjoy it, but that I'd need to take it down after that—they grow so fast, you know. At the end of the year, I told her it was time. Had a chap come with a saw, and we got it down between us, poured some kero onto the stump, and that was that. When I went in to pull a couple of drinks out of the ice box, I saw that she was cooking something on the stove."

He stopped talking then, and stood swaying a little from side to side, his fingers still touching the dead rosella's chest.

"I never told this story to a soul, but it was my birds there in that pot. Fair trade, she said, the finches I loved in exchange for her tree. I couldn't speak—damn near packed her on the first boat to America, but what can you do? What can you do? Must have been the end of 1938, because as soon as the war came, I was off. Got myself out of her way. When I met Ida, it was easy to stay away."

They stood facing each other, two tall men in the clutter of Clem's garage—although Clem was staring at the other man with a look of horror on his face. Birds in a pot? *Pets* in a pot? Who'd even think of a reprisal like that? It felt evil—and that your wife, the woman you loved, would do such a thing. *Fancy realizing you'd married someone who did a thing like that.*

He closed his eyes and pictured Elsie: Elsie holding their children, holding their grandchild, feeding the kookaburra that landed in their yard; worried for that blessed crow. He swallowed. Had he ever done a thing to enrage her so much? Had she ever sat across from him and plotted some revenge? He took a breath. It wasn't that he couldn't know: there was nothing to know. They trusted themselves with each other. They had nothing like this.

The professor shook the handkerchief into its great white square and blew his nose again. "There's no way around it, is there? There's no way of loving someone who thinks that's a reasonable thing to do."

Clem shook his head, a nasty stale taste in his mouth. "My father shot a crow once—no reason, just because he could. It seemed so cruel. I wished him dead himself for that, I think." Another previously unspoken thing said.

"Tantamount to murder, to take the life of some sentient thing," said the professor, wiping roughly at his nose. "You wouldn't have another of those beers, would you? I could well wash that story away."

But Clem shook his head again, reaching forward to pick up the bird's coffin. "I don't, I'm afraid. But let's get this one buried, and then come up for a cuppa. That's the best I can do."

In the yard, Clem set his foot against the top edge of the shovel, willing it to find a weakness in the hard, dry winter soil. They were down by the back fence where he'd buried the baby crow years before, and where the swamp had the most chance of seeping through the dirt. The shovel eased in, and Clem set about digging a small pit.

"I almost think I should say a few words," the professor whispered as he placed the coffin in its grave. "This little frame, and the ability to fly: an amazing biological culmination."

Isn't all life? Clem thought a little wildly. It felt like a moment of epiphany. He wanted nothing more than Elsie by his side right now. She'd have a better thing to say than *come up for a cuppa*; she'd have a better thing to say about the bird. She did the caring and the saying in their world.

Above, in the trees, fruit bats muttered and squawked, and a baby possum made its careful way along a telegraph wire. The other rosellas, the ones who should have cried and called for this bird, they'd all be asleep in their nests, thought Clem.

He leaned forward and scraped the dirt down onto the box.

"There now," he said as he stood up, clapping his hand on the professor's shoulder. "Come in and I'll fix us a brew." And he led the man up the familiar slope of his own back lawn, wondering at the strangeness of his coming, and the bird, and the pool game, and the night.

Sitting across from each other at the kitchen bench, each man stirred the sugar in his tea. *Did you ever ask your first wife about it?* Clem wanted to ask. *Did she apologize, explain it somehow?* He watched as the professor positioned his spoon carefully on his saucer and took up his cup, saw the way his hand shook and the tea spilled a little. *He's older than I thought,* Clem realized: maybe sixty or more. Wandering around his old neighborhood, looking for his past.

Where would I walk, without Elsie? he wondered, sipping at his own hot sweet tea. *Would I stay here or move on? Would she leave me, ever, Elsie?*

But she would never leave him; he would never leave her. *People like us*, he thought, *well, we don't*. He couldn't see himself without her anyway, and she must feel the same. Till death us do part—they'd made that promise. Clem pulled his shoulders back, proud of keeping his word.

And then he thought about the noise and the mess and the exuberant frenzy of the music she was listening to—now, he thought, *probably right now. What if some man there—?* He couldn't even imagine. *But what if some man there*—and his shoulders slumped.

"Does she often go to these sorts of concerts, then, your wife?" the professor asked out of the silence.

"Never a one before this," said Clem. "She makes me try an orchestra sometimes, or some paintings at the gallery—well, you'd know about that, with Mrs. Lewis. It's like she wants to look into another world once in a while."

"And what do you do, Mr.—?"

The question of Clem's name was so impossibly belated that he almost laughed in reply. "Me? I'm Clement Gormley. I'm at the university, Professor—maintenance, mostly; bits and bobs for the caretaker, around the grounds. I recognized you from there, as much as from around the corner." It hadn't occurred to him that the professor might not recognize him.

"Apologies, my apologies," the older man said, setting his empty cup carefully on the saucer and trying to still its rattle. "Those notions of absentminded professors—they're true, of course. They're true."

It made Clem bristle, the other man's casual claim of social ignorance, but he was courteous all the same.

"To be honest, sir—" the honorific slipped out before he could stop it, and he knew the other man would take it as his due, "—perhaps I haven't done so much work in your building. I've certainly never rehung your door or eased your window jamb." Offering the man an excuse, a way out. And then, because he couldn't resist the jibe: "You'd probably not have noticed me if I had."

"Come now, I'd like to think I'm a better man than that," the professor said, puffing out his chest with attempted bonhomie. He caught sight of the kitchen clock and shook his head. "Well, I've taken too much time from you—and given you a strange kind of night to report. Thank you for the box, and the game, and the beer, and the tea. I might stop by your back fence, if I walk this way again, and have a word or two with that pretty little bird—we all just want to be remembered in this world."

"Are you a church man, Professor?" The words were out before Clem had finished thinking them, and he flushed as he heard them, wondering at his nerve.

"Presbyterian, in the main—high days and holidays, that's all. Why do you ask?"

"The way you talk about this bird—'all creatures great and small,' I guess. It's not what I thought went with science."

The professor smiled a very small smile. "Biology can still seem wonderful even as we try to prise it apart," he said. "In New Guinea, I saw birds of paradise—the King, the Emperor, the Greater; I never made it far enough west to see the Wilson's. The Wilson's has blue skin on its head so bright it glows in the dark—you can't help but be amazed by something like that." He spread his arms wide to make a T shape from his body. "There I was in New Guinea, seeing men on their short way to dying—bullets and bayonets—when all I wanted was to sit and gaze at these extraordinarily bright colored feathers. I met Ida up there, you know, a nurse—but an artist too amongst it all; I watched the kinds of beauty she could make. We're not so hidebound, in science, to be completely blind to beauty." And he pushed himself out of his chair.

Following his visitor through the house to the front door and down the stairs onto the grass, Clem wondered if the professor meant the beauty of the birds, or of the woman who became his second wife. *Because she was beautiful, Mrs. Lewis*, he thought, and was surprised by his certainty. But he'd watched her—in the street, in the shops, or coming up the hill from the train—and there was a kind of beauty about her that he'd assumed had to do with the work she did, the constant creation of something. It seemed a risky thing to think—although Elsie was prettier. He had no doubt about that.

"We were sorry to see you go," he said, nodding up the hill towards the professor's vacated house. "I used to see Mrs. Lewis going by—she always had a smile and a wave."

"Very friendly, my wife, very friendly," the professor agreed, "and so very good at what she did. I was proud of how she changed what she wanted to do—she was a very fine nurse. She was a very fine artist. She was a very fine woman—you know.

"I don't miss the arguments, but I miss being able to stand and watch her work. That was something, you know, really something—watching a picture come into being where there'd only been blank canvas before. I never tired of it. Still . . ." He ducked back into the open garage for his hat. "She made one painting of me, as if I was back in the war, and looking every inch the soldier, which I never truly felt I was. She'd got the colors just right—every shade of green and brown, and nothing else. Even my lips were green, and my skin; I could feel the wet weight of the jungle in that frame.

"I asked her if I could have it, when we were breaking up our house. I asked her if I could take just that one—and she said no. I thought it mine by rights, being of me, but she said she'd made it, and it was all of me she'd have. She did give me another painting, a portrait of a woman—no one I knew, although for a while I tried to tell myself it was a painting of Ida herself. Her rich red-brown hair. Knew it wasn't. I hated it at first, kept it turned against the wall. But when I took these new rooms, I hung it up—for the company—and it's growing on me. The woman's smiling, just a little, and looking off to one side."

Clem smiled: he knew that look—Elsie had it, and Elaine too, although neither could ever see a similarity to the other. And then he wondered: where was Elsie's portrait now? The thought had never occurred to him; he'd always assumed that the painter would still have it with her.

"My wife—" he began, cut off as the other man went on.

"It's funny, you know, but I feel like there's some sort of camaraderie between me and this woman—two people who sat still for Ida, somehow brought together on either side of a frame." And he coughed, stepping back towards his host, and reaching out his hand, ready to shake. "Thank you," he said, "thank you for all of that. And if they ever do send you to fix my door or my window, make sure you remind me of your name. I won't mean to be rude, but I probably won't place you away from here. It's been nice to meet you, Mr. Gormley. And thank you again for . . ." His wave took in the billiards, the garage, the dark space in the yard where they'd stood together to farewell a little bird, the deep blue night sky above. "That's the color, the backdrop of my painting. An inky blue. A color that's good for the soul." He waved again, and on he went.

Clem stood a moment, watching until the other man disappeared around the corner. From across the gully he heard a train, and he wondered when Elsie would be home—he wanted to tell her about his night, and the professor, and the bird.

How did marriages fail? He'd never given it much thought—although his mother's had, he supposed, before it was resolved by his father's death. She'd never spoken of how she thought about her husband, nor of the possibility of marrying someone else.

He heard the train again as he pulled the garage door to and headed back up the stairs—he should put the kettle on again, in case Elsie was near. She'd come in, full of life and excitement, look-ing ten years younger in that pretty silver dress.

It wasn't for him, this noisy modern life.

In the living room, he flicked the switch on the record player, swept the dust off a disc in wide arcs. Frank Sinatra—now *there* was a singer. He positioned the needle, letting it drop at just the track he wanted, and the house filled with the mournful reminiscence of the middle of the night.

A world without Elsie; if she ran off, went away. If she went out on a night like this and something happened that meant she never came home—he wouldn't let himself think it might be the end of life that separated them. They were young still, and they were healthy. He'd hang onto that.

If I was the bloke in the song, sat up in some bar at a quarter to three in the morning, singing for my missus . . .

It was too much like a movie. If something happened to Elsie, Clem would be mowing the lawns and clearing the gutters and try-ing to make his own steak and kidney pie. He'd be dandling Gloria and painting the handrails and messing about in his garage. He'd be doing all the usual things—even if no one was calling from the house, "Clem? Are you down there? Are you right?" He'd be Clem, but somehow less so. Elsie sparked him into life. What more could a man ask than that?

The song finished. He walked into the darkened bedroom, and felt around for the neatly folded flannelette of his pajamas, right where Elsie placed them, every day, beneath the pillow on his side of the bed. Enough; he'd leave the door unlatched, and hear about his wife's adventure in the morning. Almost asleep, he saw the infinite possibilities of a racked triangle of pool balls scattering after the break shot. He saw Elsie, painted and framed, with the sky as the professor had described it, that rich and brilliant blue behind her head.

And in the fug of half sleep, more dream than waking knowledge, he could see the professor's painting so clearly, and he suddenly knew why. He sat up with a gasp.

That man was gazing at Elsie.

I should have bought it from Mrs. Lewis. I should have paid any price. This unbearable thought: someone else was living with his wife.

He could see the man, hat tilted, sitting and gazing in blank adoration. Thinking who knew what, doing who knew what, while she stared out beyond him.

Clem reached the bathroom and spat into the basin, catching sight of himself in the dimness of the mirror as he raised his head again. There was a wildness in his stare. He splashed cold water on his face—again, again—and made himself calm down. Other men would have seen this consequence unspool from the madness of letting their wives sit for an artist. Other men would have known what to do.

One last cold sluice of water. He didn't even know where the professor now lived. And he could hardly march around to his office and demand his wife back. He wouldn't know what to say. As for Elsie, what the devil could he say of it to her?

Clem dabbed his face dry and held his own gaze in the mirror. He remembered the physicist's words from the ferry, on the day when the pitch drop fell: *and there wasn't a blessed soul there to see it.*

No, thought Clem, standing straight and squaring himself in the mirror. *There was. This blessed soul.* And what did it matter, where a picture hung? He had the real Elsie; he had her by him.

He felt the room's walls solid around him. This house, his wife, his kids: that was what defined him. He sought no purchase on the world beyond these things.

18

The photograph

ELSIE WOKE, her head hot and her bones aching. In the four weeks since she'd been to that concert with Elaine, she'd felt on edge—it was almost a relief to be properly ill at last. She'd known Clem wasn't right to put it down to too much excitement, although the noise—the music, the screaming—had been so loud.

It was late on a Saturday morning and quiet in the house. The bedroom was wonderfully dim. Sitting up, Elsie saw a cup of tea gone cold on her bedside table and a note there too from Clem. *Gone to help Donny and Carol.* Their new house needed a bathtub. Clem was on the job.

I'll take over some lunch later on. Elsie tried to swing her legs out of bed but then had to lie back straight away, exhausted. She sipped the painfully cold tea and settled down again. Something gave way with a crackle behind her, and, patting the bed, she found the newspaper he'd left for her as well, folded as neatly as if he'd ironed it.

Exceptional Pictures Relayed of the Moon, she read. She shook her head: they'd crashed another spaceship onto the surface of the moon, and this time it had managed to send back some pictures.

Thousands of images, she read, costing millions of dollars. She closed her eyes and remembered Ida Lewis talking about this mad mission as though it was magic. *Bet you never thought you'd live to see a thing like that,* she'd said.

It's some world, isn't it? Some world, this modern world. Still, it was better than poisoning and war and plane crashes. And how would the moon look up close? What would the photographs show? It was a funny thing with photographs that they never looked quite right—the more she thought back on the portrait Ida had painted, more than two years ago now, the more she thought it was her best and truest likeness.

Mrs. Lewis. Elsie still blushed to remember the pressure of the other woman's fingers on her shoulder, the softness of the other woman's fingers on her lips.

She squirmed herself straight in the bed. *I looked myself. I looked complete.* She wished she had asked for a photo of it after all—but would a photo of a portrait be any better than a photo of a person, or would it also somehow diminish how the thing had really looked?

She sneezed, and her body relaxed. She tried not to think of the artist, the sitting, too much. Clem mentioned the portrait sometimes, wishing he'd bought it. But Elsie laughed at the suggestion. As if a house like theirs could hold so grand a thing.

"I should've come as your chaperone," he'd said just the other week, and she'd liked that idea—there she was, posed, with the artist looking at her from one direction and her husband from another. Or would Clem have found the painter painting as mesmerizing as she had? Elsie didn't like that idea quite so much.

"Clem, it wasn't that bad," she'd said, her face warm just the same.

She heard footsteps on the front stairs and thought for one mad second it was the artist, Ida Lewis, come back to visit. She blushed again.

You sort yourself out, Elsie Gormley, she thought, while she waited for a knock on the front door.

"Mum? Are you in there?" Elaine's voice.

"In here, Elaine—just push." She couldn't tell if Glory was there too—but in she came, tripping over her own tiny feet and bouncing onto the pillow next to Elsie with all the instant chatter of being two years old.

"Why are you in bed, Nan?" the little girl asked. "It's time to get up."

"Is it, love? Did you see the sunrise?" Elsie stroked the small girl's hair as if she were a cat.

"There aren't too many mornings that she'd miss." Elaine was standing in the doorway with a frown. "You all right, Mum? I wanted to ask if you'd look after Gloria."

Elsie coughed and the aches in her bones and joints sharpened another notch again. She held her breath, to make herself sound better than she felt. "Of course, of course. Just let me get myself dressed—we'll be fine." She'd have a quick sponge-down and face the day. A bit of talc, a bit of scent: she'd be all right.

She swung her feet clear of the blankets and leaned forward to stand up—knocking heads with Glory who was bending down to look at Elsie's feet.

"Ow!" The girl rubbed her forehead. "No color on your toenails. Not like Mum."

Elsie rubbed her own head with one hand, supported her weight with the other. The room had felt a little fluid around that crash. "Colored toenails?" she asked. "How fancy! Well." She pushed herself up, smiling. "That must make her a movie star!"

Elaine snorted, steadying her daughter as she stood. "I guess it puts a little glamour in my day," she said.

Glamour. Elsie sighed. She'd always thought her daughter beautiful just as she was—and Donny just so handsome. They were both lovely.

"Part of your job as a mum," Clem had said to her one day, "to think them as fair as you can."

But they were no movie stars.

Elaine seemed to be standing a long way off this morning, and as Elsie took a step forward to see her better, her shoulder rammed the doorframe.

"Mum!" Her daughter's hands shot out, one buttressing Elsie's body, the other cupping her head. "You're burning up. Sit down and I'll get you a drink." She steered her mother back to the bed while Gloria bounced all around. "Settle down, Gloria. We don't want another crash. And anyway, where's Dad?"

Elsie sat forward, felt Elaine straightening the pillows behind her back. "Thanks, love. He's up with Don and Carol—their new bath."

Elaine sniffed. "I don't think you should be here on your own— what have you got you can take? Some Veganin? I'll ring Dad and tell him to come home."

A band of tingling heat tightened across Elsie's shoulder blades in a shiver. She'd be all right, and Carol needed that new bath. But Elaine had left the room, was in the kitchen—Elsie could hear the cupboard doors, a drawer or two opening and closing.

"In the bathroom, love," Elsie called. "In the cabinet."

Gloria snuggled in close. "Poor Nan," she said, patting Elsie's arm. "I listen to your chest." She crawled onto Elsie's lap and laid her ear down flat. "Ah-thump. Ah-thump. Ah-thump." She tapped the time of the pulse across Elsie's wrist.

"That sound OK, Glory?" Elsie pushed the dark red hair back from the little girl's face. "Such a lovely, pretty thing you're going to be."

There was shouting from the road—a group of kids went riding by on their way to the river, calling and chiacking as they went.

"And we need to get a bow for all that hair." Elsie made a small plait, twisting its end to a fine point like a paintbrush as one last bike rode by, its bell clanging wildly and a voice calling, "Wait! Wait for me! Wait for me?"

"That was always your Uncle Don," said Elsie, nodding towards the road. "Trying to catch up to your mother—she was fast."

"Here." Two white pills lay like eyes in the palm of Elaine's hand. Elsie swallowed them with a gulp of water.

"I like a bike. A bike is fun." Glory sprawled across her grandmother like a knee rug, blinking at her mother with wide eyes.

"I could pedal faster than anyone." Elaine held the glass forward again for Elsie. "I was always trying to get a bit farther away. Here. Finish this."

"A bike for Glory?" The little girl had curled around to gaze straight up at Elsie.

"Of course a bike for Glory," Elsie said. "I bet Grandad already has his eye on one for you." She had a clear image of Elaine surging down a hill—wind in her hair and her face so incredibly free—but she was sure she'd never seen her ride like that. That would have been something; that would have been something to see. She squeezed her granddaughter's hand. "Let's see how fast you can go."

"Mum! A bike for Glory!"

But Elaine was refolding the newspaper, and tilting the blinds, and moving the cut-crystal canisters on Elsie's dressing table—a little to the left, and back again. It was a while before she spoke. "I'm sure your grandmother will get you whatever you want."

That flatness in her voice: it made Elsie wince.

And then: "We should get someone in here to dust."

"Oh, Lainey, leave it be—I'll do it next week." Elsie lay back on her pillows, her eyes closed. The very thought of having someone in to clean.

"Come on, then, Gloria, you'll have to come with me. No—" Elaine raised her hand like a stop sign, and Elsie, opening her eyes to see the flash of its movement, didn't know if it was to preempt a protest from Gloria or from Elsie herself. "We'll leave Nan here in peace—she needs a rest."

Elsie closed her eyes and counted—slow—to five before she opened them again. "You know she'd be all right to stay."

"Then she'd get sick or you'd be more tired. It's all right. I'll bring her back another day."

Grandmother and granddaughter smiled at each other. "Well, I'll come and wave you off then, all the same," said Elsie, pushing herself out of bed again, ignoring Elaine's remonstration.

"For heaven's sake, Mum!"

"I will blow you a kiss from the car," said Gloria, taking Elsie's hand.

"Thank you, pet."

It was cool on the front porch; the sun had not yet swung around to touch that side of the house. The three of them stood a moment in the shade, and Elsie shivered, pulling Gloria into a hug.

"I spy something in the letterbox, Glory—perhaps Mum could hold you up to pull it out?"

The girl wriggled free to skip down the stairs, and her shoes left small footprints in the springy grass.

"Post on a Saturday?" Elaine followed, and held her daughter up at arm's length. "Someone must have dropped it in. There now—run that up to Nan and we'll go on."

Elsie kissed her granddaughter on the head and watched her go, Gloria blowing the promised kiss from the car window and Elsie making a show of catching it. She waved the thin white envelope as Elaine drove around the corner, and Gloria's hand waved back its reply.

Inside, Elsie fanned herself with the white rectangle—cold, then hot; she really wasn't well—then she ran a finger beneath its flap and shook its contents free. A postcard slipped out, and a square photograph—the portrait by Ida Lewis.

As if she had conjured it up.

She squared the message between her fingers and read:

> I was sorting through my papers the other day and found
> this—thought you might like it. I still like the way I caught
> your far-off gaze. With all best wishes. IL.

No return address for a reply.

The photograph's colors weren't quite right—she could see that
straight away—and the details she remembered so clearly were no
longer visible at such a reduced scale. She couldn't bear to see herself so small. She didn't want it to feel disappointing.

She turned the photo facedown on the kitchen bench, and
pressed it down hard with her hand. She wished the tablets would
hurry up and work.

I can give this to Clem, she thought. And then: *No, I will keep it
myself.* She slipped the print into her pocket.

Turning to head back to the bedroom, her arm knocked the
letter rack from its perch on the bench as she went. The floor was
papered with notes and bills.

Leave it, she thought to herself. *You don't want to be bending
down too much. You can tidy it up later.*

But as she turned to go on again, she saw a wad of tiny white-
edged photos that had slipped free, and she reached down for
them, fanning them out like a strange deck of cards. Clem's mother.
Clem's mother's garden. The river from the wharf where Clem got
the ferry to. There was a beautiful closeup of an angel in the cemetery on the hill, and a picture of the clock on City Hall.

She flipped this last one over. *VP Day. Brisbane*, in Clem's careful schoolboy writing. And there was another of a city street, the air
full of confetti, like snow.

She shook her head: she couldn't really remember the end of the war—busy with the kids and wanting her own world kept intact. Those huge bombs in Japan: she'd wanted to keep them at bay. But here was Elaine, a month shy of four years old and climbing onto her lap—Elsie remembered that, as clear as a bell. And there it was, the horror of atomic warfare spread across the week's papers, a bomb that had *seared to death all living things, animal and human, in the city.* The worst of the nasty stuff dug up from her very own country, the newspaper had said—Elsie had wanted to cry with the shame.

She'd wanted no part of that vast event to touch her daughter and she'd quickly turned the pages. A scientist said atomic power would get man to the moon—Elsie had almost laughed at that, but the laugh became a cough as she saw another story. Some man barely reprimanded for the constant mistreatment of his children. He'd even fashioned a special whip to lash them with.

"Mother of God!" She'd never used such a phrase before and she fairly shouted it out as she pushed Elaine away from the pages and off her lap. "Who *are* these people? What are they doing?"

The little girl had taken two steps back, and was standing by the door. "It's me, Lainey, that's who it is. I'd come for a cuddle with you." So utterly matter-of-fact.

Elsie screwed up the newspaper and stuffed it into the dustbin.

"I want to see, Mum. I want to know what's there."

They were the words that Elsie registered, and she over-my-dead-bodied them at once. And Lainey slipped away, leaving Elsie scared and beset in her own kitchen. Afraid for the world and her daughter all at once. *Send her a small, quiet world and keep her safe.* She wished she believed in the power of prayer.

Nearly twenty years on, Elsie still felt sick as she remembered the scene. She should have held her daughter closer, drawn her in.

She flicked the next photograph onto the top of the pile: the inside of a shop with rows of bottles along its shelves and a window looking onto the next room. It was a chemist's shop and the photograph was taken from inside the dispensary. She brought it closer to her face. She frowned, and the creases in her forehead hurt her too-hot head. There were figures in it, a man's shoulder, and a woman staring straight into the lens. She tilted the shiny paper towards the window, trying to see something more. *Who are you? Where are you from?*

The man was barely part of it, a shoulder and an arm in a crisp white shirt or some kind of coat—the chemist, Elsie supposed. But the woman, the woman was somehow the point of the picture, looking straight at the camera with a coy kind of smile.

She turned it over and saw, in Clem's neat handwriting, just two words: *Jan, 1941.*

Jan. As in January? Or Jan, a person? Had he ever talked of anyone called Jan? Janet? Janelle? Such a tiny waist this girl had, and her hair pulled in close to her head. *Who is she, Clem? What's she doing in my kitchen, among my bills?*

Her head hurt. She wanted to lie down.

And then a coldness touched her: the idea of Clem and another girl. There might have been—there must have been. She pushed her sweaty hair back from her head: 1941. The year the twins were born.

And then her fever spiked, and she felt herself fall.

When they were courting, the sheer coincidence of having just happened to be in the same place at the same time on that street in Brisbane had screamed inside Elsie's head.

"How would I have found you?" she whispered once, frantically, when they were lying in bed together, one morning after their wedding. "What would we have done about that?"

"I'd've found you, Elsie," he said, one finger running a line from her collarbone and down, and down. "Wasn't looking for anyone else."

She heard it, all these years later. She heard that, and she wondered if it was true. Almost twenty years old she'd been—never held a man's hand before, apart from her dad's when she was a kid. What if there was someone called Jan somewhere out there now, someone who could remember her own time with Clem Gormley, wondering where he was, wondering how she let him get away?

The smile on that woman's face in the picture; it was coy, yes, but there was no mistaking it was for the camera. Maybe he had other pictures hidden away in other places. She rubbed her head. She wouldn't ask.

Pulling herself up, she reached for a box of Bex and shook the powder into a glass. She put the photographs back into their holder, hidden among the other papers, as she'd found them.

But this woman, this Jan—she'd keep her apart.

Her body swayed again as she pushed a kitchen chair into the hallway, pulled herself up to stand on the chair. She opened the little trapdoor that guarded the manhole that gave onto the dusty darkness of the roof cavity, and she slapped the photograph face down on the nearest beam.

Out of the way. Out of my way.

Then she pulled the photo of the painting from her dressing gown pocket. *And you there too.* Her secret. Safe and sound.

She balanced herself against the wall, ignoring the marks left there by her now-dirty hands and setting her feet safely back on the floor. Walking towards the bedroom, she glanced into the bathroom—Elaine had left the mirrored cabinet open, and Elsie, rather than seeing herself, saw instead an empty room, the house beyond.

Then she climbed back into bed, and she slept.

19

The flowers

"VALENTINE'S DAY," said Ben without expression. He was clipping his bag closed, getting ready to leave for the day. "The onslaught of roses." He kissed his wife. He kissed his son. He headed out the door. "You didn't shut the laundry, Lu." His voice came up the stairs. "Something's been rummaging in stuff."

One whole section of the yard was buried in a snowstorm of Elsie's doilies scattered across the grass, their white shapes bright against the green.

"Wow!" said Tom, looking down from the deck as his father went into the park. "Ta-da!"

Lucy stood and counted at least three dozen, wondering what sort of possum would do this.

They went down when Tom finished his breakfast, collecting them and shaking them and stacking them up like the thick pages of an old manuscript.

"Star," said Tom. And: "Flamingo"—pointing to a tiny pink petit-point bow.

Near enough, thought Lucy.

"And flowers—Mumma's flowers." Pointing to a rose embroidered in bright red silk thread.

"Yes, our roses." Lucy pointed to the roses by the fence.

"More roses—more roses, Mummy. Look."

There was a young man taking a huge bunch of roses, the softest, palest, gentlest pastel shades, from the back of a delivery van. Crossing the road. Coming to their gate.

"Hello?" Lucy called. "What number are you looking for?"

"Lucy? Lucy Carter? Number twelve?"

Lucy frowned. "Lucy Kiss," she said, "but I don't think they're meant for me."

The young man peered at his list, then nodded as he turned the clipboard around for her to sign. "Lucy Carter," he said again. "Number twelve. These are for you. Happy Valentine's."

Lucy Carter. No one called her that. She held the bouquet away from herself as she watched the van drive off, afraid somehow to smell its blooms.

"Pretty," said Tom, reaching up towards their lushness.

"Yes, they are," said Lucy, sitting down on the grass as she opened the card. It was typed and the printing was smudged. She read the short message: *Welcome home, love from*—an initial. Which might have been an E or an F.

"Pretty flowers," said Tom again.

"Come on. Let's put them in water."

~

Valentine's Day, somewhere back in the nineties. Lucy was sitting in the tiny university office where she was working when a courier arrived, squinting at the professor's name on the door, which wasn't Lucy's name.

"You Lucy Kiss?"

She nodded.

"Great name for Valentine's Day," he said then, angling the huge bouquet of flowers—an explosion of red, orange, yellow—onto the one piece of desk not obscured by piles of paper. "Best name I've seen today. Have a good one." And he was gone.

Lucy sat, diminished by the size, the appearance of such a thing. And then she reached for the card. *A Valentine's tribute for Lucy, who never expects such a thing.* And no name.

Her professor came in, making a show of inching around the mass of flowers. "Your boyfriend's done well," he said, twisting a petal free from one of the roses and letting it drop to the floor.

"If only I knew who he was," said Lucy, passing him the card.

"When did you find out who sent them?" Ben had asked when she told him this story. It was when they first started dating, and she told him she didn't like Valentine's Day flowers, that she'd never expect them from him.

"I didn't," she said. "I never did."

"And so somewhere in the world," said Ben, "there's a poor guy who every February remembers the year he sent flowers to a girl called Lucy Kiss, who completely ignored them. Poor bugger—he's probably never recovered from that, you know."

"One *vardøger* of Lucy Kiss might have married him," she'd said once to Ben. "In that other universe, I might have been swept off my feet."

And then, just after they'd moved in together, on the first evening when there were no boxes to be considered, no decisions about placements or possessions to be made, Lucy came home to find, in the middle of the table, what appeared to be an exact replica of that long-ago mystery bunch—reds, oranges, yellows, crayon bright.

"As if . . ."

"Yes," said Ben. "As if I'd sent you the first bunch, years before I met you." The huge smile he wore as he watched her gaze at them.

"Well, didn't you turn out romantic?" Lucy squeezed him a hug.

She twitched a single petal free and held it up, twisting it into flight as she'd watched the professor do years before.

As it dropped, she made a wish.

Now, in the kitchen of Elsie's house, she pulled a petal off the palest pink rose and pressed its softness against the dent in the top of her lip.

E or F. Elsie or Ferdi. It had to be.

She let the petal drop.

20

The function

THE HARBINGERS of doom, he might have called them. He had smelled their perfume, heavy, from the door, and he paused a moment when he saw them on the table, wondering what he might say.

"For me?" he tried.

"For Mummy," said Tom, butting against his leg like a puppy.

"From Mummy's friend?" Ben scooped his son up and set him on the table, between himself and the vase.

"Ferdi Kiss," said Tom, agreeably, and the two of them stood and stared at the bouquet, then turned as Lucy came in.

"Tom tells me that Ferdi Kiss sent these." Ben was holding his son's hand.

Lucy blushed, shrugged, and shook her head. "I don't know." She held out the card. "And it's Klim—Ferdi Klim."

Ben read the short message, saw the smudge, and shrugged in turn. "Who else, if it's not him?" Thinking, *Think fast now, Lu, think fast*, and wondering at the shape, the venom of his thought.

"It's an E," she said, straight off and certain. "It's an E, not an F. I think it's Elsie."

And he laughed at her then, so loudly that Tom joined in too. "It's Elsie," Ben said after all the noise had stopped. "Of course it's Elsie."

"I think the doilies in the yard were Elsie too," said Lucy quietly. "What sort of possum would get up to that?"

There was no more laughing then, and in the quiet kitchen, Ben turned to face his wife, wondering what he might say. There were words, phrases, flashing inside his head—like *Just stop*. But before he could say any of them, he felt Tom's hands latching onto his shoulders, the little boy hanging on and swinging free.

"Piggyback!" His voice was gleeful. "Piggyback! Make Tom fly!"

Ben reached his hands up to his own shoulders, gripping onto his son's. Those little fingers: part of him; part of her.

"Make Tom fly," he said, stepping away from the table so that the little boy dangled down behind him like a cape. "That's a very good idea." Flying him out of the room, away from Lucy, and on and on through the small square house. While his teeth clenched and his blood thumped.

They came to rest at last in Ben and Lucy's room, Ben dropping to sit on the bed and releasing his son's tiny paws. "I think I flew you all the way around the world that time," he said, feeling the weight drop away from his shoulders.

"Are you done?" Lucy called out from the kitchen. "Can I come in?"

From the bed, Ben could see the edge of the mirror—most of himself, sitting still, and Tom's feet beside him, kicking away as if the bed was an ocean he had to traverse.

When Ben was small, he and his mother had played for hours around her mirror, a freestanding thing on wide chromed feet—he'd been amazed that he could walk around the back of it and not find her standing there. He'd been amazed that there were angles from which he could see her in the reflection but not a trace of himself. Magic spots, he'd called them. *Show me the magic spots, Mum.* Making himself disappear.

He shifted along the bed and craned to look again. There were Tom's feet, swimming on, but Ben himself was invisible.

Lucy sat down beside him, as close as she could. He glanced up, at the mirror, not at her.

"Don't do this," she said quietly. "I'm sorry. Maybe it is him. But it's nothing to do with us."

Behind them, Tom had rolled over, as if to switch to backstroke.

"I have to get ready to go." Ben stood up, squarely in the mirror's frame again.

"Go?"

"Some awards thing—I did tell you. I came home to change. It's black tie."

"Right. Sure."

He pulled a coat hanger from the wardrobe and flicked its shirt so it cracked like a whip. "I did tell you," he said again.

"Yes," she said. "You did."

They were still there, the two of them, Lucy and Tom, when he came out of the shower. They were giggling and tickling, and he stared at them a moment, pushing down the strongest urge to ask why they had nowhere else to be.

It's no good looking for things that aren't there. He heard his mother's voice. *Don't make something out of nothing.*

Which was exactly what Lucy herself said when he spun around, fumbling with his buttons, and shouting that the flowers were from Ferdi: he was sure.

"Don't look for things that aren't there, Ben." She had Tom pressed in close against her chest.

He heard his own voice, yelling in response—the idiocy of this business with Elsie; the lunacy of her game. The words hung huge in the room.

"You've got your stories backwards, Ben Carter," Lucy said at last, her voice low and level. "You want to make something out of nothing about Ferdi—and nothing out of something about Elsie. Why can't they be from her?"

"Because she's a joke, a game, your crazy imagination. And you're taking it all far too far." His buttons finally fastened, he was raking through the contents of a drawer.

"I think this is what you're looking for." Lucy was standing beside him, Tom balanced on one arm and his tie in her other hand. "Don't frighten Tom," she added, and her voice was awfully low.

And she put the little boy down gently on the bed, where he practiced his frog kicks, while Lucy stood, quite calmly, fussing with her husband's tie.

"Don't ever scare him." Lucy's voice was quieter still, her fingers tying and retying the knot while Tom swam on and on.

"Well—" Ben swallowed the worst of his words. "Then don't scare me."

"Where's the do?" She patted the tie's smooth dark fabric, its knot flat at last.

"Cloudland—I shouldn't be late."

"Don't be too underwhelmed." And she kissed his cheek, as if nothing had happened at all.

It had been a magical place, the old Cloudland, a fairy-tale building up on one of Brisbane's hills, with a beautiful arch at its entrance and a sprung floor that danced with the people who danced on it. He'd never been, but in his imagination it was somewhere ideal. His mum had gone there once in a while when he was tiny, leaving him in the care of a neighbor and coming home late at night, humming to herself.

He was twenty years old and at work when she rang, astonished that the building had just gone. "Four in the morning," she told him later, "the wreckers broke it down; destroyed it all."

Like razing fairyland, Ben thought then and still thought now. When a new place opened that bore the same name—just before he and Lucy came north—he'd made a point of saying he'd refuse to visit. It seemed somehow sacrilegious. Which, he thought now, made it as good a place as any to take his bad mood tonight.

He stood perfectly still as Lucy stepped away.

"You always look good in black tie," she said.

He'd never noticed before the way normal conversation had a kind of buzz around it if a fight was being ignored. Perhaps because he'd very rarely fought.

"If you make your peace with the place, maybe we can go dancing there." She kissed his cheek again, but quickly. "But we're OK here on our own, me and Tom."

He touched his fingers to the place her lips had touched, as if to keep the kiss there. "Yes," he said, still staring at his reflection, his face impassive, his shoulders hunched. "Yes, you are."

~

In the carefully lit space of the function room, Ben found his name tag among the rows of others and clipped it to his lapel. Drinks, a few speeches, the inevitable jokes about people without Valentine's arrangements. A few more drinks, a meal, and it would be done. He nodded at some of the people he recognized—a twenty-year-old entrepreneur who designed wildly successful apps; a colleague from work; a few people from the universities—and smiled at a woman in a silky silver dress.

"Nice drop," she said, coming over to him and raising her champagne flute as if to make a toast. "Happy Valentine's."

"I don't think they're sparing any expense." He smiled. "I'm Ben." He pointed at his tag. "Now that's a dress for Cloudland."

"Felicity Smith. Events. Publicity. And no, we spare no expense." She shook his hand, her grip firm.

Felicitous, thought Ben. They batted pleasantries back and forth as the crowd grew and the canapés arrived.

"And was this the gig you wanted when you were growing up?" Felicity nodded at the newspaper's name on his tag as she held her glass out towards a waiter. She made no acknowledgment as he paused and refilled her glass, nor of his friendly smile.

Ben held her gaze as he drained his own glass. The last bubbles burst against his tongue. He could invent his life; he could make up a new version of himself, right here and now. He could tell her anything. And that might be a bit of fun. But he shook his head— at himself as much as her question—and tilted his empty glass towards the waiter.

"Of course not," he said, watching the champagne's level rise. "I wanted to be an astronaut—didn't every little boy?"

"Been to Cape Canaveral?" asked Felicity, as if everyone had.

"No," said Ben. "Although I have interviewed Andy Thomas. Why? Got any contacts?"

Felicity smiled. "I always know someone," she said. "In fact, I met a guy the other day from some mob getting up a reality show that'll send you to Mars. I could try and put you in touch, if you like—but I guess that's a one-way ticket."

"I think my wife would have something to say about that."

"Ah," said Felicity. "Your wife."

They sat next to each other at dinner. The napkins on the tables were folded like the starbursts of the doilies in his yard.

As if Elsie could have done that.

"Did you ever really try to be an astronaut?" Felicity shook out her napkin. "I don't have children myself, but what a shame for them to grow up with disappointed parents." She smiled as though she was joking, but there was a merciless chill to her voice. "Such a thing, to give up on your dreams."

Ben took a first mouthful of the rich seafoody thing in front of him. "And was it your dream to organize black-tie events and schmooze journos?" He gave a kind of smile. No need for hostilities, surely.

"I'm just saying that there are always ways, you know. I wouldn't let a thing become impossible. Why, the European Space Agency was recruiting astronauts a couple of years back. Maybe your wife would have moved to Cologne?"

"She's never been a big fan of that scent." He smiled at his own pun. "It's a grandmotherly kind of a smell."

"Perhaps she'd prefer something like this?" said Felicity, leaning towards him and holding out her wrist.

He used to do this all the time, this banter. It was easy to do it again. If flirting was a game, Ben knew he'd always played it; it was part of coaxing stories out of people.

He took a deep breath and recognized the fragrance. "Chanel. Very Marilyn Monroe."

"Well, you know how she wore it," said Felicity. "Should we try to get onto the roof somehow before the main courses come?"

As quick as that? he thought, and then—

"Ben."

He felt a hand fall on his shoulder and looked up to see the twenty-year-old man who knew how to design the best apps.

Good timing, he told himself, and meant it.

~

It was a mild night when he stepped back onto the street, with the kind of perfect pitch of balminess—sweet, warm air and the city's lights all brightly twinkling—that made him decide to walk home. He and Lucy had done it once, across the bridge, around the top of the cliffs, past the hospital, up the hill to the old cemetery and down the other side. Five miles or so—he'd be home in just over an hour. He walked onto the Story Bridge, loving the way the wind picked up as he reached the thick metal frame of its cage. Tom thought this was where his father worked—the place where stories came from—and that always made Ben smile.

It wasn't Sydney. It wasn't the harbor and it wasn't that city's famous arch. But Ben loved the way Brisbane crowded along this stretch of the river, as if it had been especially designed to look its best from this modest span of elevation. He loved the way the river described its particular line from the Customs House through the busyness of the CBD to the gardens and on past the old Commissariat Store, almost buried now by high-rise and freeway. He loved the way, at night, the lights of the buildings twinkled like Christmas. He loved Brisbane most at night; it looked like a jewel box.

It was something, coming home, bringing his family here. He'd never thought it would feel settled, or so right.

He sighed. Why fight with Lucy? He'd had just enough to drink to decide to let it go.

Coming down off the cliffs, he cut under the motorway and up past the hospital. An ambulance whizzed by, and he thought of the hospital in Sydney on the day that Tom was born. There'd been no drama in the first hours, and then total drama in the last: he'd half expected sirens and flashing lights to activate somewhere. They'd sliced his wife open—he still didn't really like to look at the scar—and it was done. Thomas, loudly come into the world.

One day in their lives, and it changed everything. Him. Lucy. Everything they were.

Then Tom turned one. And then they came here. Came home, he supposed—he'd looked sometimes for his long-gone Mum. They'd bought the house; he'd thought it would help Lucy settle in, but she still seemed so lost in this place. All this nonsense about Elsie. And now came Ferdi Klim—her past, of course, and Ben wondered, for the first time, if she might wish she'd made some other choice.

But Tom was her choice; clearly hers.

He stopped in the middle of the footpath and rubbed fast at his head with both hands.

I miss how she was. I miss how we were.

Miserable things seemed so much bigger in the darkness. And of course Tom was a glorious boy.

But Ferdi. What did he think—that Lucy would run off with him into the sunset? Family number four? Forget it. Ben knew her better than that.

A procession of empty taxis went past, each with a little speck of light bright on its roof. Ben walked on, imagining the lonely figure he made along the footpath while the cars and all their passengers rushed on by. He'd be home soon enough—up the hill, down the hill, and around beside the river. He liked the quiet dark space the water cut through the landscape too, a pause in the lights and the life.

Modest, he thought, compared to the bustle and glitter of Sydney. *Welcome home.* And it did feel more like home with three of them: he'd never seen the truth of that before.

My boy, thought Ben simply, loving his son, the very idea of him. He caught the edge of Felicity's predictable perfume at the back of his throat and hated how close he'd leaned in to smell it. Here was Tom; here was life. He was walking to his home. That was worth more than fumbling in a fire exit stairwell.

A taxi slowed by the curb, the driver leaning over towards the passenger's side. "Walking far, mate?"

And Ben reached for the door, wanting to be there already. He gave the address—*Elsie's house*, he almost said, and almost smiled.

He shut his eyes for the short drive and saw darkness flecked with starlight behind his lids, like a spray of white across a darkened lawn.

≈

He was half-asleep as he stood in the bathroom taking off his tie and fiddling with his cufflinks. He brushed his teeth and left his suit, his shirt, his underclothes, all tumbled in a pile on the floor. Lucy had left his pajamas on the towel rail, just like she did for Tom, and he sluiced himself under the hottest shower his skin could bear, relishing the warmth and the steam even on this tropical night.

Halfway into the bedroom, his hand already reaching for the covers and his eyes adjusting to the shape of Lucy sleeping in the darkness, he realized there was someone else sitting in the room—on a chair by the window, a chair he wasn't sure he'd ever seen before.

"Elsie?" he heard himself say before he realized he'd thought it. And then, more surprisingly, "Ferdi?"

There was a metallic crash as a possum leapt onto the roof of the front porch; Tom cried out in surprise and Lucy was up and moving through the house before Ben had time to hail her. He looked back at the corner of the bedroom. What he'd seen was the step stool that Lucy used to get to their highest cupboard, a furry toy of Tom's perched on the top.

"Hello, you," said Lucy, coming in again and brushing against his shoulder. "You're very late; lucky I wasn't waiting up."

He smelled her hair as she went by, its scent like a rich and familiar balm.

"I walked," he said, and he climbed into bed alongside her.

"I threw those flowers out," said Lucy in the darkness. "We don't need them here—whoever they were from." And then she turned and slept again, he was sure, her body still and one hand holding his.

Ben lay there, waiting to sleep, watching Tom's toy by the window, thinking how easily the shape of another person came in and out of focus.

21

The visit

BUT LUCY didn't sleep. She lay there still and quiet, listening to her husband's breathing and wondering what to do. The flowers had looked so perfect lying on the compost, but what had she looked like, marching across the yard to dispose of such an elegant bouquet? A lover's tiff? A breakup? An unwelcome advance? Well, whatever—she wished another Lucy Kiss had had to deal with it. Not her.

When the possum jumped again, she went back into Tom's room and sat beside his cot—*better to be awake alongside him*, she thought, fitting her breathing to his.

They were exquisite, all these moments of watching him sleep. The still point, somewhere separate from that swing between pleasure and frustration, or the different swing from fractiousness to fear. Just contentment. Just this moment. Here they were: they were all right.

I have been lucky, she thought, touching her boy's hair. She blew a kiss across the small space where he lay.

There were curlews in the park again, their calls so murderous and violent for such fine, almost delicate birds. The first time she'd heard them—the week they'd first come from Sydney—she'd shaken Ben awake: a fight; he should call the police. And he started upright, sat and listened for a moment, and then laughed at her mistake.

She touched Tom gently on the head, feeling its warmth. He snuffled a little, and stretched, and Lucy grabbed at the edge of the cot, buffeted by how much she loved him.

It still knocked her sideways.

In the outside world, there were cars on the road, the occasional plane, and the low, loud throb of a helicopter on its way to the nearby hospital. There was a burst of voices—a party ending, maybe, with car doors shutting, engines driving away. Then a blare of music and a woman's voice: "Shut up." And then nothing.

Other lives, other spaces, other times. How many mothers were sitting up tonight across this city? Chinking the curtains, she saw three houses deep in darkness—and one lit with a white square of light.

She let the curtain drop back into place, the gentle swish of its hem jarring against a different sound, something sharper—a noise like their gate, with a squeak and a click. She went through the house, checking the front door, the back door, and peering at the dim and empty street.

All the other houses she might have lived in. All the other lives she might have had. Her *vardøger*—she liked the way the word felt, like a time-smoothed stone rubbed between her fingers.

If I'd married whoever sent those flowers years ago.

If I'd married Ferdi Klim.

If I'd never married. If I wasn't here with Tom.

Standing at the kitchen sink, she saw a line of Lucys at a line of sinks, each drinking a tall glass of water. She saw rainbows darting out from the prism of each, reflecting and refracting all those other versions of herself.

And then she heard it again, the definite scrape of her gate. *There is someone*, she thought, calm and clear, and she opened the back door and looked into the darkness.

On the edge of the grass, just inside the fence, a woman was standing in a long coat. She must have been eighty at least. The coat was a bright color—pink or red—and it looked somehow textured in the night's pale light. On her feet, Lucy could see furry boots like slippers and she was holding some kind of light.

"Hello?" Lucy called. "Are you all right? Can I help you?"

The woman looked up and waved, as if there was nothing strange about standing in someone's garden at midnight in furry slippers and—Lucy's eyes resolved its details—an old chenille dressing gown. "It's all right; it's like a flashlight. They have very good flashlights, these things," the other woman said. "Makes it easy to see where you are."

"Are you lost? Are you looking for something?" Lucy leaned out from the deck, bunching the neck of her pajamas against the night.

"Isn't it nice to be out in the quietness?" the woman replied. "I'll head back in a moment."

"I could drive you—can I drive you somewhere? Or is there someone I should call?"

"My pace is still pretty good; I'll be back in a jiffy," the woman said. "I just wanted to check on the flowers—"

"Flowers?" Lucy repeated. *Elsie?* It felt almost preposterous, after so much pretending, to think this might really be true. She felt the shiver of someone walking over her grave and pinched her arm, in case she was asleep.

She was awake.

She called, "Hang on, I'm coming down." And took the steps two at a time, but the yard—the whole street—was empty by the time she'd reached the bottom and turned towards the fence.

"Elsie?" she called then, feeling a little silly and something—

cold, grabbing—that edged towards afraid. Above her the back door blew closed with a slam, and she turned and ran, unable to remember if she'd flicked the lock or not, if she'd be able to get back inside. The handle gave and she pushed the door and propped it open, her breath all the while coming fast.

At the deck's edge again, she scanned the road, the yards nearby, the park beyond, but there was no sign of movement, no sign of anybody. A curlew cried and another, further off, replied. She shivered again, and rubbed at her arms, watching the wind scuttle the clouds across the sky.

She turned and went in, careful to fasten the lock. On her way to bed, she paused and turned back to Tom's room instead. He was always the last thing she checked before sleep.

Then she stopped in the doorway: the cot was empty.

I will walk out, I will turn around, and I will walk back in, she thought, clear and slow. *He will be there; of course he'll be there.*

But the cot was still empty.

She could feel the place—a straight line across her chest—the precise point where her breathing stopped.

Ben? But no sound came; she couldn't make her voice work, like a child startled out of a dream.

Blundering back towards her own room, she collided with every doorjamb, with the edge of the sofa, with the sharp point of the sideboard that jabbed into the softness of her belly.

"Ben?" There was sound, but choked and awful.

"Where were you?" He was sitting up in bed, Tom cradled against his chest. "Tom was crying; I had no idea where you were."

Her body shook with a stammering rush of adrenaline. "I heard the gate—I was getting a drink—there was a woman by the fence— she said something about flowers—she was old—in a dressing gown—I thought it was Elsie." She was sure, she was sure it hadn't taken more than a moment.

"Jesus, Lucy, why would you go outside in the middle of the night if you heard something?" Ben shifted Tom farther up onto his shoulder, and the little boy cried again. "And this Elsie thing—for fuck's sake: it has to stop."

"There was an old lady outside. I thought she might need help. She said something about flowers—and I thought, I thought—"

"As if it was Elsie." Ben's right hand was patting Tom's back the way Lucy would, but too hard—she could hear the sting of its slap. "Any of it."

"I can take him," she said, reaching out.

"I can do it. I'll put him back."

But Tom's cries ramped up as Ben stood and made to leave the room, and he turned in the doorway, pushing his son away from himself. "All right. You do it. I was asleep."

She scooped Tom into her chest, soothing and patting. "It's all right, Dad was here for you—Dad came and got you and told you it was OK."

Tom's crying stopped, and he muffled his face against his mother's shoulder. "Cot," he said quietly. "In cot."

"I know," said Lucy.

She laid him down, tucked him in, waited until his eyes began to close. *What would I have done*, she thought, *if anything had happened?* She wouldn't let herself think what "anything" might have been.

Back in bed, she slid close to Ben, feeling for his hand. "OK?" she asked, her voice uncertain.

"Don't go out into the night if you think someone's there— what were you thinking? And Tom was crying; I can't believe you couldn't hear him. This Elsie thing—Lu, it's enough. Her, and Ferdi Klim; I'm over all of it."

Lucy kissed his hand, and turned her face against his side. It was quiet for a while—not even a curlew—and she could feel the warmth coming back to her feet.

"All right," she whispered. "It's enough."

Ben let out a snore, and the air filled with the smell of stale champagne.

Maybe I dreamed it all, thought Lucy, almost asleep herself.

Another snore from Ben, and then she was asleep. She was dancing with Ferdi Klim in a dark room to a band she couldn't see or hear. They were the only two people on the floor, while a row of Lucy Kisses lined the walls. A pendulum swung slowly overhead. A bassline thumped, and when Lucy opened her mouth to try to sing along, she found she couldn't make a sound.

22

The princess

CLEM WAS dozing on the deck when he heard a footfall on the steps.

"That you, love?" he called. Elsie was off at the butcher's.

But his daughter called back. "It's Lainey, Dad. Are you up or down?"

"Up," he said. In the kitchen, his kettle was boiling—had been for who knew how long—and he went in to pour the water into the teapot. "That's what I call timing." He stirred the leaves and set it to steep. "Time for a cup?" He smiled at his girl as she entered the kitchen.

"All right."

She was wearing a smart red dress—shirtwaist, Clem thought the style was called, with a bit of a tie like a man's.

"You look grand, love. Off out somewhere?"

Elaine smoothed the front of the skirt, sitting down carefully so it didn't wrinkle underneath. "No. Just sick of the same old house clothes."

Clem poured the tea and stirred sugar into his. "Fetch the milk for me?"

She poured milk into their two cups, and pulled hers closer, blowing on it before she took a sip. "Who was it you knew, the one who poured his tea into a saucer to cool it down?"

"My uncle Perce, that was. When I was just a nipper."

"I remember you telling us that." Elaine blew again across the tea, wincing when it sloshed over the edge. "Mum was always appalled that we might try it, me and Don. Uncouth, she called it. Like she'd know."

"Now, Lainey . . ."

She held her hand up, as if to stop herself. "Sorry. And thanks for the tea."

Clem watched her carefully. He was never quite sure what to say to his daughter. Never sure where to step. And she hadn't brought Gloria, which wouldn't please Elsie.

"Where is Gloria?" he asked then. "Asleep in the car?" He adored his chubby-legged and rosy-cheeked granddaughter—was aston-ished by how busy she could be. She was only three years old.

"She's with Gerald's mum." Elaine licked her finger, and swiped it around the top of the fine china cup so that the kitchen filled with a piercing ringing sound.

"Now, Lainey, I've told you what my uncle Perce used to say: every time you make that noise, you make a sailor die."

"What did happen to your uncle Perce?" Elaine set the cup down with such a clatter Clem wanted to check for a chip. "Where'd he go, when he sailed off over that horizon?"

Clem shook his head. New Zealand, Uncle Perce had said and there had been a card or two at first. Then nothing more. "I don't know, love," he said. "I thought sometimes I ought to find out, but I never knew where to start."

"I could go," said Elaine suddenly. "You can fly to New Zealand these days."

Clem snorted into his tea. "In an aeroplane? What sort of money is this husband of yours making?" He didn't really mean to ask—it was too forward a thing—but, really, a child of his, sitting in his kitchen proposing a jaunt in a plane.

"I suppose I could write a letter to a newspaper, or the Red Cross," he said. "That's what people did after the war." His uncle Perce must be rising seventy—if he was still alive.

There was a strange and shattering sound, and it took him a moment to realize that Elaine had picked up her cup and saucer and thrown them down, smashing them on the linoleum floor. He grabbed the dishcloth, the dustpan, and a sheet of old newspaper in what felt like one gesture, pushing the broken pieces together to make a safe bundle, and wiping away the wet mess. His daughter stood just a few inches off, some flecks of the pale tea on her shoes. The second clatter, as the pieces hit the bin, never sounded as satisfying as the first, he realized. Perhaps it was something to do with surprise. He dried his hands on the little towel Elsie kept by the stove and put his arm, awkward, along the stiff ridge of Elaine's shoulders.

"Now then," he said, trying to sound more assured than he felt. "What's this all about?"

There was no sobbing, no tears, just a thick jittery tremor that seemed to set into his daughter's frame and would not let her go. He could hear it in her voice, in the rattle of her teeth, when she finally began to speak.

"Send me away, Dad," she said. "Give me somewhere to go and something to do."

"Oh, Lainey." He pulled her close and held her—he hadn't done that since she was tiny. "Really, what's this all about?"

The shuddering was worse, and he tried to press it out of her, holding on with both his arms. He could see her fingers moving along her skirt as if she was counting, and sure enough, when she'd worked through all ten fingers, she spoke.

"I'm bored, Dad. This isn't who I want to be."

And he couldn't even offer her the household panacea of a cup of tea: she'd already had one. *If Elsie was here*—but if Elsie was here, he realized, she'd be even more at sea than him. *What about Gloria?* she'd say. *What about your lovely little girl?* Which even Clem knew wouldn't help.

"It was all your mum ever wanted, the two of you," he said. "I suppose we thought you'd be the same." He kissed the top of her head, and settled her back in the chair. "There's a nip of brandy somewhere that Elsie keeps for Christmas." He had no idea if it was sound to give his daughter a slug of it, but he couldn't see how it could hurt.

Elaine sat perfectly still now, both hands cupped around the heavy glass. "It will be better when she goes to school," she said. "Even Gerald says I might be able to get a job somewhere when that happens—a bit of typing, or a shop—if anyone will take a married woman." She drained the alcohol in a single gulp. "That's only two more years."

"What did you want to do, love?" It seemed an awful thing to ask her: he was almost frightened of the response. But it seemed awful, too, that he'd never thought to ask her before.

"I don't know. I don't even know what I might do. But I wanted more learning. I wanted more life. I wanted something beyond a quick typing speed and a bit of stenography. I didn't think it would ever occur to Mum—I knew all she wanted for me was a good man like Gerald and a handful of kids as fast as we could. Well, Gloria's enough—and Gerry is a good man. But I thought you might have helped me—you see them, Dad, you see the people at the university. You see them with their books and their ideas and their busyness. I could have tried it. I could have been smart enough, I could—"

"You could try it still, I guess?"

"I guess I could."

Clem pulled the bottle across the table and poured himself a shot. *And now this, at eleven in the morning.*

"So then, what about New Zealand?" he said after he'd downed his measure.

And she laughed. "That's easy. I just want to clear off. Get a boat, like Uncle Perce. Off I go."

It was too quiet in the kitchen. Clem hadn't a clue what he ought to say next. He thought about ringing his son-in-law at work. He thought about ringing Don. He thought about how to keep Elsie away.

He said, "It'd be a shame to waste that nice frock on a yacht, love. I'm sure we can think of somewhere better you might wear it." He needed someone to come up with a plan; he needed someone to have the kind of bright idea that would surprise her, take her in. If Ida Lewis was still around the corner, he thought suddenly, he'd march Lainey around there and get her to talk to the girl about changing what she wanted in the world.

That painter and her husband: he hadn't thought of them for months.

"You know your mum was once a model?" He could see the painting now when he closed his eyes—still wished sometimes that it was his to own. "She hasn't led such a dull life as all that."

"A model? Mum? For magazines?"

That stopped her in her tracks. Clem gave a smile. "No, for that painter, Ida Lewis. There's a portrait of her."

"A portrait of Mum." Elaine drained the second shot. "I don't believe it. Well. Maybe there's hope for us all."

Clem followed the line of her gaze to the point where it sheared off into the nothingness of the backyard. Was it secrets she wanted? Was it mystery? Was that life?

"What about the university?" he said. "I don't know the first thing about getting there to study, but there must be a way to find out."

Elaine shook her head. "I'm sure there's nothing I can do," she said—defiantly, he thought, as if she almost enjoyed being defeated. "Just chin up, carry on. It will be better for Gloria once she's at school too."

"Is it not what you thought, then," he asked, "being a mother?" He'd never asked Elsie what she thought of it all—you could see how she felt, the way she beamed and bustled and organized.

"It's not anything, Dad. That's the trouble. I don't feel anything. Everyone says Gloria's lovely, and I can see she is—she smiles; she doesn't fret; she's well behaved. I see the others—see how much they love their children, and how happy they are for all that. I'm not . . . it isn't . . . I just want something else."

She closed her eyes and sat like that a while. When she was very young—Clem remembered—she'd thought this trick made her invisible. He wondered now if she still did.

Something else, he thought. What world would he conjure, if he could give her something new?

"When I go into town with my friends," Elaine said, her eyes still shut, "Mum thinks it's all silly teas and hairdos and gossip—I know she does, Dad. But they *do* things, those women. Two are training to be teachers. One is training as a doctor. One goes bushwalking—on her own—and draws pictures of the plants, the rocks she sees. They take courses and hear lectures—they read things and think things. Their world—" she opened her eyes and frowned at where she was, "—is not like this. And Gerald's lovely, and Gerald says, get a hobby. But a hobby . . ." She was smacking the flat of her hand against the side of her head; the noise was awful. "A *hobby* is not what I need."

He was with her then, stilling her hands and holding her close. He took deep breaths, the way he and Elsie used to when the kids were small, and hurt or scared, and needed to be calmed down. It took longer than it used to, but at last he heard her breathe in time with him.

"Do you remember when Gloria was just born?" he began, shushing her when she started to reply. "Of course you do—but do you remember, we had a princess come to visit? She came to open one of the new university buildings. Princess Alice; I got to shake her hand. She was very beautiful, I thought, and very clever, they said too. And I thought that boded well for our new girl."

"Oh, it will be different for her." The cold tone of Elaine's voice made Clem flinch. "All the great change in the world—I'm not yet twenty-five, and my life's laid out for me already. Those teenagers shouting at the Beatles last winter, they'll have it; they'll have it all. They'll have a whole new world. Me, I was there with my old mum." She shook her head. "And she's back, you know, your princess—I saw it in the newspaper. Back to make a fuss about the women at your university. Where I am not." These last words sharpened by the pause that emphasized each one.

"I didn't know, love. If you'd said something while you were at school, if you'd ever said anything, maybe we could have—well, we just didn't know . . ."

"No," said Elaine. "You didn't." But she took hold of Clem's hand from her shoulder, and she held on. "It's all right," she said at last. "I won't buy a boat and sail off. And I won't do anything daft. I like leaving Gloria with Gerald's mum—she doesn't make the fuss of it that Mum does. All the questions of why I don't want to spend my time with Gloria; all the comments about what I'd rather do instead."

It wasn't right for her to talk about her mother that way, Clem knew that. He wanted to raise Elsie up again in her daughter's mind. He wanted a way to defend her. That was his job.

"She took good care of you, your mother. You mustn't deny

230

her that. More care than I'd ever seen a person take." He paused a moment. "She loves you," he said. Elaine should know that but he wasn't entirely sure. "Don't you ever let that go."

And Elaine did smile as she stood up and came around to stand behind him, kissing the top of his head as he had kissed hers. "I know you love us, Dad. And I'm sure that Mum does too. We're just two different people, she and I." She kissed his head again. "If it's OK, I'll have a lie-down, before I go." And she went to her old room, shutting the door with a snap.

Clem eyed the brandy, poured himself another half. He missed his kids. He missed their childhood. He missed the weekends ranging around in the bush and along the river, finding bits and pieces and working out what use they might be. Donny would suggest one thing, Elaine another, and somehow they'd find something the three of them agreed on, and work out how to make it together.

While Elsie stayed at home and fed the mangle. Such a different experience of their childhood to mine, he thought, *but she never seemed to think she'd missed out*. He'd take Gloria fossicking when she was bigger—and Don's kids, now that Carol was in the family way. They'd want rockets, not bikes and trikes, he supposed: there were so many things shooting up in the air. But guns, they'd still be a winner—particularly now this new war in Vietnam was getting off the ground. Little boys always wanted guns.

War: Elsie kept her children safe from all of that, wouldn't even let its stories touch their world. "You take the best care of them, Else," he'd said, standing with her by a bonfire of newspapers when the war ended, when they still lived with his mum, when the twins were so young and so small.

"Give us a hand with this shopping?" Elsie called now from the foot of the stairs, and he went to meet her halfway, reaching for her string bags of parcels.

"You've got enough provisions for a world expedition," he said with a snort. "You planning on going trekking? Expecting World War Three?"

Elsie set her things down on the table. "Don't you make jokes about war, Clem," she said, and so sharply that he leaned forward fast to kiss her cheek.

Let's keep her away from all that.

"Well, where would you go, Else, if you could go anywhere?"

"Like your uncle Perce; off into the blue?" She laughed, patting down her rumpled hair. "I'd go everywhere," she said. "I'd see the world. There must be so many places that don't look like this." She paused; he could see her hunting for the most exotic place she knew the name of, in the spirit of the game. "Well then—Tashkent!"

And he kissed her again. "Then I'll take you, Elsie Gormley. You and our restless girl Elaine."

"Is that Lainey's car out the front?" she said then. "Is Glory here?" Already heading for the hall.

Clem shushed her from the doorway, swinging her around like the beginning of a dance. "She's having a little lie-down, love—one of those shocking headaches, I think. Gerald's mum's got Gloria, and she's just gone in for a rest."

Elsie sat down, pushing off her shoes under the table. "I'll take in a drink and a facecloth," she said.

Clem nodded. "She'd like that." He wasn't sure how much of the morning he should share.

"Is it flu, do you think?" Elsie asked, moving to fill a glass of water that Clem knew was for Elaine. "It'll probably go to Gloria if it is, and then we'll have her sick as well."

But he knew she loved that too—the soup and the blankets and the hugs and the baths.

"It's not flu, love. Glory's fine." He watched Elsie go with the water towards the hallway. The props of affection. "Go on in, but go easy on her. She really is a bear with a sore head."

And then he heard her, in the usually empty room, doing her best. "Here you are, Lainey: don't sit up, love. Just pop this on your forehead and have a drink when you need it. You've done the right thing, you know, coming home. Here you are. Try this now. Safe and sound."

And he loved her for it. She was the center, the heart of his world.

23

The curlews

IT WAS late spring when Clem died—pneumonia, like his dad, and his last days so miserable as he worried this would turn him into the one man he hadn't wanted to be.

"If I could've gone any other way," he'd whisper, holding fast to Elsie's hand until the cough broke up his words and broke his hand free from his wife's, his fingers flexing and fluttering against his own chest like a tiny bird.

Talking himself into it, she thought, terrified that that might indeed be what he was doing. But she patted and soothed and said, "You'll be up and about in no time, Clem. There are too many chores that want doing."

He was only fifty-four, and suddenly all the plans they'd thought of making were too late. Elsie had marked a story about a cruise in one of her magazines and mentioned it one weekend. Clem had clipped an ad from the weekend paper for a little runabout—twelve foot of zippy hull—and left it on the kitchen bench. And Elsie, who'd never thought of such a thing, found herself imagining skimming across the surface of the bay, anchoring off a sandy beach, wading ashore, making a little fire, cooking some sausages, and pouring a thermos of tea. Cruising, either way.

Now, he was diminishing before her eyes, his lungs racked and his nerve just about gone.

"Wanted to see the world with you, Else," he said one morning. "Wanted to take you to Tashkent."

His words fell into a cough that Elsie tried to mop away—drink this, swallow that, and *shh, don't think of such things now.*

The doctor gave him some medicine and not much of a chance; Elsie kept telling him he'd be up and about in a jiffy.

And then, lying by him in the middle of one night, she dropped off for a moment listening to his broken run of breaths and, opening her eyes, in a silence, knew, just like that: he was gone. She took his hand, but all the life and warmth had gone from it, and it felt strange, and solid, and nothing like skin or pulsing blood or anything to do with a person.

Let alone Clem.

Still, she held on. She held on, as if she could push all the loving she was supposed to do for him in their next ten, twenty, thirty years together, into the wake of wherever he'd gone.

Neither of them were church people. In the quiet dark of twenty minutes past two in the morning—she could see the luminous green hands of the little clock Clem kept on his bedside table—she wished for the first time that she was. There'd be some comfort in believing in a hereafter. But the world was so still and quiet this morning that she wasn't sure there was anyone left alive in it but her.

She got out of bed, pulling on her dressing gown and pausing as she went by Clem to kiss his cool, smooth skin. In her world, Clem was always that young man looking up at her from the bright sunshine of a Brisbane afternoon. "Let me help you there," he was saying, holding up his hand as she swung down from the still-moving tram. Fifty-four, and dead, was no part of her image of him.

In the lounge room, she fumbled with the telephone. The black Bakelite receiver felt heavier than usual and she stood for a moment with her finger above the dial, wondering who she should call, and why. Dialed the first two digits of Don's number, and hung up. Dialed the first two digits of Elaine's. Pushed the cradle down to clear the number, and listened to the purr of the dial tone.

Not like anyone can do anything, she thought, replacing the receiver and heading back to bed. She wished she knew what she should do, awake and alone. Knitting, reading, watching—you could make a vigil out of each.

She climbed across Clem's still, quiet body and settled herself cross-legged, the way her children and grandchildren always sat when they were waiting for her to read.

"So I can read to you," she heard herself say, and she reached over for the novel she was halfway through, flicking on her tiny bedside light. She'd read to him this past week, on and off, pushing them both through a difficult book she'd picked up in a second-hand bookshop in the city, where the lady had called it a classic. "Iconic, even. *The* great Australian novel, I'd say." It was about some bloke trying to make the best way in his world. It wasn't in a hurry—that was like life, she supposed—but she wanted to see how it went in the end.

"It's lovely, the sound of your voice," Clem had said. "Reckon I could stand any of your hard books like this." She wished she'd thought to read aloud to him before. Now she'd just have to plow on on her own.

Every so often, Elsie liked to read a hard kind of book, or take Clem to hear some classical music or see some paintings in the Exhibition Building. "I think we should, love," she'd say, as he shook his head and made a joke about being out of his depth.

Wanting something different, something exciting: it was to do with Ida Lewis and the size of other lives.

Holding the book open now with one hand, she let the other rest on Clem's immobile torso as she scanned to find her place: "'The man returned to his chair on the edge of the room, and looked at the blank book, and tried to think what he would write in it.' Remember Stan Parker," she reminded her husband. "There was his wife, rummaging for something in a cupboard, and she found a notebook that she'd thought to give her son. Then Stan Parker asks her for the book, says he might make notes in it, or lists."

She cleared her throat self-consciously and went on:

The blank pages were in themselves simple and complete. But there must be some simple words, within his reach, with which to throw further light. He would have liked to write some poem or prayer in the empty book, and for some time did consider that idea, remembering the plays of Shakespeare that he had read lying on his stomach as a boy, but any words that came to him were the stiff words of a half-forgotten literature that had no relationship with himself.

Shakespeare, she thought. *It's always Shakespeare.* When she was a girl at school, she'd tried to read one of the plays—*The Comedy of Errors*—but got no further than the first few pages. People separated at birth, one mistaken for the other, no one recognizing anyone: you wouldn't credit it in life. Yet it was only ever Shakespeare and the Bible that clever people said you should read. Shakespeare and the Bible and now this book about Stan Parker.

She set the book down again; she knew how this Stan Parker felt, and she felt for him. Here she was, in the deep in the hours of darkness, in the middle of the most shocking thing that had ever happened to her—her husband dead on the mattress beside her—and she too wished for a poem or a prayer.

She thought of the painter again.

"I want to tell you something, Clem Gormley," she said then, as quietly as she could. "About that painting you were set to buy."

She knew what had seduced her: it was the sight of the one part of the artist's body she'd been able to see—her right arm—rising and falling in great, majestic sweeps as she blocked in the pure blue.

"Cerulean blue," she told Clem now, remembering the word, savoring it. She kept the tube of color in the bottom of her crystal jewelry box at the back of her dressing table, and she uncapped the lid every so often, sniffing its pungent, oily smell.

"And then she'd stop and swap brushes, and I'd see the tiny busyness of her hand making this intricate picture of me. There was another version of me coming out of the movements, big and small, of her arm. And it made, it made me feel, well . . ." She was blushing even now. "It made me feel adored."

She picked up her husband's heavy hand from where it lay on the quilt, and kissed it. "There was nothing in it, nothing but a single kiss—I kissed her hand. And it's been worming away at me ever since. More than ten years, Clem, on the brink of telling you."

Where was she now, the Elsie in the picture while this Elsie blushed and held her husband's hand. Once in a while, she let herself dream that the Elsie in the painting was off with Ida, on her adventures, together somehow. Now, with Clem's strange-feeling hand in hers, it occurred to her for the first time that the canvas might be anywhere—she might be hanging on her own in some dark hall, or filed away and forgotten, out of sight. And then it also struck her that she, the real Elsie, might now go anywhere too.

She swallowed a sound like a sob, and heard an echo of it in the night: the strange and mournful shriek of a curlew. It was impossible not to interpret the sound as grief or loss or suffering. *That is the right noise to make now*, she thought, fierce and alone.

The clock's hands had crept on an hour: the night was unbearably long.

Maybe everyone had that one thing that would tempt them—in her case, the sight of an artist's arm rising and falling as it brought a new version of her into being. And if you caught sight of that, in the right place at the right time, then some new bubble of possibility opened out, and some extraordinary thing unfolded.

Some people walked in; some people turned away.

What if I'd turned away when he put his hand up to me on the tram? What if I'd said, "I'm right, thanks," and swung down unassisted, on my own? There in the nighttime, Elsie felt as if her children and her grandchildren were fading a little, less secure.

Or what if he'd married that Jan? She gripped his fingers, knew their shape.

I must let the kids know, she thought then, and sat still, afraid to move in case her husband's body disappeared while she was gone. No. She didn't want Stan Parker's life. She wanted to hold on tighter to her own.

Somewhere in the darkness, the curlew called again and the sound worked like an alarm, propelling Elsie through the house towards the kitchen, where she lit the gas stove and shifted the kettle onto its bright blue ring.

"I'll just make a cuppa," she called, as she would have done if Clem had been awake, if he'd been alive, and found herself taking two cups down from the hooks above the bench. Which was when she cried, and cursed, and realized, for the first time, the full size of what had happened.

Her husband was dead. There was such force in that sentence, and she felt her hand grip the pretty cup until its handle snapped in two.

She cried some more, splashing the kettle's boiling water in a wide arc across the table, its mat, a box of pictures she'd been sorting, and her own left hand—so that she could only call out and cry harder again. She grabbed the box, as angry with it as if it had caused her husband's death, wanting to hurl it away.

That woman, Jan: she'd shoved her photo right up in the roof, well away, with that wretched portrait too. She should shove the rest of them up there as well. Tears flowing and her mind a kind of frenzy, she dragged a kitchen chair into the hallway and stood on it, ramming the box into the cavity's darkness.

Look at yourself, Elsie Gormley. Look at the state she was in. She stood there crying for all she was worth, her face snotty. Reaching up to steady herself against the manhole, her hand brushed the slivers of those two other prints and she pulled them down. She wiped her eyes as she stared at the photograph, the painting.

It must have been the light, or the darkness, or the crying, but she almost thought that both pictures were pictures of her. *You can come down now. He's gone.* She'd found something powerful in the threat of this Jan sometimes: a thing to push against, a thing to fear when she wanted to rail against Clem for some minor, inconsequential thing. It had been a kind of strange relief to think something hard and horrible. And now that made her cry even more.

Off the chair, in the kitchen, she held her hand under a gush of cold water. Outside, behind the hill's ridge, the faintest line of silver was coming up, like one of those Beatles songs about the sun.

Here it comes.

She'd been singing it to her smallest grandchild, Don and Carol's new boy. *Little Clemmie.* And she hummed a little now to calm herself as she went back in to Clem.

"I'm going to go out," she said, as she usually would. "I'm going to walk down to the river and back. When I come home, it will be morning, and I'll . . . do whatever you need me to do."

In the still-dim bedroom, she fumbled for any clothes—the grubby green pants she usually wore in the veggie garden—and tied a scarf around her bed-squashed hair.

In front of her mirrored dressing table, she paused, picking up the pretty bottle of cologne Clem had given her for her last birthday, squirting a little of it on one wrist and pressing it gently against the skin of the other. How did it work, dying? Did everything stop at once, or did your senses peter out at different times? Would he smell this scent, this rosy blossom?

She dabbed a spot of the perfume in the center of her husband's cool forehead and let her finger rest there for a while. Even its fragrance smelled sad. She knew she'd never wear it again.

He had loved her without question and he had loved her without pause: she was certain of that. He had thought the best of her always; he'd brought her the one life she'd wanted. Who would she be now, she wondered, without him? Who was Elsie Gormley if Clem Gormley's idea of her was no longer alive?

~

The river was as busy as ever, folding over itself along its rocky edge and running fast and thick in its center. How clear the waters used to be—there had been beaches farther upstream where people went for swimming parties. Now, the water ran a thick and impenetrable brown.

That's what she should have asked Ida Lewis, she thought suddenly; she should have asked the proper name for that color, something less disrespectful than "mud." Then *olive, cutch, sap green*—these words crept slowly from some lost crevice of her mind. Was she starting to forget?

She watched the water rush and surge, watched the way the mangroves' branches twisted and twined along the opposite shore. There was something to be said for a certain vague scattiness—how heavy to remember all things. She'd walk on through the gravestones, she thought, with no particular purpose. And then she'd make her way home.

As she rounded a corner in the graveyard, a gust of wind puffed through the trees and a flurry of jacaranda petals rained down, so bright against the dimness of dawn. They looked like a glimmer of fireflies.

Beautiful, she thought, and heard her own voice: "Beautiful and brilliant." She climbed to the top of the cemetery's hill, turning to look at tombstones here and there like someone in a showroom. Would he like a slab, or a headstone? Something ornamental, or a poem? Or just his name—*husband of Elsie*—and the dates?

At the end of one row, she pulled up. Ahead of her was a fine granite monument, highly polished and divided in two. The left-hand side recorded the birth and death of a man born not much earlier than Clem, she noted, and dead just this year passed. On the other side, the stone was smooth and blank, and she realized for the first time that that would be *her* space, the space for the wife, now living, who must ultimately die too.

She spun around fast, her eye caught by another divided stone in the next row over. The husband dead in 1936; the wife—Elsie almost cried out at the impossibility of it—dead just two years ago, in 1971. Her mind boggled at the math: thirty-five years that woman had had to live without her husband alongside her. Thirty-five years of missing him, and living. She wasn't sure which was worse: the certainty that she too would die also, or the idea that she might have to wait so long.

It seemed an impossible wait.

She noticed nothing on the rest of her walk—no people, no places, no time. So she was surprised to find herself almost back where she had started and dazzled, for a moment, by the glare of the sun against the glass wall that formed the end of Ida Lewis's old studio. The property had changed hands so many times in the past years; Elsie hadn't kept track of everyone who'd come and gone.

Standing on the verge to cross the road, she closed her eyes and saw the painting. It was funny, but when she thought of herself, she always thought of Clem alongside her—or if not Clem, one of her children, or her grandchildren now. She was never alone, not really, but in that neat rectangle of a painting, that was how she'd

242

been caught and pinned. On her own, completely on her own, as she felt she was, this morning, for the first time.

Perhaps that was all there was to the difference between her and her daughter, Elsie thought, staring at the shiny glass until her eyes began to smart. Elsie had always thought of herself in the context of other people—her own mother; her husband; her babies; their children. But Elaine thought of herself in the context of herself—or that's how Elsie saw it. *Maybe it's to do with being younger*, thought Elsie. Maybe everyone thought that way now.

So maybe I'll call Elaine first; she was closer to her dad. Then I'll call Donny, and that undertaker up on Ipswich Road. Or do I have to call a doctor? I'll call the doctor first, and then the children. Someone will tell me what to do. And although she was walking downhill, her feet seemed to slow and stumble against the mountain of tasks that might be ahead of her—letting people know, and clearing things out, and bothersome things with banks and government departments and the university and so forth that she'd never had to think about before.

Coming up the back stairs, she saw the fly screen door pushed open and thought for one moment that the whole thing had been some mad dream and that Clem, awake, was moving through the house now, getting ready for his day. But she knew as she stepped over the threshold that it was her own panicked absentmindedness that had left the door like this and that Clem would be lying on the bed where she'd left him.

As he was.

Three months later, when the water rose and the river spread out and out until her suburb and so many of its houses were deep within its stream, Elsie stood carefully in a neighbor's little aluminium runabout—exactly the specifications that Clem had thought of getting—and watched the high tide wash against her windowsills. She'd lost her wedding dress, her furnishings, her books; she'd been entirely unprepared. The only thing she'd managed to do well, she knew, was find Clem's bit and brace to bore seventeen holes, each the width of a broom handle, into the floor of the rooms of her house.

The photographs had been the worst loss. She'd left the house with an overnight bag and a box of the papers she'd need—about the bank, about the house, and her will. On top of that she'd balanced two more boxes, which she thought held the family's photos—from her own childhood, through her wedding, the birth of the twins, and on through the rest of their lives. The last photo she had of Clem, his hands holding the deck's railing at the back of the house as if he was on a ship in a gale.

And then, standing in the spare room at Elaine's, up on the ridge, as the water rose and eddied on the floodplain below, she'd opened both boxes and found them full of packets of veggie seeds.

"I must have picked up the wrong ones," she'd said over and over.

Elaine sighed. "I thought you'd be more prepared, Mum," she said. "It didn't occur to me that I should check."

Gloria stood quietly offering her grandmother a handful of photos that she'd had fixed to the frame of her mirror. "You can have these, Nan: they're a start."

Gloria, last Christmas. Gloria, by Elsie's new Eiffel Tower rose, planted straight after Clem died and now in bright pink bloom. A younger Gloria, wedged into the crook of Elsie's elbow, the two of them reading a book.

"I wonder which book that was?" Elsie peered at the image. "Can you remember, love?" But Gloria shook her head.

"I'd have sent Gerry down if I'd known you were in such a mess," said Elaine.

"I thought the rain would stop," said Elsie. And standing in

Elaine's spare room—*without so much as a hand towel laid out for me*, she thought—she had an image of moments of her life floating and swirling on a cool, clear lake, and then washed away, swept into some vast plughole.

When the waters ebbed and she could go back to her house, the boxes of photographs were the first things she rummaged for. The water had carried one across the room to the back door and dumped it there, lid still on, but saturated by muddy muck. The other one she never found.

"I read that you could wash photographs, Nan," said Gloria, standing behind her, peering around. "You wash them and put them onto blotting paper. I'll clean the bath out—we can put them all in there. I could go and get some blotting paper, if you like."

But it felt as though the whole city had been washed away, and Elsie didn't like the idea of Gloria, almost twelve, tripping through some muddy, busy street, looking for a stationer whose shop had probably been turned into a mound of mush.

"We'll make do, love," she said, watching Gloria carry the precious carton to the bathroom. She'd stayed there all afternoon, changing the water, dipping the images—every time Elsie walked in she saw her history floating to the surface of that crystalline lake she'd imagined: her wedding, her mother, her husband, her children. She tried to take a photo of the bath itself and its aquatic mosaic, but there was no film in the camera. When Elaine took Gloria home, Elsie pulled the pictures out of the bathtub, impatient, and set to drying them with a towel, crisp and efficient, wiping off the emulsion from their surfaces and rubbing away most of the pictures with it.

Gloria took over the delicate photographs after that first day, salvaging what she could and insisting that she would go into town—on her own, on the bus—to buy some blotting paper. By the time she came back, Elsie had bundled the lot into the garbage bin.

"Oh, Nan." Gloria hugged her hard, her lanky preteenage arms tight around her. Then: "I had an adventure with this—" and she waved the thick white paper. "I even met a boy—don't tell Mum!" Her brave trip on the bus, with a map, and navigating several city blocks and meeting a boy who'd been as lost as she was.

"He was looking for the shop I wanted; he wanted things for a rocket he was making." She barreled on. "He'd watched *Apollo* on the television, like we did—you and me and Pop."

"I think quite a lot of people watched *Apollo*." Elsie smiled.

"He lives over on the north side," said Gloria as if Elsie hadn't spoken, "and he said his house was so high up a hill that they didn't even know there'd been a flood. I said, how could he not? It was on the telly, like the moon!"

"Just us with our water views, darling," Elsie said. "What was his name?"

"Alex—isn't that nice? I like names with an *x* in them. They sound special. He said it was a secret name; he said he'd never told another living soul."

Elsie laughed. Her girl would grow up all too soon. This time together—for all its messy and smelly mud—a time like this might never come again. She heard Elaine's car in the drive.

"We won't tell your mum," she reassured her granddaughter. "And maybe you'll see him again."

Gloria smiled, kissed Elsie on the cheek, and ran down the stairs.

"I'll bring her back tomorrow, if you want her," Elaine called.

And Elsie called back, "Yes, yes, always."

She watched the car go around the corner, watched the wind play in the trees. Leaning down, she opened the lid of her rubbish bin, shaking it from side to side to cover the pile of splotchy images as the sun caught their still-white edges here and there.

24

The candle

IT WAS the kind of morning when the sun shone so brightly that the park's leaves looked moistened, their greens alive with such a polished shine. Such a day, thought Lucy, should go smoothly, but here was Tom refusing to eat his egg and objecting to every conceivable thing. Lucy was trying to be patient while he slammed his head around one way and then the other to keep his mouth beyond her reach. She'd tried encouraging, cajoling, and distracting in the space of fifteen minutes. She'd talked about the lovely things they'd do when this breakfast was done.

And then her own mood slammed from patience to exasperation like a yacht's boom, and she was furious.

She was tired and she was cross and it was not yet eight in the morning. They'd had a possum in the roof the last three nights. Ben had finally wrangled it down through the hatch and into the yard at midnight. Which was when Lucy, waiting to go back to sleep, had heard another noise, and realized that their possum must have been a mother. Their possum had had a baby. And now the baby was alone and in their roof.

Up the ladder every half an hour leaving fruit and water and peanut butter, she felt sick at the thought of the separation they'd wrought.

"It's a possum," said Ben, more than once. And: "We can deal with it tomorrow." And: "I've had enough of this."

She didn't want to know if he meant her fussing with the ladder, or the possum, or something more. But if a baby creature died on her watch, that meant she had no guarantee of Tom's safety. She'd known that with the clear and dangerous logic of the middle of the night.

When day came, the fruit and peanut butter were still arranged along the beam, just as she'd left them. And then Tom had wanted as little of his breakfast as her stowaway marsupial.

"Don't worry about it," Ben kept saying. "He'll get hungry later on. Don't make such a fuss."

At that moment Lucy heard her own voice, sounding like some malevolent, cursing thing. "I. Don't. Want. To. Be. Here." She spun around, grabbed her bag, her sweater and sunglasses, clattered down the stairs, and left Tom's terrible noise behind.

Why not? she thought. If Ben could decide he'd had enough of something, so could she.

It was terrific, this potent mix of elation and rage.

She stood at the edge of the park behind her house, her fists clenched. *I will walk around the block*, she thought. *I will feel better. Then I will go home.* And she went around once and then again, ignoring her own house on both loops.

On the third circuit she saw in the shadow of one of the park's trees the old woman in the dressing gown.

Of course it was Elsie, Lucy thought as she stepped towards her. Who else would she conjure up now?

"I'm Lucy," she said. "We live in your house, over there." She was suddenly aware of silence all around her. She couldn't hear Tom's cries anymore, nor the sound of any birds or any cars. Perhaps she'd stepped out of her own world.

"You live in my house?" The other woman's voice was very loud. "That can't be right. Surely I should be living in my house." And she leaned forward. "Is your name Jan?"

"No. I'm Lucy," said Lucy again. "I mean, we bought your house when you moved out. Listen, did you ever send me any roses?"

The older woman frowned. "Roses? My husband never wanted to grow roses," she said, "and the ones I planted when he died just never thrived." Her voice was small and sad this time.

Lucy touched her arm, her own eyes filling with tears. "I'm so sorry. The last thing I meant was to upset you."

"Please go away," said the other, older woman in the same tiny voice. "I'd like to come back to my home."

And Lucy went away, through the park, along the path and all the way up to the train station, blinking hard and rubbing at her head. It couldn't be Elsie; not really. She must have imagined it all.

~

Elsie watched her walk between the trunks of all the fig trees; watched herself, years before, in Lucy's footsteps; her daughter on the same path; her daughter's daughter too.

What had Lucy said about roses? She hadn't had a thank-you for those yet.

These girls. Where were their manners? Now, why could she not find her keys?

~

When the first train to pull in was one that went to the airport, Lucy smiled as she got on. Maybe today she'd have gone as far as Paris. If only she'd picked up her passport.

She pushed her glasses up onto her head and wiped her eyes, her cheeks, her chin. *I'll just go into the city*, she told herself, *and then I'll get off this train and come home.* But she knew she was going to the end of the line, and when the train pulled into the domestic terminal, she knew she was going to walk inside and buy a ticket. She stood on the concourse, squinting at the board.

Newcastle: she could turn up at her sisters'.

Melbourne: she could take a taxi to her dad's place.

Sydney: she could go and see her mum.

She took a breath. If she was running away, she would run to Astrid's mother, to Linnea—just like she did when she was seven years old.

Hobart: that's where Linnea lived now, where all her Christmas cards came from. It was no less crazy than anything else Lucy had done this morning.

"You're lucky, the direct flight leaves in just over half an hour," said the woman at the service counter. "Now, what about luggage? It's a rush, but we could get it on."

"No," said Lucy. "I don't have any."

"And a return date?"

"Just one way." She felt invincible. She waited for someone to ask what she was up to. She waited for someone to ask, *Are you OK?*

"How are you paying?" asked the woman behind the counter, busy at her screen.

Lucy remained invincible all the way onto the plane, and when her seat belt was done up low and tight, when her handbag was stowed under the seat in front, she pulled her phone out of her pocket and called home.

The machine picked up and she exhaled.

"I'm all right," she said. "I'm sorry. I'm on a plane. I'm going to Hobart. You're lucky it's not Paris." She heard her own weak attempt at a laugh. "I'll call you when I get there. I love you. I do love you both so much." The "do" was wrong, she knew. They would never have thought to question that she did. But it was said now. It was done.

And then she turned off her phone, leaned towards the plastic window and the warmth of the sun, and closed her eyes as the safety demonstration ran its course.

"If you are traveling with a child or someone who requires assistance, secure your own mask, and then help them," said the announcement.

"First rule of parenting," as her father always said.

She felt the plane surge, pushing into pure acceleration. And as the ground fell away, the amazing rush of what she'd done fell away too. Now she felt panic; now she feared catastrophe. *Don't ever scare him*, she'd told Ben.

What had she just done?

She scrunched her eyes shut and swallowed some tears. Then she slept the deepest sleep she'd had for months.

It was years since she'd been to Hobart; she'd gone once as a student, with Astrid, and they'd spent two weeks hiking around the edge of the island before fetching up at Astrid's mother's new place for the respite of comfortable beds and hot food and long, long showers. "Look south," Linnea had said as they stood on the steps of the post office. "There's nothing between here and Antarctica."

She'd have gone that far now, if she could.

Off the plane, Lucy headed for a taxi, fumbling in her bag for her phone, for Linnea's address. She wasn't sure if it was the same house she'd visited, all those years before. She wasn't sure what she'd say when Linnea opened the door—*if she's home*, she thought for the first time.

"This address," she said to the driver, "is it central, or further out?"

"About as central as you can get," said the man, "give or take," and off they went.

She glanced up and saw the huge bulk of Mount Wellington pushing high behind the town.

"This is going to sound odd," said Lucy, "but has that mountain always been there?" She had no recollection of seeing it the last time she'd visited.

"About forty million years or so," the driver said, "give or take."

As she raised her phone to take a photo, it started to ring—not Ben, but a number with Tasmania's code.

"Hello?"

"Lucy? Sweetheart? It's Linnea. Your husband just reached me—terrible reception down here and I was out walking. Where are you? Are you all right?"

"I'm in a taxi," said Lucy, as if this was a perfectly normal conversation, a perfectly normal day. "I'm on my way—should be with you in . . ."

"Fifteen minutes," said the driver, "give or take."

"Fifteen minutes."

"I'll see you then," said Linnea.

Above the city's pretty waterfront, the taxi stopped at a tiny cottage with huge, lush roses along the fence and a deep porch. Linnea opened the gate and pulled Lucy into a hug, hanging onto her and managing to get some money across to the taxi driver with her other hand.

"No, no," she said as Lucy began to protest. "Nothing to say about it—it's my pleasure. It's good to see you. Let's get you inside, and have a nice cup of coffee, and we can see what we need to do next."

"Thank you, Linnea," said Lucy, standing still on the garden path, as if the words required a certain solemnity or moment. "I didn't know where I was going—and then I thought of you. I'll have tea, if you've got it, if that's OK."

Linnea smiled as she pushed the front door open, and Lucy saw the way the house opened out to a wide, light room at the back made almost entirely of glass. There was a deck, a garden, and a perfect view of the Derwent beyond. "You should bring Tom and

Ben down for the yacht race," Linnea said, taking her arm and following her gaze. "It's magnificent sitting on the deck as the sails rush towards the finish line. All that effort; all that spectacle."

Lucy walked across the room towards the view. Out on the water, there were boats making their way along the river, tacking one way, going about, and tacking again. There were so few yachts on Brisbane's river, Lucy thought. You could sit and watch a whole reach and see no boats on the move.

"Coming from the airport, when we turned the corner and saw the mountain, and now this; everything seems beautiful today."

"Perhaps that's because you're here unexpectedly," Linnea said as she cleared some papers away from a table beside Lucy. "Perhaps that changes the way things look. Swing it round." She pushed at a chair. "You don't have to stop gazing."

"I could sit here forever," said Lucy later, taking her tea and cradling the mug in both hands.

"You're very welcome here." Linnea let her hand rest on Lucy's head. "You always will be. But I think your lovely husband and your beautiful little boy would have something to say if I kept you that long. Do you have pictures? I haven't seen him since the one you sent when he was born—and he must be, what, twelve months, fourteen or so?"

"He's coming up to two," said Lucy, reaching for her bag to pull out her phone. "Here: I took one of him last night before he went to bed." She was astonished at how bright and real her son looked in the photo. He was so far away. "Linnea," she said quietly. "What have I done?"

There was a single beat of silence, and then Linnea spoke. "You've come to visit me," she said briskly. "You probably need a rest—most mothers do. There's nothing else to say. You don't even have to decide how long you're here for. Now, drink that up while it's still hot."

Lucy reached for the tea, feeling seven years old again. But as she shifted in her chair, she knocked her bag down, spilling its contents across the floor—her wallet, her glasses, a plastic car, and a packet of sultanas.

"Oh," she said quietly, spinning the car's wheels. "Oh no."

"I'll run you a bath," she heard Linnea say, brisk again, and she heard the water while she sat driving the little red car up and down her thigh, hating herself. It seemed no time had passed before Linnea called to her, "Come on, Lucy, it's ready." As if she were still just a child herself.

"Tom always asks if he can take his cars into the bath," Lucy said then, setting the toy down on the table. But then the bathroom was magnificent too, with a softly-velvet neck rest and a window angled to take in the river's sweep. She chose one yacht from all the traffic on the water and watched it ply across the bright blue span.

The rest of the day skated by, and Lucy settled herself again in the chair by the window, watching the change in the afternoon's light.

"All right," said Linnea at last, taking the chair next to her. "Let's make a plan. How about I keep you for three days—long enough for you to have a break, but short enough that Ben won't get too scared. They get scared, husbands; it took me years to work that out, and I'd lost three of them by then. Take your time, drink my tea, but tomorrow we're going on an excursion to the sea cliffs you walked along with Astrid—do you know, I think that's almost twenty years ago? We'll take a boat along that coastline, so you can see what you were walking on. And the next day, we'll run out to the new gallery and I can have you at the airport for the six o'clock flight back through Sydney. I told Ben you'd get a taxi home—too late for Tom to be on the road."

In the middle of the river, another small yacht tacked and turned, and as Lucy watched it, her finger traced its line. She'd drifted from the sound of Linnea's voice entirely; the cliffs, the gallery, something about sending her home. She didn't want to think about any of it now.

"How many husbands did you have, Linnea?" She was watching her yacht muddle a turn and send its sail out wet across the water when she realized her friend had stopped talking.

"Just the three—the first one, and then Astrid's father, and then the one after that. I talked myself out of them, you know."

"Why did you talk yourself out of them?"

"I didn't mean to, the first time. He left because he didn't want a child—fair enough; and I was so sure I was right. He made leaving seem so simple. When I'd married him, I'd believed all that death-do-us-part stuff; I believed we would go on forever. When he up and left, after five or six years, nothing felt like it needed to be permanent, or like it could be. I'm not saying that's right." Linnea held her hand up towards Lucy's frown. "I'm just saying that's how it felt. I never bothered to try to hang on to Astrid's father—I was really just in love with having Astrid—and I knew too many women who thrived as single parents to be daunted by that. Then the next bloke, after you girls were grown up—well, he was very nice, and the wedding was fun, but I don't think I ever expected it to last either. I was sick last winter and he came to see me—brought me some soup his new wife had made. I thought that was rather chivalrous, in a twenty-first-century way."

Without her thinking about it, Lucy's fingers were working at her wedding ring, turning it so that it slipped up towards her knuckle, and then back down.

"Tom's gorgeous," she said. "I should have been more patient."

"Probably," said Linnea, "but they can make it tricky sometimes." She paused, pushing a photograph across the table towards Lucy. "This is Astrid now—well, last Christmas. America," she said, before Lucy could ask the next question. "Manhattan—but Manhattan,

Kansas. She works as a ranger. There's something special about the grass, apparently. I was planning annual trips when she told me she was moving to Manhattan—but it was the wrong one. I suppose we talk once a month or so, but we're not really close. I always liked it when you came round to play—and later, when you were bigger. I understood the things you were interested in: music, poetry, travel. I could suggest things that you thought were fun. But plants and plants—that's all there was for Astrid. Perhaps it's genetic: they named me for some great-great-somebody's obsession with Linnaeus."

From deep inside her memory, Lucy saw Astrid, six or seven years old, frozen in the middle of a game of make-believe. "Come *on*, Astrid," she heard herself saying. "We're *supposed* to be getting these babies into a bath." While Astrid crouched down on the garden path that Lucy had designated as their playhouse's bathroom, staring at a tiny yellow flower.

"Look, Lucy, it's a buttercup—but can you see? There's something odd about it. I think it's a different sort of *species*." As if this was some great thrill.

"It's different how?" Lucy held her position, her imaginary baby propped against her shoulder, her foot and hip jutting impatiently, the way her own mother stood when she didn't want to be kept waiting. "What's a species?"

"*Ranunculus lappaceus*—the common buttercup. I've got to get my book—come *on*, Lucy, this is much more important than your silly game." And Astrid had run inside calling, "Mum? Mum? Where's my plant book? I think I've found something *interesting* in the garden."

"Does she have kids?" Lucy asked now, placing the photograph of Astrid flat on the table and tracing the flick of her hair. "I should know that, but . . ." So familiar, yet so long out of touch.

Linnea shook her head. "One of our many points of difference—not that I mind her not having children, although that would have been lovely. But I asked her once about it; she'd had some boyfriend for a while, and she was heading for her thirties. I just wondered if it was something she'd thought about, in among the seeds and the soil, you know. And she said . . ." It took Lucy a moment to look up and realize that Linnea was trying not to cry. "She said she hadn't liked childhood that much and wasn't interested in doing it again. I might have had a few regrets about things that happened but, you know, I always thought that we had *fun*." Linnea wiped at her eyes with her sleeve. "What a thing to say."

"I had fun," said Lucy quietly. "I had the best fun with you two." The Astrid of the photo was almost smiling, pale sun on her face, and one hand reaching off to the side, presumably to hang on to whoever was standing there, not included in the image.

"Is she happy?" Lucy asked. "Don't you miss her?" If Tom ever said such a thing to her—but then she couldn't imagine anything would cut her off from him.

Except when he wouldn't eat an egg on toast, and you ran out the door.

Linnea shrugged. "There's a new guy," she said, taking the photo back and stroking one finger along its frame. "He has a daughter. We're civil now, at least—for a couple of years we didn't talk. But that was no good; it made it worse. Now, well, we keep in touch. But it's not the old age I'd imagined." She reached out and touched Lucy's knee. "Another reason I'm pleased to see you."

Lucy took Linnea's hand. "I always thought you were a wonderful mother," she said. "I always wished my mother was more like you. And I probably said something just as terrible to her along the way. Maybe we're always just cruel." She closed her eyes, picturing Astrid in the photo. "It'd be nice to catch up with Astrid—I always think of her when I see buttercups."

"She'd love to hear from you." Linnea let go of Lucy's fingers. "When you go home, you do that."

"Home"—just that one word, and Lucy cried, sobbing out a muddle of flood and Elsie and Ferdi and flowers and break-ins and possums and more.

"I used to be so good at moving to new places," she said when she'd run to her end. "This time, it's felt much harder."

"The Elsie thing," said Linnea after a moment. "What do you think that is?"

Elsie was an idea, a comfort—Lucy knew that. She pulled her wedding ring off her finger and set it spinning on the table. "At first it felt friendly," she said, "like she was welcoming me there. I liked to think we'd been chosen for her house or it had chosen us. I guess I just took it too far—she can't have been standing on the footpath in the dead of the night, or in the park this morning, can she?"

Linnea leaned back, her arms stretched above her head. "Well, I wouldn't want to leave if it were me," she said. "Would you? 'They can carry me out in a box,' as my grandfather used to say. Perhaps they're both hard things, coming into new lives, or going out of old ones."

And as Lucy reached to stretch too, she saw, outside the window, Linnea's neat lawn, trimmed and tidy. Its surface was spotted with buttercups, like clusters of stars in the grass.

~

The next day, engulfed in her slicker on the sightseeing boat, Lucy felt exhilarated by the salt and the speed.

"It feels better, getting off the land for a while," she said, and Linnea nodded, pulling her beanie down over her ears.

"I love these cliffs. That's what you went stomping on with Astrid." Her whole face was lit up, and as Lucy turned to look at the edge of the land, she understood why.

Behind her, the skipper was deep inside geology—she heard the words "dolerite" and "sandstone," "mudstones" and "granites" as she took in the landscape in front of her. "They're so tall," she whispered, trying to remember how high she must have felt as she'd walked this coast all those years before.

"Three hundred meters, the highest ones," said Linnea. "I love it when we've got the best or biggest something—and these are the highest sea cliffs in the southern hemisphere. Look at that, the way the rock changes so sharply, the way the dolerite shines. I forget how glorious it is when I'm not here."

Lucy tilted and craned her head, trying to take it all in. "My husband's got this thing about space travel," she said. "The Americans made the first orbit of earth on the day he was born. Anyway." She took her time, aware that she was reaching for some new idea. "It's this, isn't it. It's like the first images of the planet from outer space; you forget where you are—the big picture—when you're stuck in your kitchen or your backyard or your office. You forget how breathtaking it is, and how beautiful."

Linnea held her hand. "I thought you'd like it," she said.

~

It was four in the morning when she woke in Linnea's spare bed, and the house was quiet and dark. Her body was stiff from being buffeted on the water and she swore as she frowned at her watch. Reaching for her phone, she called Ben's number, and waited.

"Lu?" he said, the phone not quite close enough to his not-quite-awake mouth.

"I want to come home."

"Great." He coughed. "What time is it?"

"Four? Sorry. Linnea took me on this amazing boat trip—you should have seen the cliffs. I fell asleep in the car coming back, but I wanted to talk to you. And to Tom."

"He's just here—you want me to wake him?" She could hear the joke in his voice—the thing you never do, wake a sleeping child.

"What do you mean he's just there? Is he OK? Is everything all right?"

"Sure," said Ben. "I brought him in when he woke up earlier. Seemed reasonable—we could both use the company."

"I wish you were here." Lucy twitched the curtain at the window and the brightness of a streetlight flooded in.

"Me too." Another cough. "Are you OK?"

"I wasn't ever really not OK," said Lucy carefully. "You know, I make too much of things sometimes."

"You don't say."

"You do too."

"Yes. I do."

Through the window, Lucy could see the light spots of the flowers in Linnea's smooth green grass. "Wasn't 'luminescent' one of your favorite words?"

At the other end of the connection, Ben laughed. She loved to make him laugh: things were all right.

"It's four in the morning," he said. "Go back to sleep. And your possum's gone home too. I got it out last night—another adult. There was no baby. I'll see you when you get here—it's tonight, now. It's tonight. You're almost home."

"Yes," she said, "almost there."

~

She was on edge for the rest of the day, from the moment she woke and saw daylight. She sat with Linnea eating breakfast and on they went, through the morning, through the gallery, the artworks Linnea wanted her to see.

A room of all-white books. A waterfall that spelled out words. A snaking hall of prints.

Lucy took her friend's arm. "Linnea?" she said. "I really just want to go home."

"One more thing." And Linnea steered her into a dark, quiet room.

At its center, a single flame burned, steady and perfect. There was something hallowed about the dimness and the silence. Lucy stared at the fixed point of the candle's flame until her eyes had multiplied its image again and again in the darkness. Then she blinked and the flame collapsed back into itself.

There were no other Lucy Kisses in the darkness. There were no Elsie Gormleys in her world.

Blow out the candle and make a wish, she thought, and as the idea formed, she made herself take a step back. *This is always here*, she thought, *just like the cliffs*. And she felt the calm happiness of her stolen day in Paris—but not when she was in the gardens, or thinking about children. Where else had she been?

She closed her eyes and saw there one of the museums she'd visited that day. A pendulum swung through wide, clear space, a pendulum that etched out the spin of the earth. The near, the far, the in, the out of the plumb bob's graceful sweep.

But that wasn't what she'd loved about it. Not the arc. Not the motion. Not even the way it traced the Earth's movement, right there for her to see it on the ground. What she loved was the fixed point up above as the world turned below.

Wherever I go, thought Lucy, blinking in the gallery's deep darkness, *wherever I am, this is here, and this candle is alight*. She closed her eyes again, and the candle's afterimage glowed brighter still.

Anchored. Centered. Safe.

There had always been that point.

Coming out, she found Linnea and they made their way to daylight and the last leg of her trip.

"And when you come again," Linnea said, "when you bring your boys, we'll take them up Mount Wellington and find another view to see."

Lucy kissed Linnea at the terminal, thanking her for everything, and suddenly embarrassed by the manner of it all.

Linnea hugged her. "Any time," she said. "Any time."

From the plane, she called home.

"Nearly there," she said to Ben.

"Nearly here," he said to her.

Then she tapped out an email to Astrid—*out of the blue* and *the state I was in* and *after all this time* and *your mother, so kind*—and heard the satisfying whoosh of it heading towards Kansas as the flight attendant closed the plane's last door.

Off we go, she thought, and realized she was excited.

The plane pushed itself up off the ground and swung around, heading up, heading north, heading home. Lucy took three straws with her drink and laid them out across the tray table like fiddlesticks. One. Two. Three. Ben. Tom. Lucy. She straightened them, aligning their tops and bottoms as best she could.

She'd have a cleanup when she got home—all those boxes, all those lives, and all those doilies. She didn't need any of them anymore.

And then she sat sipping her drink, occasionally moving one of the three straws laid out in front of her. The ice cube slid into her mouth with the last of the liquid and she held it there, savoring its coldness. She was in that summertime pub; she was in Paris. She was in one of those moments when something content and complete hummed through her body. She relished the edge of it now.

As the plane nosed towards Brisbane's runway, Lucy watched the clouds, fine stripes laid across the nightlight view like trails of gossamer spiders' web. The spiders were still down there, spinning their proprietorial banners, as vast and as many as ever. The trees, the green was all still growing, although autumn was coming on now. The river cut the city with its capricious line of darkness, its snaking switchbacks winding in from the coast. It was a beautiful, beautiful thing.

There were stars above, and dotpoint lights below—she was closer each minute to home. Then the plane's wheels bounced against the tarmac and she had arrived.

As the plane surged along the runway, the nocturnal landscape rushing by, Lucy tapped at her phone. There were two new emails in her inbox. One from Linnea, so pleased to have seen her: *come again, any time.* The other from Astrid, during the American night with a daughter—*my partner's,* she said—who had a temperature.

Amazing to have your message, amazing to hear from you. I've missed you—well, time flies, they say. Want to hear about you and your boys and your life. Can't believe you saw Mum. She always was so fond of you. Take care of yourself back at home. And let's not let it be so long.

Outside the plane, the warm air of the tropical night wrapped around Lucy and the streetlights glowed. Back there, behind her, down south, the high cliffs still loomed and the candle still burned—where she wasn't. Because she was here.

When she was small and at home on a rare sick day, she'd never quite trusted that her classroom would be there, with the day and its lessons going on, if she wasn't. "Solipsism": nine letters. Of course Ben had known the word.

It was how the rest of the world felt sometimes now that she was someone's mum. As if almost everywhere and everything else had disappeared. Sometimes, that wasn't so bad.

Overhead, a few stars pocked the city's glare.

"No bags?" The taxi driver stood with the boot of the car propped open.

"No bags," said Lucy.

"And where am I taking you?"

"Home," said Lucy.

She would go home. She would go in. She would hold them both—Ben and Tom—as close as she could. She would shut the door and fold them, safe, inside.

Her house. Lucy's house.

Lucy's home.

25

The planetarium

HE'D NEVER heard anything like the sounds Tom made when Lucy left—they were profound: vast and guttural. They were pure anguish and abandonment, and it took all his focus and fortitude to stand in front of their barrage, let alone stop himself joining in, furious and unhelpful.

Ben had no thought of running after Lucy. He thought: *So, this is how people leave.* The way his father had.

But then there was Tom, and the bawling, and Ben stepped inside the noise and felt as frightened and as angry as his boy. He counted to ten, slowly, the way he knew Lucy did, drawing his breaths out a little further each time until they felt smoother and more free.

"Tom," he said, "come here, love." And he gathered him into the circle of his arms. "She's just tired, mate, and a bit cross. You know how you have a tantrum sometimes? That's what Mum's doing now, I reckon. But it's all right—she'll be fine, and we're all right."

He could say these sentences, no problem, but deeper down Ben seethed. *This mess, this stupid mess*—and what business did she have making their boy so upset? *Don't ever scare him.* Huh.

Tom snuggled into his father, sniffing and wiping his snotty nose across Ben's shoulder—the sort of thing he thought would send him spare before he had his own child. But he held Tom, and patted him, and shushed him. And the sky kept moving past the sun.

He rang the office and told them Tom was sick—"yes, Lucy too. Lucky it's almost the weekend." And then he peeled away Tom's sticky pajamas, and his own snotted ones, and got the two of them under the hottest, strongest shower Tom could stand. "Wash it away, Tom, my man. Let's wash it away and feel better."

They were in the shower when Lucy rang from the airport.

Hobart, thought Ben, replaying the message. Well, there was no Ferdi Klim in that part of the world, as far as he knew. And no Elsie either.

He found Linnea's number in Lucy's address book and made an uncomfortable call—"My wife's run away; she's coming to you." You could rely on people to be polite about the strangest things. Then he built a complex train track with Tom—"I reckon we could go three layers here, and how about a figure-of-eight?"—and watched the small boy loop and whiz his engines round and round.

So this is parenthood, he thought. *You behave better than you might for the sake of your kid.* He wanted to shout at Lucy. He wanted to hate her. He wanted to hold her and demand the old Lucy back, the way she used to be. He wanted to tell her, once and for all, not to worry about every catastrophe that her busy mind could imagine—for herself, for Tom, for a baby possum. He wanted no more imaginary friends—nor long-lost real ones. *Us. Here. Now*, he thought. *That's all.*

He watched Tom select rolling stock for his favorite engine: his precision, all his care.

The back door slammed.

I do not hear you, Ben shouted inside his head at Lucy's Elsie. *This is our place. You do not belong.*

"Who there, Daddy?" Tom's trains were paused along their tracks.

"It's just the wind, love, just the wind," said Ben. "I'll get you some toast now, Tom. Some raisin toast, and milk?"

When the food was done—Tom, ravenous from no breakfast, ate three slices—they sat a while and leafed through different books. Picture books. Atlases. "Where's Mummy?" asked Tom, and Ben pointed to the island hanging off the bottom of Australia's distinctive-shaped continent. Nothing unusual. Make no comment. As if she always flew away. And then came home.

And then: "Space book," said Tom, and trotted off to get it.

It was a big book with heavy cardboard pages and so many flaps and foldouts—huge numbers, vast distances—and he dragged it across the floor to set it at Ben's feet. They read about the Big Bang, those deceptively simple-sounding words, and a number it was easy to say. ("Thirteen-point-eight billion years—that's almost fourteen billion, Tom," as if rounding up those extra millions was neither here nor there.) They read about the planets, which Tom practiced naming, and the sun, which he told Ben was hot "like the toaster." Ben read through all the bits of information, lifting all the flaps and unfolding all the foldouts. He held his phone up to the bright blue sky and showed his son where the constellations were, still there, hiding behind the daylight and ready to shine through at night.

"I thought that was the most amazing thing when I was little," he said, almost to himself. "The stars are always there, you see; the stars are always there." He watched his son's determination as Tom padded back into his bedroom and returned with a bucket of different colored balls, a flashlight, and a wide black towel.

"Planets," he announced. "And night."

"Have you done this before?" Ben asked, smoothing the towel across the back of the sofa, where Tom indicated it should go.

"Mummy did," said Tom, pointing. "Universe." He placed the flashlight carefully on the sofa's arm and clicked on its beam. "Sun," he said, pointing to its brightness. Then he went back into his bedroom and came out dragging a bucket full of spaceships, a bucket full of luminous plastic stars. "Rockets," he said, pointing at one bucket. "Milk way," pointing at the other. "Now we can play," he added, smiling.

"Yes, we can," said Ben. This magic; this creation—this was better than a day in the office, no matter what story he might get to write. His rage and fury began to fold down into something that ached now for Lucy. As long as Lucy was all right; as long as Lucy was all right, everything else was all right too.

And then came the idea of kindness. Just give her this break, this respite.

"I'll take the shuttle," he said, driving it along the runway of a stripe in the rug and then whooshing it high over Tom's head and all around the room, while his little boy giggled and laughed.

His mother had helped him make a cardboard rocket, Ben thought. *But my wife made our boy the whole universe.*

~

It took seven rounds of "Twinkle, Twinkle" for Tom to settle in his cot that night; Ben had never had to sing for such a long time, and he could hear his voice croaking in the darkness towards the end.

"Come on, mate," he said as he finished for the last time. "I reckon that's enough starlight for anyone. You close your eyes now and think of all the nice things we'll do tomorrow—might go to the planetarium: what do you think? The big room where you can see all the stars? Or we can just make another one at home together here."

"OK." Tom yawned. "And Mummy home?"

"Couple of sleeps. And you and me, Tom, we'll have an adventure while she's away."

"OK."

Just say it's normal, and it is, thought Ben. But he poured himself a whisky when he went into the kitchen, and he sat with it, out on the deck, looking out at the trees and up at the night.

The house was awfully quiet.

Wonder if Elsie's husband sat here, waiting for Elsie, the two kids asleep in their beds. He took a long sip. *Wonder if Elsie ran away?*

Perhaps it was always the same: the frustrations, the misunderstandings between people, and the noisy freight of family. Or perhaps Clem and Elsie would have looked at Ben and Lucy and wondered what aliens they were.

"You think so much about things, you young folk," Lucy's dad had said once, listening to them worry away at the pros and cons of some decision or another. "Us, we just got on and did it—I'm not saying that was right all the time, but we must have saved a lot of energy."

Ben took another sip of his drink and watched two possums spit and hiss, facing off on the high electrical wire. Spoiling for a fight.

Another sip now while the possums shrieked, and he pulled out his phone, scrolling through the numbers he'd dialed that day until he saw Linnea's. But he kept his thumb away from the imperious green button.

"Give her time," Linnea had said. "You don't sleep, you know, when you've had a kid. Not properly. No one ever tells you that. You're always primed to wake up, in case someone needs you in the night."

He wanted his wife to come home.

Flicking away from the keypad, he found his camera roll and worked backwards from his pictures of Tom's galaxy earlier in the day, all the way to older shots, before his son was born. Lucy with her belly stretched taut and a smile from ear to ear. Lucy with her hands under her own weight as if she was cradling a melon. He drank again, and scrolled forward: Tom, so small, nestled in the crook of Lucy's neck. Tom, so small, cupped safe in Lucy's hands in a shallow bath. Tom, so small, fast asleep in a cot that looked huge.

It was the one useful thing he remembered from the classes they'd had to take before they had him. "If you're having a bad day," the midwife had said, "take a moment to flick through some photographs. You never take photos of your bad moments—so when you flick through some of the happy things, you let yourself remember there'll be other lovely times."

"This too shall pass," Lucy had murmured.

"Well, yes," said the midwife. "Not the parenting; that never stops. But whatever noisy mess you find you're in."

Back inside, he turned on his computer, opened the folders of photos and moved through them until he found Lucy before Tom—without even a hint of Tom, or an idea he might come into being. Lucy years ago, when there was just the two of them, beginning to be themselves. The years they'd been together now—almost spoilt for time together on their own.

God, she was beautiful—she still was, of course, with her red hair and her lovely olive skin. He could remember being astonished by her when they first started dating. She'd seemed radiant, so full of life and certainty. He could remember the first time he kissed her; it was the only first kiss he could recall.

"Well, there you are then," she'd boasted, a little bit proud, when he'd confessed that, after years of them together.

Here they were, their first New Year's together. Someone had a place with a view of Sydney Harbour. There was champagne. There was seafood. There were fireworks. There was Lucy, part of a group of pretty young women leaning in towards each other with their glasses, all of them doing more in their lives than they'd ever imagined, and loving it.

Lucy had never been more glorious. There she was, smiling, wearing a dress that left her beautiful back bare. If he thought of her out of nowhere, he realized, he thought of her on that night; she'd buzzed with some potent combination of contentment and potential.

"It's so arbitrary," she'd said at one point. "Who says it's December thirty-one that the year flips? Who made these decisions? Some pope somewhere? A king? An astronomer?"

"Either way, it's a good excuse for kissing." Ben heard this sentence as clearly as if it had been said in the room with him now, and turning in his mind's eye to the man standing next to him on that night, more than a decade back, he knew who had said it. Ferdi Klim, a woman on each arm and another one trying to find a handhold.

"Should've been an octopus," he'd said, catching Ben's eye. "So you're the new boyfriend?"

"I am."

"Nine letters," said Ferdi. "I heard you think you're good at this. A. R. S. E. C. Y. O. T. T."

"'Astrocyte,'" said Ben, taking them both by surprise.

Now, Ben shook his head. *How did I even know that word?*

Moving back and forwards between the photographs, Ben found Ferdi's sleeve here, his shoulder somewhere else, the back of his tall frame, stooping down, talking to someone or maybe kissing them.

He was there; he was there all the time.

He closed his eyes, trying to draw more detail from the darkness of his mind, and he remembered Ferdi and the three girls somehow hailing themselves a taxi a few minutes before midnight, disappearing up the road in a flurry of honking horns. At the last minute, Ferdi had turned to kiss the eponymous Lucy—"how can I not, with that name?"—and they'd held on to each other for a few seconds.

"Of course I'm staying here," Lucy had said, one hand hanging on to Ben's. "I've done my time—you're going off. You're over there." The taxi; the girls.

The power of being chosen: he'd forgotten that great glow.

I am lucky, he thought, looking at his pictures again. *We're together, and we're lucky.* Draining the last of his whisky, he watched the screen change through its slideshow, watching one Lucy dissolve into another one, and stay much the same in each. He made the usual list of resolutions—to be more patient; to be more present; to be more kind. They were easy to make on his own.

There was a crash from the cavity above the ceiling and a possum poked its nose out from the top of the linen cupboard. Ben knocked his chair in his haste, leapt for the ladder and the towel he'd left nearby.

"You're all right; I've got you. You're all right." The possum's body quivered as he wrapped it close and carried it outside. One less thing for Lucy to worry about. Ben crawled into bed and slept soundly, with the sense of a job well done.

And when Tom cried out the next night—after more trains and excursions and more food than his father had ever seen him eat—Ben was up in a moment, ignoring all the edicts and directives as he transferred the boy to Lucy's empty half of the bed. Where he slept beside him, settled and deep, undisturbed by his mother's late call.

When Ben woke that Sunday morning, they'd slept through the birdsong, he and Tom, and the morning was heading for seven.

26

The time lapse

IT WAS bright when Elsie woke, and later than she'd expected. After more than a year in this room, its brightness still surprised her. They'd caught her wandering—the trips of her mind; the trips that she took. They said they were going to move her to the building next door.

"More secure, Mum," said Don, "and just one room."

A terrible sense of entrapment: she wouldn't speak of it.

She barely spoke again.

She stretched, and stood, and went into the shower—where she slipped and fell. This time, she heard a crack.

"Hello, Elsie?" called the young girl who came by now each morning. Elsie could never remember her name. "Are you right? Big day today—you're moving out."

And as she heard herself reply—"I'm not here"—she felt the world move beneath her, tipping her into its blackness. In its dark silence, she realized, she could no longer hear Clem's loud clock.

When she woke, she was in a hospital room with the sheets too tight across her feet. Three young men in white coats were talking to her children.

"Ah, there you are, Mrs. Gormley," said one of them, noticing her gaze.

And where else would I be? She smiled politely, trying to follow their sentences through words like "intracapsular" and "hemiarthroplasty." None of it sounded good.

"You had a fall, Mum," said Don.

"Broke your hip," said Elaine.

Well, then, thought Elsie. The doctors looked so young standing there, smiling at her. "No more nighttime flits." She closed her eyes, her whisper no more than a breath.

"Sorry?" The one standing closest to her—the one holding her chart—looked over the top of his glasses.

"She doesn't say much anymore," her son said softly.

"Her mind wanders." Her daughter's voice was crisp. "She was lucky not to break anything when she fell the first time, back at home."

"She's doing well for her age," said her son, holding her hand and squeezing.

His voice—all their voices, come to think of it—shook and shimmered, as though the room was a kind of echo chamber. *Ah, reverb.* Like Don's grandson had said.

Perhaps I'm not here, thought Elsie, *the way they're talking. When did Donny get so old?*

"We were due to fly out this evening," said Elaine then. "Flying to London, to see Gloria—for a big show of her pictures."

"You go," said Don. "Mum would want that. And tell Gloria to come home soon—if she can." Nodding at Elsie in the bed. "Thick as thieves they were, Mum and Glory. It would mean the world to her."

She could feel them watching her while she lay between them, very still, her eyes closed.

"She looks so still—like a statue." Elaine's voice was softer than usual; that was nice.

She heard her son's voice: "Yes."

"There was a painting," Elaine was saying. "We found that photo—remember? You thought it looked like Mum, but I said no."

And then she heard a woman sniff. Was Elaine crying?

"But it was. It was a portrait Ida Lewis did of Mum."

Don's voice now. "That painting? That was Mum?"

"It was. By Ida Lewis. Gloria saw it in a magazine somewhere. She's trying to find out where the painting is. I made a copy of the photo for you too."

The sound of paper being pulled clear of an envelope.

"That's a lovely thought, Elaine." Don's voice was gentle. "It makes her look so grand, though, don't you think?"

"So much more than Mum."

Elsie could feel some pressure against her other hand, and when she opened her eyes for a moment, she saw her daughter's hand pressed lightly on her own. "Imagine, a glamorous secret like that."

Elsie blinked, and saw Elaine, skipping alone along a path while Donny walked beside his mother, held her hand.

"Dad told me about it—not long before he died. But I didn't think it was real. As if Mum would get to do a thing like that."

My daughter Elaine, thought Elsie clearly in the dimness of her mind. *All the things she didn't do.* And as she settled to think about this, she caught the scent of roses, sweet and thick.

Perhaps one of her children had brought them. Or perhaps it was the roses the new woman—Lucy, wasn't it?—had planted. She could see them too, as she lay here. She could almost taste their smell. Those roses. And the garden did look lovely: even Clem would be impressed.

"Attar of Roses." Elsie's voice was almost silent.

"She got exactly the life that she wanted," Elaine said. "I spent all my life living it too."

Elaine, in the darkness, quite close by.

≈

In the hospital at night, it was never truly dark. There were lights here and there, and bright buttons on machines. There were brilliant strips and tiny bulbs; globes and flashes and other lights. In the smallest hours of the morning, someone was likely to wake you—to check something or measure something. To make sure, Elsie suspected, you were still alive.

She didn't sleep. There was too much noise, too much coming and going. And the pain in her hip was quite sharp. Instead, she floated on her own river of thought, in and out of different times, different rooms, different pieces of her life. Here was Clem. Here was Ida. Here was Glory.

Such a long time since she'd left home, since she'd fallen on the green carpet and lain there, watching the day's light move around the house.

"You take your time in going," Clem had always said when they left a movie, left a party.

Elsie said: "There's always one more thing to say." This had to be the longest leave-taking of all. And he must be miles ahead now. *How will I ever catch up?*

What would it be like, Elsie wondered, when she did come to the end? There'd been nothing to it for Clem—breathing, breathing, and then not. At least she trusted it to be calm. Almost forty years he'd been gone; she wished she believed she would see him again, in some other place, on some other side. But then she realized she had seen him daily these past years—as long as she'd been floating on this tidal, turning time. Here he was now, stepping up to the side of the tram—she leaned down and smiled at him as she caught his hand.

"I'm going to marry you, Clem Gormley," she said.

He smiled and said, "I know."

She pulled herself up a little higher in the bed and caught a glimpse of something moving in the window that gave onto the corridor—her reflection, she supposed, or maybe some other, more mobile version of herself. Once, in the middle of the night, she'd looked in the window of her old house and had the shock of seeing someone standing on the other side. Lucy: that was her name. Elsie had made Carol send those flowers and Elaine had been so cross at how much they cost.

Now Elaine was strapped into the metal cylinder of an aeroplane and flying halfway around the world; Elaine, who for one moment had held her hand. And maybe Gloria would come home—Glory, who might find Elsie's painting. *Hang on; hang on.*

It all moved too quickly, like the lights flashing in her room right now. She could feel how terribly quickly the world turned. She could feel herself falling through space.

She tried to move her thumb. There was no movement.

And then she stopped. She wasn't sure if her eyes were open or closed—but somehow, if she tipped her gaze a little to the left, to the right, the time lapse of her life was running from a different spot. Time lapse: that was a phrase that Glory had taught her. She'd shown Elsie some of her own sequences the last time she was home: plants blooming; the earth moving against the night sky; tides rushing in and out.

"Time lapse photography, Nan," she'd said. "You compress time—take a single shot every couple of minutes, and then run it together like film." She had another project that showed dresses being made, the fabric seeming to leap through the stages from cutting to sewing to fitting to catwalk in less than a minute.

That was what life felt like now.

Inside Elsie's body, blood was not quite getting to where it needed to be. She wouldn't walk again; she wouldn't talk. She couldn't press the button hard enough to tell anyone it was happening. So she shifted her gaze inside the night-sky dome of her mind and watched different parts of her life pass by. Through a window she watched people dance. She watched a tram move along a street. She watched a painter mix her colors. And the night spun into day and the rest of the time still to come.

It wasn't so bad, she supposed. She'd just lie here, quite quietly, and wait.

Maybe this was how she'd finally get home.

27

Lucy's house

BEN WAS planting more trees in the yard when the car pulled up. *Who's this?* he thought as he watched the woman in the driver's seat check her reflection in the mirror, fuss about with something in her lap.

Probably someone for the neighbors, and he shook some potting mix into the hole he'd dug for the tallest melaleuca, wetting it down before he eased in the plant. He'd lost count of how much they'd planted in the three years they'd been here. Paperbarks, honey myrtles, tea-trees, ficus, eucalypts, more. The trees made a crescent of different greens around the edge of the big corner block.

The particular judder of a closing car door: Ben looked up towards the road again. He rarely heard that sound without the memory of Lucy slamming shut an orange taxi door late on a Sunday night and running across the grass to where he stood. "Here I am." Her voice light; her smile wide. "Here I am. I've come home."

He closed his eyes; it still made him smile.

"Hello?" The woman was standing on the curb. Her dark red hair glowed bright, like Lucy's, but her clothes were very stylish, very fine. "Excuse me—do you live here?"

Ben wiped his hands and blinked. "I do," he said. "Yes. Can I help you?" She could have been one of the other Lucy Kisses, snuck through to this one's world. Her *vardøger*.

She took another step towards him. "It's a strange thing to ask," she said, "but my nan lived here—and I—"

"Elsie? You mean Elsie Gormley?" He shaded his eyes. "We bought the house, three years ago, from her."

"Yes, Elsie Gormley. She died last week and I—" And then the woman was crying, without trying to wipe at her tears.

"I'm so sorry," said Ben, unsure if he should offer a handkerchief or reach out a hand. He glanced back at the house, half expecting its shape to have changed with this news. "Would you like to come in? Could I get you some water? Some tea?"

The woman smiled. "No, thanks. My uncle said you'd done wonders with the garden; I wanted to come by and see."

Ben nodded at the digging and the planting. "We've got a kind of forest out here now," he said.

"There used to be a kookaburra Nan fed," said the woman. "I don't suppose he still comes round?"

"No—although I think he did, right at the beginning. We haven't seen him for ages, though my wife's always hopeful he'll come back." Ben made another gesture towards the house. "You're sure I can't get you a drink?"

The woman shook her head, and stepped into the shade. "But I wouldn't mind just stopping for a while," she said. "I loved it here, when I was a kid. All the stories, things to do—there was a swamp at the back, you know, spotted with blue hyacinths. My grand-father used to take me foraging in there—plants, things that people had thrown away; I guess it was a bit of a dump. But I thought it was like having a treasure chest over the fence." She looked along the side of the house and down to the park that had replaced the swamp. "You were all right in the last flood?"

"We were fine."

"It went under in seventy-four, you know," she said, and Ben nodded.

A chocolate-colored myna bird hopped across the grass, and the woman laughed. "When did they get here?" she asked. "It was all the other kind of small grey noisy miners in my day."

"They've been coming the past year or so," said Ben. "Our boy's been watching them move down from the hill."

"He was a baby when you moved in, wasn't he? I remember Dad telling me that. I thought Nan would like it that the house had a new family."

"Yes. He's four now," said Ben. She was very glamorous, standing there in her smart black clothes—the longer he looked, the less she seemed to look like Lucy. He was conscious of being grubby from the dirt.

"Elsie lasted a long time," said the woman. "She was ninety-three. She had a stroke a couple of years ago, and wasn't really with us since. I meant to come home more, you know—meant to bring her here and see if you'd mind if she had a look around. You never know if that's a good idea."

They both shrugged.

"We'd have been happy to see her," said Ben. "For a long time we thought of this as Elsie's house. My wife used to imagine her coming back to visit in the middle of the night."

"I wouldn't have put it past her," said the woman.

The myna bird hopped across the branches of one of the callistemons, roughing up the thicker bark with its beak, and balancing as the thinner twigs swayed beneath it. At the apex of the tree, it pushed off, and flew into the sky.

"Wouldn't you love to be able to do that?" said the woman, as she watched its curving flight. "I know they're pests, but they're just so rich a color. They're part of the starling family—or that's what we call mynas in England. I think starling is a much nicer name."

"Do you live there?" There was something round and polished in the sound of her voice—it reminded him of what he remembered of his own mother's.

"For years," said the woman. "I left Brisbane as soon as I could—never really got on with my mother. But I felt very sad to leave Nan."

There was a clattering inside the house, and a great shout, and Lucy and Tom came down the front steps, each with a rocket. Lucy was singing about starmen and Tom was making the crackling sounds their rockets needed to blast off.

"Tom, Lu," called Ben. "Come here a minute. This is Elsie's granddaughter." They dropped their arms and their game, their blastoff, paused.

"You've got some lovely rockets there," said the woman, nodding at the toys. She crouched down next to Tom, holding her hand out towards the dark green spaceship he held, a tube of cardboard with a plastic funnel on the top. "Would you mind if I had a look at this? I've always fancied making a rocket, and you look like you've done a good job."

Tom passed it to her. "This one can go all the way past the end of the last universe," he said proudly. "Mum and me tested it the other day."

"That sounds like an impossible mission." The woman laughed. "Are you good at impossible things?"

"Yes, I am," said Tom with the certainty of being four. "Mum and me see impossible things all the time. We saw a pitch drop thing that had taken *thousands* of years—"

"Well, not thousands—thirteen or so," said Lucy, resting her hand on his head.

"We saw it slowly in real life, and then we saw it speedy on Mum's phone. We saw a whole year in *ten seconds*." Tom's voice was rising and his face was one great smile.

"Ah, time lapse," said the woman. "That's one of my favorite things. You know, my grandfather saw one of those drops of pitch fall—imagine that: the right place, the right time."

"Mum says maybe when I'm finishing school, I can maybe see the next one." His face clouded. "I'm not even at big school yet."

"Well, it's good that you've got rockets to keep you busy while you wait." The woman smiled. "I met a boy once in this very city who told me he was building a rocket, and I mean a *real* one. I used to wonder how that voyage went."

Ben brushed at his face as if something had landed on his skin; he had the sense of having tripped and stumbled, although he stood stock still in his own yard.

"Ours are always highly successful voyages," said Lucy, looping her arm through her husband's. "But will you come inside and have a cup of tea or something? It would be lovely to hear more about your nan. I used to talk to her—I mean, pretend to—when we first came." She blushed. "We had a run-in in the end."

"Is that why she sent you those roses? My mother was appalled by how much they cost."

The woman laughed as she handed the rocket back to Tom, but Lucy and Ben stood suddenly silent and still. Ben shivered, and some great silence chilled the world. He felt Lucy's fingers tighten on his arm.

"I won't come in, thanks. I'm on my way out to the airport— flying back to London today," Elsie's granddaughter said, her voice breaking the pause. "I just wanted to see the place before I went. I was so relieved you hadn't demolished it—little cottages like this, they turn them into concrete monsters these days."

"Concrete monsters?" Tom's eyes blazed out to wideness. "*Real* monsters? Like the real rocket you talked about?"

"Not really," said his dad, pulling him in against his legs. "It's just an expression. There are no monsters around here."

Then the silence widened around them again, and the sun shone hot and bright.

"Can I ask you a favor?" The woman spoke after a moment. "Would you mind if I take a quick picture of the house, just to keep, before I go?"

"Of course not," said Ben. "I can take it for you if you like, so you're in it?"

"Yes." Lucy felt in her empty pocket for a phone. "And if you could take one of the three of us too—we don't have many of us three here together. Ben? Have you got your phone?"

He nodded, holding out the small device to their guest.

The woman smiled. "Of course," she said. She pulled a phone from her own pocket, fiddling with the switch. "Sorry," she said. "It's my nan's phone—Mum says it's got some of Nan's photos, stuff that everyone thought had been lost. Sorry," she said again as she fumbled with another button. "I'm still figuring out how it works."

"It's like mine—" Lucy reached for it, and Ben saw her start. "It *is* like mine," she said slowly, turning towards her husband. "Look. I had this cover and then . . ."

"Yes," he said quietly. "I see."

"Don't know how Nan ended up with something like this," said the woman, passing the phone to Ben and standing at the foot of the stairs. "One of my cousins' kids must have got it for her. And I should warn you, I hate having my photograph taken—you'd never believe I take pictures for a job."

Ben tensed his hands to stop them shaking as he stood to frame the shot.

They swapped positions then, Lucy, Ben, and Tom ranged up the stairs and Elsie's granddaughter framing them on Ben's phone. Ben felt his throat catch each time he swallowed—with excitement or fear, he wasn't sure which.

"That's lovely," the woman called, "and another?" Snapping five or six times. The garden beside them was bright with flowers, red and white.

Passing the phone back to Ben, the woman took a deep breath and combed her fingers through her hair. She was taking in every inch of the house's exterior—he could almost feel it being sucked towards her gaze.

Gloria, he thought suddenly. *Her name is Gloria. She knows my real first name is Alex.* He stared at her, wanting to say something—wanting to say, *It's you; I think I know you; stay a while.*

"All right," Gloria said. "I'd better push on. Thanks for the photo—and for planting all these trees. It looks like an oasis."

"We love it," said Lucy.

"Our home," Ben said, looping his arm around his wife's shoulders and holding her close. "Or Lucy's house. As it should be."

"That sounds all right too," called Gloria, halfway towards her car. Somewhere overhead, a kookaburra called, and she looked up to see it sitting on a cable beyond the yard, its feathers hunched and its tail swaying slightly to keep its balance.

There you are. There you are. Safe and sound.

She waved once as she drove down the street, glancing in the mirror to see the bird launch itself across the sky, and three people—Lucy, Ben, and Tom—together on the grass, looking down at a picture of themselves.

Acknowledgments

This project has been assisted by the Australian Government through the Australia Council, its arts funding and advisory body, and I'm profoundly grateful for the grant which first allowed it to find its way. In 2014, I was awarded a *Griffith Review* residency at Varuna to complete a later draft of the book—many thanks, also, for that.

My ongoing thanks to Jane Palfreyman, Siobhán Cantrill, Louise Cornege, and everyone at Allen & Unwin in Sydney, and to Sarah Cantin and Judith Curr at Atria in New York. Thanks to Jenny Hewson and Federica Leonardis at Rogers, Coleridge & White, to Zoë Pagnamenta and Alison Lewis at the Zoë Pagnamenta Agency, and to Alice Whitwham at Elyse Cheney Literary Associates.

This novel grew from "Elsie's House," a short story published in *Griffith Review 34*, and I'm very grateful to that journal for the support and space it gives my words. An earlier version of "The Crow" was published in *The Best Australian Short Stories 2012*. Several editors gave me the chance of writing articles and reviews that fed directly and indirectly into this book: thanks to Ian Connellan, Marieke Hardy and Michaela McGuire, Stephen Romei, Julianne Schultz, Susan Skelly, Sally Warhaft, and Susan Wyndham for those opportunities.

The epigraph comes from the poem "III. De Libero Arbitrio" by John Burnside, copyright © Penguin Random House UK, and is reproduced here with the permission of United Artists LLC on behalf of John Burnside.

The poem quoted on page 118 is from "The Story" by Michael Ondaatje and published in *Handwriting* (Toronto, Ca: McLelland and Stewart, 1998), copyright © 1998 by Michael Ondaatje and reprinted here by permission of Michael Ondaatje.

The quote on page 237 is from Patrick White's *The Tree of Man*, copyright © Patrick White 1955, reprinted with the kind permission of Jane Novak.

This book has been fed by all sorts of conversations. For these, as much as for all sorts of practical, philosophical, and literary support, many thanks to Hugh and Violet Armstrong, Alexis Beebe, Harriet Beebe, Sue Beebe, Tegan Bennett Daylight, Lilia Bernerde, Helen and Kerry Bierton, Jemma Birrell, Ruth Blair, Ili Bone, James Bradley, Sarah Branham, Leah Burns, Ian Bytheway, Susan Clilverd, Sally Cole, Matt Condon, Angela Dean, Clare Drysdale, Chris Dudgeon, Daniela Flynn, Bill Genn, Stuart Glover, Marilyn and Les Hay, Alison Holmes, Bruce Ibsen, Afro Inglis, Annette and Michael Jarrett, Edwina Johnson, Shelley Kenigsberg, Matthew Lamb, Dick Leeson, Eleanor Limprecht, Stewart Luke, Rachel Mackenzie, Alison Manning, Robyna May, Jen McKee, Richard Neylon, Kim Offner, Denis Peel, Sean Rabin, Larah Seivl-Keevers, Robyn Stacey, Andrew Stafford, Fiona Stager, Thomas Suddendorf, Mark Tredinnick, Cory Unruh, Ally Wakefield, Stan and Janette Warren, Hannah Westland, Sarah Weston, Geordie Williamson, and Charlotte Wood.

For their attention to these words, particular thanks to Krissy Kneen, Gail MacCallum, and Kris Olsson, and to Clara Finlay, Ali Lavau, and Virginia Lloyd.

Most important, my thanks and love to Nigel Beebe and Huxley Beebe, who've had to live with this book for a while.

About the author

ASHLEY HAY's work includes fiction, narrative nonfiction, journalism, essays, and reviews. Her novels have been longlisted for awards including the Miles Franklin and the International IMPAC Dublin Literary Award, and shortlisted for categories in the WA Premier's Prize, the NSW Premier's Prize, and the Commonwealth Writers' Prize, as well as the Nita B. Kibble Award.

Her second novel, *The Railwayman's Wife*, was awarded the Colin Roderick Award by the Foundation for Australian Literary Studies, and also won the People's Choice at the NSW Premier's Literary Awards. It was also published in the UK, the US, and in translation.

A former literary editor of *The Bulletin*, she contributes to journals including *The Monthly* and *Griffith Review*. Her work has won awards in Australia, the UK, and the US, and has been anthologized in collections including *Best Australian Essays*, *Best Australian Science Writing*, and *Best Australian Short Stories*.

She was editor of *Best Australian Science Writing 2014* and was awarded the 2015 Dahl Trust/ABR Fellowship, for which essay she won the 2016 Bragg UNSW Press Prize for Science Writing.

She lives in Brisbane.